The Gold Scent Bottle

Dorothy Mack

SIGNET
Published by New American Library, a division of
Penguin Putnam Inc., 375 Hudson Street,
New York, New York 10014, U.S.A.
Penguin Books Ltd, 27 Wrights Lane,
London W8 5TZ, England
Penguin Books Australia Ltd, Ringwood,
Victoria, Australia
Penguin Books Canada Ltd, 10 Alcorn Avenue,
Toronto, Ontario, Canada M4V 3B2
Penguin Books (N.Z.) Ltd, 182–190 Wairau Road,
Auckland 10, New Zealand

Penguin Books Ltd, Registered Offices:
Harmondsworth, Middlesex, England

First published by Signet, an imprint of New American Library,
a division of Penguin Putnam Inc.

First Printing, April 2000
10 9 8 7 6 5 4 3 2 1

Printed in the United States of America

250

After the dance . . .

Max was maneuvering Abigail around the entrance opening into the corridor as they talked. "You stand in no need of practice, my sweet. That last number proved you are an accomplished waltzer already."

"Thank you for the compliment, Max, but I fear I am too short to make you an ideal partner."

"Nonsense, a small girl can partner anyone."

Something in her smile, gratitude mingled with disbelief, caused Max to cast prudence aside yet again. There was nothing save a large Chinese urn holding a fern screening them from those passing the entrance to the great hall, but Max gave in to a desire that had been gaining in urgency throughout the evening, and kissed her parted lips, pulling her against him as he did so. The element of surprise worked in his favor initially, and he savored the sweetness of those soft lips. . . .

Coming next month

COUNTERFEIT KISSES

by Sandra Heath

Sir Gareth Carew was quite smitten by the attentions of London's lovely new arrival–until he recognized the charmer as Susannah Leighton, the woman who blamed him for the loss of her family's fortune. But can he win back her trust–and her love?

0-451-20022-5/$4.99

BURIED SECRETS

by Anne Barbour

"One of my favorite authors."–Mary Balogh

Love was for poets. Marriage was for fools. That was pretty much the philosophy of dashing rake Christopher Culver–until a scandalous spinster named Gillian Tate aroused his curiosity...and captured his heart.

0-451-20023-3/$4.99

THE NABOB'S DAUGHTER

by Dawn Lindsey

Anjelie Cantrell was the most sought-after heiress in Jamaica–and the most infuriating. Lord Chance is afraid the girl is more interested in mischief than marriage. That is, until their hearts were shipwrecked...

0-451-20045-4/$4.99

To order call: 1-800-788-6262

Chapter One

He'd scarcely stepped into the overheated reception room with his comrades when he spotted her in the center of an admiring group of men. There could be no mistaking that distinctive blond hair, so fair as to appear silvered in the candlelight; and the fluttering fingers that accompanied her animated speech struck a familiar chord in his memory. As did his accelerated heartbeat and the burning sensation in his chest.

Four years since he'd set eyes on her and nothing had changed, Max acknowledged between despair and disgust. He clamped his teeth on a groan and resisted an urge to turn tail and leave while he struggled to marshal his forces. *Everything* had changed, he reminded himself savagely. Four years ago Felicity Stanton had been the toast of the town and his promised bride. Today she was the Countess of Dalmore—his stepmother—and the mother of a three-year-old child, the half sister he had never met.

Four years ago he had been carefree and twenty-three, the age Felicity was now. He'd also been credulous and trusting. Neither description would fit him today. Knowing Felicity had proved a liberal education.

Unaware of her enlarged audience, Lady Dalmore threw back her head in a well-remembered gesture and produced a trill of delighted laughter, the silvery sound carrying to the blue-coated trio just inside the wide doorway.

"Old Whitey, bless his black heart, was in the right of it for once when he promised we'd see all the real stunners at Mrs. Cathcart's."

Claypoole's reverent whisper and the accompanying pinch on his right elbow jerked Max out of his memory-induced daze, aided by another low voice on his left.

"The question becomes how do we wangle an introduction to that glorious creature?"

"Nothing could be simpler, my dear chap," Max said, removing his elbow from his other friend's grasp. His glance still nailed on the woman holding court in the corner, he made a small adjustment to his sleeve band and set off in her direction.

His companions, demonstrating the ability to react swiftly to changing conditions peculiar to men of the military fraternity, subdued their disbelief and followed close on his heels.

The beautiful young woman, doubtless sensing movement on the periphery of the group of which she was the focus, looked over her shoulder as the trio approached. Max, all of his faculties at battlefield alert, grudgingly awarded her full marks for presence of mind as she quickly disguised the shock—and perhaps dismay—evident in her initial reaction to his sudden appearance. She produced a brilliant smile and a little squeal of delight as she dashed across the remaining space to greet him with both hands extended.

"Edgeworth," she cried, giving him his title, "how wonderful to see you, but how naughty—and typical—of you to spring up out of the ground with no advance notice of your intention to return to England."

Max accepted the invitation of those outstretched hands, raising first one then the other to his lips in a theatrical gesture that gratified Felicity, sparked jealousy in her glowering admirers, and impressed his friends. The little smile on his lips mocked the situation while his mind registered her cleverness in presenting him as a thoughtless dolt. His smile rivaled hers as he replied with obvious gallantry, "And how typical of you to outshine every other lady in the room, Felicity. You have not altered in the least degree in four years. You are exactly as I remember you from our last meeting."

Lady Dalmore's smile remained steady, but her glance narrowed during this speech. Max transferred one of the hands he held to his arm and maneuvered her around closer to his fascinated comrades. "May I present some friends to you, my dear Felicity? The giant on your right is Captain Claypoole, and the bearer of the magnificent military mustachio is Lieutenant Wilcox. Gentlemen, this lovely lady is the Countess of Dalmore."

Both officers executed graceful bows, but the younger spoiled the effect somewhat by jerking upward, his puzzled eyes winging back to Max. "Am I mistaken? You did say Dalmore?"

"Nothing wrong with your ears, Freddy," Max assured him coolly. "I have the singular honor of being entitled to address Lady Dalmore as 'Mama'."

The countess paid no heed to the muffled guffaws and ripple of increased interest animating her audience, but turned her attention to the red-faced young officer, saying sweetly, "If you are well acquainted with my husband's son, Lieutenant, you will know that he likes to have his little joke. I am delighted to meet you and Captain Claypoole, and shall now make you acquainted with these other gentlemen." She proceeded to name the five men who had remained in close attendance throughout the interruption provided by the arrival of her stepson and his comrades.

Max's interest was not so invested in the identity of Felicity's admirers that he missed the hint of sarcasm in her designation of him as Captain Lord Edgeworth, but he allowed nothing to disturb his bland response to the mass introductions. Any initial awkwardness in the situation was banished when one of the civilians, who had been inspecting their uniforms, asked if they belonged to the 18th Hussars. When Captain Claypoole allowed this to be the case, the newcomers were besieged with questions about the costly Battle of Toulouse that had taken place at Easter just as Napoleon was abdicating his throne. It seemed everyone present had been acquainted with someone who had fallen in this wasteful final battle of the Peninsular campaign.

Max was content to leave the answers to his comrades while the greater portion of his brain was given over to reviewing and evaluating the extraordinary coincidence that had produced this meeting on his first night back in London with the woman he had joined the army and fled the country to avoid. The time that had elapsed since he'd walked so unsuspectingly into this room could not be more than five or ten minutes at the outside, but he felt he'd been standing here for an eternity trying to keep his gaze from fixing on Felicity's lovely face. Steely discipline kept his hands at his sides, although his collar was choking him and his ears felt as if they were on fire.

Felicity looked cool as a cucumber in a diaphanous pale blue gown that revealed the masterly sculpture of her body with each movement. He knew it was small-minded of him to resent the ease with which she had dealt with the potentially embarrassing encounter, but the knowledge did nothing to mitigate the unworthy emotions raging in his breast. He concentrated on the monumental task of unclenching his teeth and relaxing his jaw before permitting his eyes that had been directed unseeingly at the group of men to return to his former fiancée.

What he'd intended to be a brief impersonal glance quickly confounded him as he met a look from large light blue eyes that threatened his good intentions with its intensity. "Where is my father tonight?" he blurted, mentally running for safety by shifting his gaze, darting blind eyes about the room as he sought to regain his equilibrium. This process was unexpectedly aided by Felicity's soft laugh in which he detected recognition and amusement at his plight.

"Dalmore is where most of the peers of the realm are tonight, of course, dining with the Tsar of Russia in the Guildhall. And if rumor is to be believed, also with the tsar's sister, who disdains our English practice of excluding females from such occasions. Surely you have noted how thin of company all London's drawing rooms are this evening?"

"I . . . this is our first evening in London," Max admitted. "We were aware that Alexander was here on a visit of state, as well as the King of Prussia and General Blucher, but had not heard that the grand duchess was also in England."

"Oh, yes, Catherine has been here long enough in advance of her brother to dissipate all the good will our citizens bore him by her haughty manners and ungracious reception of the Prince's efforts to honor her."

"You have met her then?" Max asked, not out of genuine interest, but from a desire not to dwell on the meaning of that look they had just exchanged.

"In a manner of speaking," Felicity said dryly. "Catherine is not overly interested in members of her own sex, although she has cultivated the Princess of Wales and Princess Charlotte to annoy the Prince."

"But surely it is only proper that all the visiting dignitaries should pay their respects to the heir at least?"

"It is common knowledge that Charlotte has been at loggerheads with her father over the proposed marriage with the Prince of Orange, and, in fact, has been trying to squirm out of the contract by stipulating that she never be forced to live in the Netherlands and that she have complete control of her movements between England and the Netherlands. The Russians are not best pleased with the proposed alliance either and would be delighted to see it broken off. The would-be bridegroom has not helped his cause by getting disgustingly drunk at every function he has attended during the sovereigns' visit."

Max might have encouraged her to expand on the subject of the palace intrigues, but Felicity forestalled him by taking his arm in a proprietorial clasp while she begged her admirers to excuse them for a bit as they had a lot of family news to catch up on. This request was accompanied by a luminous smile that sought and shed its benevolence on each man present in turn. To a man her admirers stood up straighter, swallowed their disappointment, and voiced their complete understanding and acceptance of the situation. If Max had needed any proof that marriage and motherhood had not diminished his former fiancée's potent attractions, this display would have supplied it. It certainly added to his wariness as he followed her through a series of stifling rooms thronged with richly dressed humanity. He caught scraps of conversations here and there and was conscious of a considerable amount of feminine laughter before Felicity led him through a small door into a deserted hall—nearly deserted, he corrected himself mentally. Blinking in the sudden dimness, he saw a man and woman vanish around the bend of an ascending staircase just before Felicity opened a door and gestured him inside.

The room they entered was quite small; one glance was sufficient to discover that its furnishings consisted of one table desk holding an oil lamp, one straight-backed wooden chair, and one settee upholstered in what appeared to be a dark green brocade.

Felicity glided over to the settee and seated herself. Max

remained standing even after she'd patted the cushion beside her in a smiling invitation. The smile did not waver as she said brightly, "There, now we can talk without having to shout over a dozen conversations."

"I should not have thought there was much we had to say to each other, Felicity."

"Max!" she protested on a little laugh. "After four years? Much has happened to both of us. We are not the same people we were then. We shall have to get acquainted all over again."

He stood regarding her steadily without expression while silence filled the space around them like acrid smoke, replacing the air. At last Felicity looked away, her eyes darting about the room for a moment before coming back to him as she said hurriedly, "At least you must let me say I am truly sorry if I upset you by breaking our engagement at our last meeting."

"*If* you upset me by throwing me over for my father? Is there some doubt in your mind about that?" he asked in tones of exaggerated wonder.

"We were both so young then, Max," she replied with a pleading little gesture of one hand. "We had been acquainted for only a few weeks, we didn't really know our own minds. When I met your father I realized that I needed someone older . . . with more experience of life—"

"Also wealthier and in full possession of a title and estates," he added pleasantly.

She flinched and sent him a wounded look. "Max, this terrible war has changed you. You have grown so hard."

"Also older and with more experience of life."

"I can see that." Lady Dalmore rose from the settee in one fluid motion and erased the distance between them, touching the blue and silver sash of his uniform with the tips of her fingers as she glanced up at him from under long lashes, adding in seductive tones, "And dangerously attractive too in your dashing regimentals."

Max fought to keep his features impassive and unlocked his jaws to say softly, "And what of you, Felicity? Do you find being Lady Dalmore everything you hoped?"

"Yes, of course," she replied quickly. "Dalmore is an estimable man, and he treats me like a queen. I just wish he did not have such a dislike of living in town. We have scarcely arrived at Dalmore House before he is pining to get back to Oakridge. It certainly cannot be the superior society there that pulls him, for I must tell you I find our neighbors dreadfully provincial in outlook." Her features, which had taken on a discontented cast, brightened, and she slipped her hand under his elbow, smiling up at him. "It's marvelous to have you back, Max. We'll do all the things we used to enjoy together, riding and driving—recollect that you once promised to teach me to handle the ribbons. I shall hold you to that," she declared gaily. "Even the most stiff-necked matrons would not dare to criticize, for you are family, after all. We'll—"

"Felicity, you cannot possibly suppose that I shall be living at Oakridge." It was too close a thing to decide who was the more dumbfounded at the moment, Max thought with grim humor—he at the notion of living under his father's roof in forced proximity to the woman he had hoped to marry, or Felicity at the idea that he might decline such a treat.

"Your father will be devastated," she protested. "You must not imagine that because he has married me there is any lessening of his affection for you or that he would not gladly welcome you home. Indeed, he has pored over all the reports from the Peninsular these past years, dreading to find your name on the casualty lists."

The sweet earnestness of her manner would have been touching under other circumstances. A reluctant smile at the obtuseness, whether real or feigned, of the female of the species crossed Max's lips. "I have an estate of my own from my maternal grandfather, as well as his town house, Felicity," he said, gentling his voice. "I assure you my father is cherishing no expectations that I shall return to Oakridge except for the occasional visit."

The eagerness drained out of the countess's face, and her pretty mouth took on a provocative pout. Max slipped a finger between his throat and suddenly tight stock, stretching his chin upward before rushing into speech. "Naturally I shall be calling at Dalmore House in the next day or two to see my father—" He broke off this conciliatory speech, raising his eyebrows in mute question as Felicity shook her head from side to side.

"Unless you don't mind rising from your bed at the crack

of dawn tomorrow, I fear you won't see your father. He has scheduled his usual early departure from town. We'd have left by now had he not felt obliged to attend this dinner at the Guildhall."

Listening intently, he heard the note of petulance in her voice change to excitement as she continued, "But you must come to us in the next fortnight, Max. There will be a number of guests staying at Oakridge, so it will be much livelier than usual. Please do not fail me or disappoint your father."

Inarticulate protests eddied violently in Max's brain, but failed to coalesce into a coherent, much less civil refusal, and he heard himself weakly promising to make one of the upcoming party at his ancestral home. Immediately, the realization that he had trapped himself sent a jolt of anger and resentment through his veins. He was curt with Felicity in pursuing his paramount goal of escape, inventing a second engagement for himself and his comrades as he led her out of the suffocating little room. After the damage had been done, he achieved a measure of glibness, rattling on about plans to meet other friends at a popular gaming house as they passed a couple standing in the shadow of the staircase, locked in a passionate embrace. All Lady Dalmore's practiced cajolery failed to produce an agreement to change his mythical plans. In order not to appear boorish, however, he allowed himself to be presented to his unknown hostess and spent fifteen minutes doing the pretty to an attractive woman whose lithe body, vivacious manner, and skilled use of cosmetics all contributed to maintaining a youthful appearance that did great credit to her determination to keep nature at bay.

Max's discreet head signals brought Captain Claypoole and Lieutenant Wilcox to the area presided over by Mrs. Cathcart, eventually resulting in an open invitation to frequent her saloon from that hospitable lady whose interested gaze returned with flattering regularity to Captain Claypoole's tall athletic figure. Max reiterated his claim to a later appointment, pointedly ignoring the indignant expressions that appeared briefly on his comrades' faces before they added their apologies to his and took their reluctant leave.

A few moments later, when the former soldiers were

back on the pavement, Captain Claypoole grumbled, "What was the idea of dragging us out of there with a hoaxing tale when we were being so royally welcomed?"

"I'm sorry, but I could not bear the heat in there another minute," Max replied, patting his handkerchief over his damp forehead as he strode forward.

After an exchange of startled glances, his friends followed, suiting their steps to his. "At least we were bidden to return at any time in our own right," Captain Claypoole said, "without needing the sponsorship of Whitey or his lordship here, he with the delicate constitution."

Max grinned. "*You* certainly were welcome, Clay. Unless I am greatly mistaken, our charming hostess was quite taken with you, do you not agree, Freddy?"

"Yes," Lieutenant Wilcox replied, "but that still leaves us standing on a street corner on our first night in town—our only night in town, I should point out, Max."

"I told Felicity we were going to meet some friends at a gaming house." Max glanced across the intersection where they had paused. "There used to be a popular place, Merryman's, where the play was not too deep about five minutes from here. We might try whether it is still in business."

His friends being amenable, they set off for St. James's and found the establishment Max remembered still operating at the same location. A quick look at the players filling the rooms tonight revealed that the management had not changed its policy of catering to a youthful clientele rather than seeking out those with deep pockets. After a second, more careful look at their surroundings, Max would have taken his oath that nothing else about Merryman's had changed either. The furnishings looked exactly as he remembered them if one made allowances for the fading effects of four years of accumulated dust and grime on the walls and fabrics. It even smelled familiar. One deep breath convinced him of the unwisdom of repeating that exercise. His lips twisted in wry recognition that he had grown more rather than less fastidious after four years of foreign filth.

Though they were not shy about expressing their disapprobation at finding those in attendance exclusively masculine after the delights of Mrs. Cathcart's rooms, Captain Claypoole and Lieutenant Wilcox soon settled down at the tables to play with enthusiasm.

Max's emotions were multilayered that evening to say the least. He was relieved to see his comrades enjoying themselves, particularly since he had dragged them away from a delightful evening of flirtation at Mrs. Cathcart's. He was conscious of a burgeoning restlessness that he strove mightily to suppress throughout their time at the gaming house. The extraneous inner struggle resulted in lapses of concentration at play to the detriment of his purse. He frittered away his time wandering from table to table until he caught himself again losing track of the play.

Afterward, Max attributed the final disconcerting aspect of his first night in London to a combination of annoyance at his inability to keep his mind on what he was doing and sheer recklessness. At the time, however, it seemed like a simple case of boredom that caused him to accept an invitation to a game or two of piquet from a young man who, like himself, stood idly watching the action at a crowded faro table where Max's friends sat engrossed in play. It was not until they were halfway through the first rubber that it gradually dawned on Max that his opponent was a deal younger than he had first assumed. His deferential manner and youthful lineaments would have betrayed him earlier had Max not been so preoccupied with his own thoughts.

By the time Max had won the first rubber by a large margin, he had assessed his opponent's skill and found it wanting. He strongly suspected the youth was underage also. A suggestion that they discontinue the contest in favor of seeking a place at the faro table was met with resistance, nor would the younger man agree to lowering the stakes they had agreed on. Seeing that he had wounded the youth's pride, Max subsided and set himself to the task of reversing the natural outcome of the contest without further bruising this awkward pride. This was easier said than done, given that the cards persisted in falling in his own favor at the same time that his opponent made egregious errors in his discards. He slowed down his own consumption of wine to a standstill, grateful at least that the lad did not become noticeably foxed during their session of piquet.

By the time his sleepy comrades came seeking him, Max had reduced the boy's losses to just over three hundred pounds, but he still felt like a Captain Sharp fleecing a flat when the youth paled and swallowed hard before excusing himself to speak to a friend hovering in a near corner of the room. Max waved his own friends away to lessen the embarrassment of the coming scene and waited impassively until his erstwhile opponent returned with a thin, anxious-looking youth of his own age.

"I regret that I have insufficient funds to pay my losses tonight, sir . . . Captain," he said with an attempt at dignity that was belied by a hoarse quality to his voice. "I shall give you my vowel for three hundred and ten pounds now and will call upon you tomorrow if that will be convenient?"

"Certainly." Max bowed in acknowledgement and accepted the paper held out to him by his vanquished foe. "Now, if you will excuse me, my friends are waiting."

He was turning away when the youth said urgently, "A moment please, Captain. I do not know your direction, or your name, for that matter."

"Remiss of me. I am Edgeworth, late of the 18th Hussars. I will be staying at Stephen's Hotel in Bond Street for the next day or two. And you are . . . ?"

"My name is Roland Monroe of Broadlands near Richmond. This is my friend Percy Basingstoke."

Max and Mr. Basingstoke exchanged bows and murmurs, and, there being nothing more to be said, the trio dispersed with Max rejoining his friends a moment later, a slight frown rippling his brow.

"Taken to plucking the pigeons, have you, Edgeworth?" Captain Claypoole asked as they went down the steps to the street.

"A half-breeched babe more like," Lieutenant Wilcox put in sapiently. "If that was a chit he gave you back there, I'll wager you've seen the last of him."

Max's frown deepened. "I'd be glad to think you correct, Freddy, but the cub refused to avail himself of the opportunity I gave him to escape without exchanging identities. He was obviously well bred and well mannered. I fear some poor papa will be the recipient of a shamed confession tonight. It was my fault for not realizing how young he was right away."

"I still think you've seen the last of him; in fact, I'd be willing to put up my jeweled Spanish dagger against Allegro that you never see him or your winnings again."

Max laughed. "Still trying to steal my horse, Freddy? Allegro stays with me. We've been through a lot together; it would be like selling my brother to part with him."

"Very touching, if you had a brother. I'd swap mine for a mule," Captain Claypoole said, pulling his two engrossed comrades back to the safety of the flagway as a high-perch phaeton took a corner too closely. "I hope the hotel's brandy is better than Merryman's wine. I need to get the taste of that swill out of my mouth."

The subject of Max's regrettable experience in the gaming house was allowed to drop as the three friends made their way back to Bond Street, where the ensuing session of reminiscing about their communal past, accompanied by copious amounts of the hotel's best brandy, continued deep into the night.

Max awakened to unnervingly bright sunshine and a head that reacted to every sound from the street below like a gong being struck by steel hammers. Struggling up onto his elbows, he learned that movement was no less painful than sound this morning—or afternoon. He had no idea of the time as he gazed with a jaundiced eye about the hotel chamber, noting the disorder he'd created disrobing last night at whatever ungodly hour he'd parted from his comrades. *Lord,* even his eyeballs hurt! He closed his eyes, which didn't help, and sank back into the pillows with a groan, but there was no further relief to be gained in bed. Sleep was impossible while a jumble of thoughts chased around in futile circles inside his head.

His friends were to leave London today for their homes. If they were in anything approaching his sorry condition right now, he did not envy them the ride. He had a long list of matters to attend to himself in the immediate future before the next phase of his life could begin, the most crucial being to open his town house and replace the carriage and horseflesh he'd sold before leaving for Portugal four years earlier.

Driven by a compelling need for some sort of initiative, Max sprang up into a sitting position and instantly regretted his impetuosity as the hammers attacked his head anew. Letting out a hissing breath, he eased his burdensome body off the mattress and walked gingerly over to the washstand, kicking his shirt and one boot aside in the process.

Looking in the mirror had definitely been a mistake, he decided a moment later. With his heavy growth of beard and puffy, red-rimmed eyes he looked like a debauched pirate. By the time he'd recovered from the shock of dowsing his head with cold water, however, Max felt semi-human again. Human enough at any rate to kick himself figuratively for having sent his batman, Gibbs, a London native, home to his family yesterday. The idea of shaving himself in cold water in his present state held no appeal.

Max was searching in vain for a bellpull when a knock on the door heralded the entrance of the one person on earth he would sincerely welcome at the moment.

"Gibbs! That ugly phiz of yours looks prettier than an archangel's to me right now. If that is hot water you are carrying, I may fall on your neck in gratitude."

The jug-eared batman set down his burden on the washstand and made a slow visual reconnaissance of his master's person and the messy room. A wide gap between his front teeth was revealed by his grin, but he held his tongue as he started to set the room to rights.

"Did I ever mention that I prize your taciturnity above all your other sterling qualities? Remind me to raise your wages," Max said, plopping down into a chair and clutching his aching head as he prepared to put himself into more capable hands than his own.

An hour and a half later, his pressed and precise appearance a credit to his batman's skilled ministrations, Max stood on the flagway outside the hotel, watching the backs of his two comrades as they headed for the stables. His somber mood did not accord with the brief and casual farewells they had just exchanged. This then was the final act that defined his military career. The men he had lived in the closest proximity with and fought beside for four years and depended upon for all human contact for weeks at a time would henceforth occupy not the center but the periphery of his life. Only now did he realize how little consideration he had really given to how he would spend the next thirty or forty years. He told himself it was probably too soon to experience a sense of expectation or enthusiasm for the future. That would come in time. For the moment it was enough to think about getting some food into his stomach. Things would look more promising when the hollow feeling was relieved.

Max was enjoying a second cup of coffee and perusing a newspaper when Gibbs appeared at his table, soft-footed as ever. "There's a cove wishful to have a few words with you, Captain."

Lowering his paper, Max beheld his erstwhile piquet opponent. His first thought—that Freddy would have lost his prized dagger—faded as he noted the tense set to the young man's features and the box he clutched in his gloved hands. "Ah, good afternoon, Mr. Monroe. Please sit down." He gestured toward the other chair. "May I offer you some coffee?"

"No, no thank you, sir." The young man shook his head as if to clear it of extraneous matter, and launched into speech. "Lord Edgeworth, I have come to tell you . . . to explain that . . . that although I cannot honor my obligation to you at this time, I plan—"

"Are you of age, Mr. Monroe? It is not my custom to play cards with minors," Max said bluntly with the intention of releasing the youth from his self-inflicted purgatory. He could see that he'd erred as the lad's chin ascended and a surge of red flared across his cheekbones, but any resentment he might have felt at such frankness was well cloaked in dignity.

"I attained my majority last week, sir. The evening at Merryman's was by way of a celebration actually," he added with a twisted attempt at a smile.

"A costly celebration, but the fault was mine. I was rather preoccupied last night and failed initially to assess your youth. I propose that we cry quits and shake hands, Mr. Monroe." Max rose to put his intention into effect, but youthful pride intervened again.

Mr. Monroe stepped back while holding out the box he carried, shaking his head. "No, sir," he said firmly. "It is a matter of honor and I would like you to take this as a pledge that I will redeem my vowel in the near future." When Max made no move to accept the box, the young man set it on the table and fumbled with the lid, eventually removing a charming, heart-shaped gold and enamel scent bottle with dove-shaped stoppers. "I know it may not be worth three hundred pounds, but it is very choice, as you can see, and it belonged to my mother," he said hurriedly, returning it to its nest when Max stood still, frowning silently. "You mentioned that you would be staying here for only a night or two, sir, so I shall be obliged if you will give me your permanent direction."

Max sighed. "Curzon Street," he replied, conceding defeat.

The youth's eyes, which were an unusually deep blue verging on purple, lost their anxious expression, and his rather narrow jaw relaxed its grim set as he bowed in acknowledgment before taking his leave immediately. His stature was no more than average and his build was slender, but his straight back resonated dignity as he walked away from the brooding man by the table.

Max sighed again in resignation and picked up the box after replacing the lid. As he moved slowly toward the hotel staircase, he reflected that his return to England was already complicated in ways he had not foreseen in Spain.

Chapter Two

The reedy young man in an ill-fitting tan coat visibly wilted in the face of the lady's withering reproach.

"I thought better of you than this, Percy. I counted on you to keep Roly from doing anything foolish—at least," she amended, from a wish to avoid owning to unreasonable expectations, "to keep him from sinking himself utterly beneath contempt."

Stung by this final charge, Mr. Basingstoke attempted a feeble defense. "I s-say, that is coming it rather too strong, Gail. I tried to keep Roly from going to that gaming hell, suggested we might take in a show at Astley's or even go to see a turnup at the Fives' Court, but he would have none of it—had the notion to double his blunt at the tables. You know how mulish Roly can be when he takes a notion into that thick head of his—well, of course you do or you would not have begged me to keep him out of the clubs in the first place. *You* know he has no head for cards, *I* know it, but what's the good of that when Roly don't know it? At least I stuck with him as I promised you I would, but how you expected me to keep him from losing everything once he'd got himself into a game of piquet has me stumped. And I couldn't very well tell that captain he'd challenged that Roly never remembers what cards were played and in . . . invar . . . always bets on long odds, could I?" Mr. Basingstoke stopped to draw a breath, the aggrieved note in his voice giving pause to the young lady listening intently.

"No," she sighed, "I don't suppose you could do that. Once he'd gotten into a game—although I hold that military man grievously at fault for engaging to play with an obvious halfling—he was bound to lose his money. But," she added, her own grievance still rankling, "he lost money he did not *have,* and you could have stopped him from resorting to thievery at least."

"Thievery!" Mr. Basingstoke gaped at his antagonist, a slender, petite brunette who barely came up to his shoulders, when she leapt out of her chair as though unable to contain herself any longer. "What are you talking about?"

"What would *you* call taking property that doesn't belong to you to secure a debt?"

"What property? All Roly did was sign a chit and promise to call on Edgeworth the next day."

Abigail's suspicious gaze softened in the face of her old friend's obvious bewilderment. "So he did not tell you what he intended to do? I beg your pardon, Percy, for ripping up at you like a shrew."

Mollified by the lady's apology and the remorseful look in her large blue violet eyes, Mr. Basingstoke blushed, stammered, and demurred. "No, no, perfectly understandable . . . upset and all that, but you still have not told me what property Roly stole."

"He took the gold scent bottle my mother left to me, the one thing of value I possess in the world."

The enormity of the crime or perhaps Abigail's valiant attempt to still her trembling lips struck Mr. Basingstoke dumb for a few seconds before he expostulated, "Well, if that don't beat the Dutch! Roly knows how much store you set by that trifle—no, not a trifle, of course, that *keepsake* of your mother's. Stupid thing to do too because Edgeworth didn't ask him for a pledge of security. Of course," he added with painful honesty, "Roly more or less told him he would pay what he owed the next day, which he couldn't do, naturally. No way to raise the wind that quickly."

"No way to raise it at all! Where is Roly going to come by three hundred pounds honestly?"

"Surely in the circumstances your father would . . . ?" Mr. Basingstoke wafted the delicate suggestion into the air.

Abigail batted it down. "My father paid Bertie's debts when he outran the constable a few years ago, but that was because Bertie is too valuable with the horses to let him languish in Newgate. Bertie has been working off the debt ever since at little more than a groom's wage, according to him. Also, Papa warned Roly on a number of occasions that he could not expect to be rescued from his follies. Papa despises Roly because he prefers music to horses, so you see there is no way Roly will be able to redeem my scent bottle in the foreseeable future—or ever if he persists in trying to emulate those whom Papa refers to as wealthy wastrels."

Mr. Basingstoke, looking more uncomfortable than ever at these frank family revelations, cleared his throat and admitted, "One or two of Roly's friends are peep o' day lads, but I would not call them wastrels precisely. Always ripe for a lark, of course—well, so is Roly for that matter—but perfectly honorable, I assure you."

"From what I have heard of their 'larks,' they seem to me to be a worthless lot," Abigail declared roundly, "and I fear they will be the ruination of Roly. Sometimes I wish he were not my twin so I could turn my back on him and simply dislike him as I do Papa and Bertie."

"Now, now, you don't really mean that, Gail," Mr. Basingstoke said, tugging at his collar. "Family after all . . . blood thicker than water . . . that sort of thing."

"I most certainly do mean it," Abigail insisted. "Just because they share the same blood does not prevent my father and elder brother from being mean-spirited bullies with no interests beyond horses, and my father is a clutch-fisted tyrant too, who begrudges every penny that doesn't go to the horses.

"Look at this room!" She directed her friend's gaze with a wide gesture encompassing the large saloon, its beautiful proportions and high ceiling diminished by the shabbiness of its furnishings. "This is where we would receive company—if we ever had company, that is," she continued in bitter accents. "Do you know there has not been a woman over that threshold since Mama died eight years ago, nor a penny spent on furnishings or repairs? Look at the peeling paint everywhere and the chipped paneling and threadbare carpet. I work my fingers to the bone to keep it clean; it is a constant battle just to get them to remove their stable boots before coming inside. On several occasions I have begged Papa to let me buy some paint and I would do the work myself, but he refuses to spend the money. I have to account for every penny I spend to run the house, so I've not been able to save anything from the housekeeping money.

"You have been to the stables, Percy. If there is any truth in you, you will have to concede that the horses live better than I do. The stables are kept in a high state of repair and cleanliness, and as for the horses, there is never any mending of *their* bridles and cloths, but just look at this old rag I am wearing! Papa considers it quite good enough for another five or ten years!"

This challenge reduced Mr. Basingstoke to a state of red-faced panic, his mouth agape and his vocal apparatus paralyzed. He stared bemused at the angry girl defiantly displaying a much-darned brown skirt gripped between her fists, her eyes bright with unshed tears.

"Well?" she demanded, thrusting out a small foot clad in a well-worn slipper. "Am I as well-clothed and shod as the horses at Broadlands?"

"I . . . I'm sorry, Gail . . . I guess I never really looked at you before and—"

"You nor anyone else! I might as well be invisible!"

"*No,* no, that is not what I meant!" he said, desperately earnest. "When I look at you, I don't see an old brown dress. I see the face I've preferred to all others for as long as I can remember."

Compunction shafted through Abigail at this simple tribute, and the tears threatened to become a reality. "Oh, Percy, please forgive me. I am the greatest beast in nature to rip up at you this way when you are the only true friend I have in the world."

"No, no, I am a dolt for not noticing how matters stand here. No sisters, y'know, but I do have a mother; should have known that females set a lot of store by such things as clothes and furniture and . . . and such falderols." He waved a vague hand to include the room's contents in his summation. "Speaking of m'mother, she has always been very fond of you, ever since your mother used to bring you and Roly to Glendale to play when we were children. Perhaps she could speak to your father about—"

"Thank you, Percy, but I would never dream of putting Lady Basingstoke in such an invidious position, and it would not serve in any case. You may recall that when I was about seventeen your mama generously offered to take me about a little socially, just to local gatherings at the homes of people my parents had always known, like the Lawrences, and Papa flatly refused. He showed me the letter Lady Basingstoke had written him and read me the riot act for putting her up to it—which I had *not* done. It was just your mama's generosity and good nature that had prompted the offer, but Papa said he would not be beholden to anyone, and I was better off staying at home than being condescended to by those who looked down on us for breeding horses for a living. I still shudder to think of the brusque terms in which he likely couched his refusal. It was months before I could do more than bow to Lady Basingstoke in church, I was so mortified.

"The only person who ever had the slightest claim to being able to influence Papa was Mama. Since she died, he seems to mistrust all of humanity. I should be covered with shame if he were to say something cutting to your mother, who has always been so kind to me. I'd never be able to look her in the face again."

"Well, it was just an idea. I'd like to be able to help you," Mr. Basingstoke replied, looking more unhappy than ever.

"You *can* help me, Percy. That is why I asked you to come today—to beg you to help me to get my scent bottle back."

"You know I'd do anything in my power for you, Gail, but my pockets are to let until quarter day, which is why I was unable to assist Roly, and I won't have three hundred pounds even then."

"How can you think I would try to borrow money from you, Percy, when we both know I could never repay you?"

The disclaimer failed to achieve its intent of reassuring Mr. Basingstoke, whose wariness increased visibly as he waited for the ax to fall.

"It's really quite simple. I intend to ask this Lord Edgeworth to return my scent bottle, but I have no way to get to London. Will you take me to see him, Percy?"

Mr. Basingstoke's jaw dropped, and his first attempt to speak produced no articulate sound, but then he sputtered, "Have you lost your senses? You cannot ask Edgeworth to return a freely given pledge of security."

"Of course I can. I shall simply explain that Roly had no right to offer it in the first place since it belongs to me."

"Where is your loyalty?" Mr. Basingstoke demanded, aghast. "You'll make Roly look like a fool—or worse."

"He *is* a fool—and worse," Abigail returned calmly. "Where was his loyalty or his honor when he took my scent bottle?"

Mr. Basingstoke could not refute this point, and his feeble attempts to change Abigail's mind fell on deaf ears. She looked both adamant and mournful as she declared, "I was sure you would help me. You said you would do anything for me, but I see I have asked too much of you. Never mind, I apologize for taking up so much of your time. I shall find another way of getting to London."

Goaded beyond endurance, he gave his childhood friend a decidedly unfriendly look. "Very well, I'll take you to London lest you do something even more crack-brained on your own. I swear there is nothing to choose between you and Roly when it comes to mule-headed rashness."

"Oh thank you, Percy. I knew you would not fail me. I do not even know where this Lord Edgeworth lives," she confessed.

"He said he was staying at Stephen's Hotel for a couple of days—beyond that I have no idea of his direction."

"Then we must lose no time in finding him. Do you think Lady Basingstoke would object if I told Papa that she had invited me to spend the day with her tomorrow?" Abigail asked diffidently. "I feel terrible about involving her in a deception, but I expect Papa would think it strange indeed if I were simply to propose junketing around with you for hours on end."

Mr. Basingstoke kept to himself any thoughts on Mr. Monroe's probable reaction to having his daughter absent herself from her home in the company of someone he would doubtless stigmatize as a young wastrel. He promised blithely that his mother would be happy to be of service in a good cause and, when Abigail drew back in alarm at the idea of divulging the sordid affair to a living soul, assured her that he would give his parent an expurgated account of their errand that would not reveal her brother's folly.

Seeing that her fervent gratitude embarrassed her old friend, Abigail subsided and meekly promised to be ready to leave when he arrived the next day.

Over the next few hours Abigail suffered severe pangs of conscience on Percy's behalf for embroiling him in her troubles. Despite her vehement denial of his charge of disloyalty to her brother, she could no longer deny to herself that by telling this Lord Edgeworth that Roly had taken her scent bottle without permission, she would be betraying her twin for the first time in their lives. The dreadful irrevocability of the proposed course frightened and tormented her.

Abigail wished passionately to talk to Roly, but he sent word late in the afternoon that he would be staying with a friend for a few days. She had been all but ready to cancel the expedition to London when this message arrived. It acted like a bellows on the dying embers of her fury. She did not hesitate to ascribe her twin's action to moral cowardice, a desire to avoid her wrath and a well-merited dressing down. She went to bed in a rage without writing to Percy, only to lie awake half the night agonizing over her own perfidy should she seek out her brother's creditor. When she did finally sleep, however, her dreams were of her mother disappearing into the mist carrying the golden bottle, her back implacably turned to her pleading daughter.

Abigail awoke unrested but with a renewed resolution to do her utmost to retrieve her inheritance. Not even for

Roly could she risk losing her mother's gift to her. In some corner of her heart there was shame at her selfishness, but it did not lessen her determination. When her father questioned her stated intention to spend all day at Glendale, she told him the story she and Percy had agreed on, that Lady Basingstoke was feeling below par and desired her company.

By the time she climbed into Percy's curricle in midmorning, Abigail felt steeped in wickedness, having now added perjury to her list of sins. Not surprisingly, this mood undermined her value as an entertaining companion. After several of his conversational sprouts had withered in the desert of her monosyllabic responses, Mr. Basingstoke became exasperated. "I don't know how you expect to talk Edgeworth out of that scent bottle when you cannot even string two words together about the weather or the scenery," he declared, fixing an indignant eye on the silent girl beside him.

"Oh, Percy, I am so sorry," she replied in swift contrition. She shook her head as if to clear it of all thinking matter and smiled up at her companion, her large eyes beseeching his understanding. "I have been feeling so miserable and . . . and *wicked,* but as of this moment I mean to enjoy this lovely day and driving with you and simply getting away from Broadlands for a few hours."

She was as good as her word, gently encouraging Mr. Basingstoke to describe her father's new hunter in minute anatomical detail. Before another mile passed, they were back in the state of easy intimacy fostered by a lifelong friendship. Abigail began to take in the passing scene, sighing with pleasure at the intensely green fields and hedges. A sense of well-being stole over her in the presence of softly moving, herb-scented air under a blanket of blue sky clotted here and there by creamy puffs of cloud. Nor was she unmindful of a delicious aura of freedom, almost of escape that hovered over the swiftly moving curricle despite the unpleasant nature of her errand. When was the last time she had been farther than two or three miles from Broadlands? Months? Years more like, she realized. Her spirit took wing as the curricle bowled along behind Percy's well-schooled greys. Her head swiveled as though a ball on her shoulders, so loath was she to miss any of those sights peculiar to the city environs. For a time she forgot the reason for this rare outing in her pleasure in the quickened life beat of a city.

It was not until they had left the environs behind and were in the city proper that she reluctantly turned her mind to her quest. "Where did you say Stephen's Hotel was located, Percy?"

"Up ahead in Bond Street," Mr. Basingstoke replied, feathering a corner with an automatic precision that brought an admiring smile to his companion's lips. "It's mostly for the military, or the army, I should say. Naval officers generally patronize Fladong's in Oxford Street. As you can see, I dispensed with my groom today—no need to broadcast this excursion any further—so we shall have to leave the curricle at a stable yard. We may take a hackney if you object to walking."

"How could I object to walking on such a lovely day? Besides, I already feel terribly guilty about putting you to so much expense on my account. I have an idea—why do you not set me down in front of Stephen's Hotel, and you may return for me later? That way you will not have to engage the services of a stable."

"Have your wits gone begging, girl?" Mr. Basingstoke demanded, slack-jawed. "A fine figure I would cut letting you saunter unescorted into a hotel full of soldiers. Your father would have my guts for garters if word of such a thing ever got back to him. Now, do you have any more bright ideas to offer?"

"No, Percy."

Abigail's uncharacteristic meekness earned her a suspicious glare, but she preserved an air of innocent gravity, and presently the pair set off on foot in perfect charity, their squabbles forgotten.

Abigail's good spirits received a severe check twenty minutes later when upon inquiry at Stephen's Hotel, they were informed that Lord Edgeworth was no longer a guest of that establishment. Subsequent questioning failed to elicit any further information. The hotel porter, reluctantly declining a *douceur,* was obliged to admit that his lordship had failed to provide news of his destination when he'd departed on the previous day. Abigail, oblivious to the interested glances directed at her by several young officers lounging about the lobby, gazed blindly at her escort with eyes held wide open to contain the incipient tears.

Mr. Basingstoke gave the trembling fingers on his arm a reassuring squeeze and bundled her out of the hostelry before her distress could bring unwelcome notice upon them. He walked her rapidly away in a silence that lasted until Abigail, having regained her composure, asked dully, "Where are we going?"

"To the stables. Stands to reason Edgeworth had a horse and a servant with him when he arrived in town. Servants talk. Might glean something helpful there."

New hope flared in Abigail, only to flicker when her companion warned, "Mind you, if he was heading out of town, which is the most likely thing, we shall be at point non plus. You'll have to obtain his direction from Roly and press your suit by letter."

Fortunately for Abigail, their luck was in. One of the ostlers in the stables, his memory aided by the coin Mr. Basingstoke held out, recalled that Lord Edgeworth's groom had said as how his master lived in Curzon Street. He did not know the number but, after cudgeling his brains, triumphantly pronounced that he recollected as how Gibbs, the batman, said it was a good house except that it sported a ridiculous purple door.

Armed with this information, the pair set their feet westward toward Curzon and in due course arrived at a fair-sized brick house much in the style of its neighbors except for a rather distinctive front door. "Would you say that was purple?" asked Mr. Basingstoke. "It looks like muddy brown to me. Besides, it is obviously closed up—there is no knocker on the door. Perhaps we should continue on toward Shephard's Market."

"No, that door is purple, or was before it faded. I am persuaded this is the right house, and it is very likely, you know, that there has not been time yet to put up the knocker if Lord Edgeworth only opened the place yesterday." She spoke with an assurance that evaporated when repeated loud knockings by Mr. Basingstoke, who had removed one of his gloves for the purpose, produced no response from within.

He suggested again that they continue down the street, but Abigail urged, "No, let us go down this alleyway first,

Percy. Mayhap we will see some signs of life at the back of the house."

Suiting action to her words, she entered the alley next to the house, trailed by her reluctant companion. "Look, Percy," she said excitedly, "that window is open several inches. The house cannot be uninhabited."

"Yes, it could. Might simply have neglected to close it tightly. All the others on this side are closed. Just an oversight most likely."

"Percy, will you boost me up so I may look inside?" Abigail asked in her impulsive way. She gave a giggle at her friend's appalled expression, but begged, "Please, Percy, there is no one about to see us. If the room is shrouded in holland covers, we'll know it is still untenanted and that will settle the matter for today."

Mr. Basingstoke was still inclined to argue but, as so often in the past, proved incapable of resisting the entreaties of his old friend. In the end, still muttering darkly, he bent down and gave her a leg up.

Abigail, peering inside, emitted a muted squeal. "Percy, I can see it! My scent bottle is standing not ten feet away on a table." Her voice shook with excitement. "Can you boost me up farther? I am going to get it."

Mr. Basingstoke, automatically complying with her request, stopped suddenly as the second part of her speech plunged into his brain like a knife. "You can't climb into someone's house!" he expostulated.

To his horror, Abigail had already pushed the window up several more inches and was scrambling over the sill as he spoke. As she pulled her foot out of his grasp, his previously dormant survival instinct came alive, and he leapt to grab the leg disappearing over the sill. He succeeded in getting his hand around her ankle as he jumped, but with disastrous results. Abigail pulled against his grip and in so doing lurched off balance into a small stand holding a silver urn of some sort that tumbled off, landing with a reverberating crash on the wooden floor beyond the carpet.

Outside the house Mr. Basingstoke started at the sudden noise and froze in his tracks, all senses alert.

Inside the house the man sitting at a desk in his bedchamber also heard a distinct sound of metal ringing on a wooden floor rising from somewhere on the entrance level.

* * *

Max was alone in the house, having sent his faithful batman to the Registry Office to interview prospective servants. He had intended to perform this task himself today, but the appearance of two letters from Oakridge in the morning post had robbed him of all initiative, whereupon he had delegated the chore to Gibbs.

The past few days had been spent attending to the myriad details pursuant to reestablishing himself as a civilian English town dweller. After a visit to his bank, where he picked up the keys to his grandfather's house, he'd headed for Long Acre, where he'd ordered a new curricle and a perch phaeton from Hatchet's. Next he had arranged to hire vehicles and cattle as needed until he could accept delivery. After these vital matters had been attended to, he was free to tackle the enormous task of acquiring a civilian wardrobe. He'd begun, for want of current information, by splitting his custom between Weston in Old Bond Street, long favored by Mr. Brummell, and Schweitzer and Davidson nearby in Conduit Street, who enjoyed the Prince Regent's patronage. He'd allowed these establishments to guide his selections of what was currently enjoying a vogue, with the caveat that he would accept no garment, however fashionable, that impeded his free movement.

Armed with fabric swatches, he'd then spent tiring hours in St. James's outfitting himself with every accoutrement from hats to handkerchiefs, with special emphasis on his boots, which he'd always had from Hoby's ever since he'd entered society. A glance to his right disclosed a pile of unopened boxes and packages reposing in the corner of his bedchamber. He and Gibbs had had all they could do late yesterday to make the ground-floor study livable and search out linens for their own bedchambers.

Any memories he'd had of this house dated back to when his mother was living. To his knowledge, his grandfather had not used it personally after his daughter's untimely death, renting it out for the Season until his own demise two years ago while Max was in Spain. Fatigued by his unaccustomed labors and shopping, Max had slept like the dead on his first night in his new home, but with morning, memories had started trickling into his mind, and the letters from Oakridge had opened the floodgates.

His father's letter, which he read first, had been short and to the point. The earl had stated his relief at his son's deliverance from the dangers of war and his disappointment at not seeing him immediately on his return to England, offering as excuse the information that he had not learned of Max's return until the following day when he was already halfway home. He went on to express the hope that he would have the joy of seeing his son at Oakridge at his earliest convenience.

Max had reread this epistle, frowning over its implications. On the surface here was a man, a father who wished to see his son. A very simple situation, except that nothing but the most formal of messages had passed between them for four years and in none of these infrequent communications had there ever been a direct reference on either side to the fact that the parent had married the girl the son desired. From the moment when Felicity Stanton had told him she preferred to marry the earl, Max had not set eyes on his sire. In the beginning he had not even admitted the possibility of future meetings between them. He had come through that nightmare period of the soul when all he could feel was the pain of betrayal by the two most important persons in his life. Life had gone on—although not a normal life, unless one considered the state of war to be normal—and the primacy of the betrayal had receded; at least it was no longer with him constantly, although he could not conceive of a time when he might be able to put it entirely behind him. There was no going back, but he would like to see his father again if for no other reason than to define his present feelings toward one who had been both parent and friend to him in the years after his mother had died.

Max had experienced an inexplicable aversion to opening the letter from his stepmother. He had trained himself not to admit Felicity into his thoughts. Their past had held a fleeting promise of ecstasy that had come to nothing—worse than nothing, since the ending had been so cruel. Even now it was imperative to limit their meetings for the sake of his peace of mind. That meeting at Mrs. Cathcart's had been entirely disquieting, but he'd avoided a mental evaluation of it, throwing himself into the mundane business of preparing himself for his new life. Only an idiot could imagine that this ostrichlike policy could continue into the future, however.

It had taken the best part of an hour to overcome his reluctance to learn what was in Felicity's mind at present, but eventually he had slit the wafer and unfolded the single sheet. It was a circumspect communication, he decided, not much longer than his father's. She'd addressed him as her dear Max, claimed pleasure at the prospect of introducing him to his little sister, reminded him that he had promised to join the other invited guests at Oakridge shortly, and cheerfully declared her intention of including some eligible young ladies for his appraisal since he was not getting any younger. It contained nothing that would worry the most jealous husband, offend the strictest cleric, or set up the backs of the highest sticklers among society's dowagers.

Max read this charming effusion with ironic detachment and contrasted it to Felicity's almost seductive behavior at the Cathcart evening party. He had pushed the events of that evening out of his mind, but now he deliberately recalled the way Felicity had crowded close to him and talked gaily of the things they would do together at Oakridge. He had not believed then that he had imagined the element of invitation in her manner, and he did not believe it now. Granted that his own response to her beauty and appeal had been hot, sudden, and shaming, but it had not arisen in a vacuum. Even at that moment, part of his brain had been questioning the propriety of his stepmother's behavior as a young married woman. Though he'd tried to banish the incident from his thoughts, he had found her mere presence at Mrs. Cathcart's surprising, and her seeming intimacy with a woman whom he'd pegged as outside of society was disturbing. He had not been so bemused by the allure of his former betrothed that evening that he had failed to note among the other guests several lapses of the public decorum society demanded between members of the opposite sex, even if the whole world knew them to be lovers in private. Was his father aware of this odd connection his wife had formed?

It was at this point in his mental reflections that Max went over to the Chippendale highboy in search of the key to his grandfather's wine cellar. A quick survey of this amply stocked room provided an additional reason to be grateful to his maternal grandparent. He returned to his bedchamber with a bottle of fine old brandy that he proceeded to sample as an aid to creativity while he attempted to compose a letter to his father.

He was engaged in this activity when the pounding on the entrance door began. No one knew he was here, so he ignored the sounds while he tried to phrase an acceptance of the invitation that would not reveal his reluctance to subject himself to the sort of ordeal it did not require much imagination to foresee. If he'd had the good sense to provide himself with a wife before returning home, he would not be in this predicament now, he raged mentally as his labors continued to be unproductive.

After a few minutes the pounding on the door stopped, but the welcome silence did not produce an inspiration. All he could think about was the complete awkwardness of his position when he went back to his ancestral home, even though the presence of houseguests would provide some distraction.

The next assault on his ears caused him to leap out of his chair, overturning it in his haste. The pounding had been outside—*this* racket was inside his house. Max dashed from his room without stopping to put on his coat. As he ran down the stairs, he was straining to identify the source and location of the metallic noise, which had stopped before he reached the ground floor. The only room where the holland covers had been removed was the study, and now that he thought of it, he recalled opening the window in there after smoking a cigar last night.

Max flung open the door to the study and stopped, transfixed in disbelief as his eyes located a small figure—*a girl*—about to swing one leg over the windowsill.

"What the devil is going on here?" he cried. *"Stop right where you are!"*

Chapter Three

When the door opened, Abigail cast a terrified glance over her shoulder, but her only response to the question and command from the fierce giant in shirtsleeves was to redouble her efforts to go back out the window, hampered though she was by the scent bottle and her skirts.

Her escape was brought to an undignified end by a none-too-gentle grip on her shoulder. In her panic Abigail struggled wildly, kicking out at her captor. His colorful oath told her she'd inflicted pain, a grave error on her part as she realized the next instant when she found herself imprisoned between his hands gripping her tightly above the elbows.

"Whoa there, my fair housebreaker, not so fast."

That brought her head up in a hurry. "I did not break into this house," she denied hotly. "The window was open."

"Ah, a hair-splitter as well as a thief."

Abigail was dimly conscious of a note of amusement in the giant's voice, but she raised her chin a trifle and stared defiantly into cool grey eyes. "I am not a thief. This scent bottle belongs to me."

"By dint of the fact that it is—temporarily—in your possession, I apprehend?" He glanced at the bottle held between her hands against her bosom.

"You apprehend wrongly, sir. It has been in my possession since my mother willed it to me on her death eight years ago. If you doubt my word, I can show you the tiny scratch I made on it with sewing scissors when I was a child."

"Who are you?" The grey eyes had grown intent, roaming over her face and person in an intrusive manner that demanded great resolution on Abigail's part to endure with a semblance of composure.

"My name is Abigail Monroe. Are you Lord Edgeworth?"

"Yes." He was frowning now as he released her arms. "I thought those eyes looked familiar. Mr. Roland Monroe is your brother?"

"My twin, actually."

"Did he send you here to steal back his security pledge?"

"*No!* Roly does not know I am here. He—"

A loud knocking at the entrance door made Abigail jump.

"Ah, that would be your accomplice unless I miss my guess."

"Percy is not my *accomplice!* He kindly drove me to town so that I might explain the situation to you and beg you to return my property."

"But then you decided stealing it would save tiresome explanations? I see." His voice was perfectly affable, but Abigail's fingers itched to slap the nasty little smile from his mouth.

"Gail, are you all right? Who is in there with you? Open this door, or I shall get a constable!"

Lord Edgeworth had seized Abigail's wrist and pulled her into the entrance hall with him at the beginning of this speech. Now he threw open the door.

"Mr. . . . Basingstoke, is it not? How do you do? Do come in, unless you would prefer after all to round up a constable to join our merry little party?"

Seeing Percy's chagrin in the face of Lord Edgeworth's sarcastic civility steeled Abigail's spine as nothing else could have done. An icy calm stole over her, and she vowed to show no weakness in front of this supercilious bully. She'd die before affording him one more instant of enjoyment at their expense.

"May I have my wrist back, sir?" she asked coolly, adding, "I assure you I shan't try to escape."

"It would grieve me to cast doubt on a lady's veracity, so I'll just relieve you of your burden for the moment," Edgeworth replied, plucking the scent bottle from her grasp as he released her wrist. "Shall we adjourn to the study, where you may tell your . . . story in a modicum of comfort?" He stepped back, indicating the way with a sweeping gesture. Abigail, head high, stalked ahead of the men and reentered the study, smarting over his slight emphasis on the word "story."

"I believe you will find this settee tolerably comfortable, ma'am," said Lord Edgeworth, still playing the gracious host. Percy, who had not uttered a word, plopped down beside her, casting her a look of anguish as he did so.

"You must forgive me for receiving you in shirtsleeves. As you have doubtless observed, my house is as yet unprepared for visitors. Regretfully, I am unable to offer you refreshment."

"Did you finish the brandy then?" Abigail asked with a deplorable lack of prudence.

"Gail!" moaned Mr. Basingstoke, finding his voice at last.

Both antagonists ignored him. "Are you suggesting that I am drunk, Miss Monroe?" Lord Edgeworth asked softly.

"Why no, sir," she replied kindly. "A trifle above your bend, perhaps, but certainly in possession of all your faculties."

"Well for you that I am, my girl, for you betray your youth and lack of breeding with every word you utter."

"Sir!" gasped Mr. Basingstoke.

"And I collect your sarcastic pretense of hospitality under the awkward circumstances reflects *your* good breeding?" Abigail shot back.

"Tit for tat, Miss Monroe," he acknowledged, bowing. "And now perhaps we might get down to those 'awkward circumstances' to which you alluded? Does this little gold bottle really belong to you as you claimed earlier?"

"I can attest to that, sir," Mr. Basingstoke spoke up manfully. "I am solely to blame for this sorry situation, not Gail . . . Miss Monroe."

"No, Percy, you are not to perjure yourself for my sake." Abigail turned to the viscount and said with painful honesty, "Mr. Basingstoke did not wish to bring me here today, but I traded shamelessly on our long friendship to persuade him because that bottle is my mother's gift to me, my inheritance. Roly had no right to pledge it as security for his debt to you. I thought, hoped, that you would understand and return it if I could explain the situation to you.

"The rest I don't believe I *can* explain," she said frankly, her cheeks reddening. "No one answered our knock, and we feared the house was unoccupied—the knocker was off the door. I saw the open window and reasoned that if the covers were off the furniture it would prove the house was tenanted, and I could come back later. I made Percy boost me up for a look. When I saw my scent bottle in here I simply . . . simply felt I *must* get it back."

Abigail's voice, which had started out steadily enough, was shaking badly at this point, and she looked at Lord Edgeworth helplessly "I . . . I still don't know how I could have done such a thing, and I do apologize most sincerely." Her pride sunk in mortification, she could no longer bear the viscount's impassive examination of her countenance. Her eyes fell to her gloved hands clasped tightly together in her lap.

Lord Edgeworth had not taken his eyes off her face during this lengthy confession. He continued to stare at her wordlessly until the throbbing silence in the room almost reduced her to a fit of screaming. She bit her lip fiercely, conscious of Percy shifting his weight beside her as her eyes were drawn as if by magnetism back to the lean, dark-skinned countenance of her adversary. She would not grovel, she promised herself, and sat up even straighter.

"So you would throw yourself on my mercy, Miss Monroe?"

Lord Edgeworth's voice was as dispassionate as his features. Abigail did not accept the invitation in his pause, remaining mute, and after a charged moment while Percy cleared his throat, the viscount went on, "I am not prepared to act on your request at this time, Miss Monroe. If you will return tomorrow with your brother, I shall give you my decision then."

Consternation flared in her face. "B . . . but that is not possible, sir. My brother is away from home at the moment and—"

"When does he return?"

"I don't know—he said he'd be gone for a few days, but I don't even know where he is."

"I do," Mr. Basingstoke said, rising to his feet. "I'll give him your message, sir. I daresay they can be here before noon tomorrow."

"But, Percy, I . . . I don't—"

"I think we should be going now, Gail. We've intruded

on Lord Edgeworth's patience long enough. With your permission, sir, we'll bid you good day."

Lord Edgeworth replied in courteous terms and proceeded to see his uninvited guests to the door.

Aware of the glances that had passed between the men deliberately excluding her, Abigail had nothing to do but mask her resentment at being reduced to a nonentity under a cloak of silent dignity as she and Percy took their departure.

The drive home was nothing less than a trial of endurance for Abigail. Nothing could serve to throw disharmony into stricter relief than the narrow confines of a curricle. Once they were beyond earshot of any audience, Mr. Basingstoke did not scruple to favor his old friend with his poor opinion of her actions and general demeanor during the late unhappy incident. An innate sense of fairness forbade Abigail from mounting an effective defense, and the bitter knowledge that she was deeply at fault for allowing her anger at Lord Edgeworth to betray her into unbecoming and ill-bred conduct denied her the relief of retaliation.

Time and distance took the edge off her consuming fury at the viscount, but this was replaced by desolation at the growing realization that she had forfeited the esteem in which Percy had formerly held her. She sat mute and miserable throughout the drive, impervious to the lovely scenery that had so delighted her that morning as she wearily replayed the day's events in her mind.

For the first time she had acted against her twin brother's interest for selfish reasons, and she was well served now that her rebellion had resulted in humiliation and failure. Roly would be furious with her of course but, unlike Percy, he was in no position to claim the high moral ground, she thought with a returning flicker of spirit. There was ample opportunity to nurture a little flame of hope that all was not yet irretrievably lost since Percy seemed bent on ignoring her existence once he'd had his say. Whether he was busy with his own thoughts or simply indulging a fit of the sullens, she could not tell from covert sideways glances at his unassuming profile. It seemed prudent not to invite his attention lest she provoke him into ringing another peal over her.

Abigail reviewed the confrontation with Lord Edgeworth, wincing inwardly at the appalling breach of delicacy she had committed by implying that the man was foxed. Sheer retaliatory nastiness must have prompted that infelicitous remark, though she had certainly smelled brandy on his breath when he had grabbed her and thwarted her escape. He was a detestable brute who delighted in putting her in the wrong, actually inviting her with his provocative taunts to cast off civility's guards to tongue and temper. She had accepted the invitation in no uncertain terms, giving free rein to both, to her eternal shame. And then he'd had the effrontery to lecture her on good breeding! Still, he had not quite closed the door on her hopes for the return of her scent bottle. She must not lose sight of that in her dismay at his insistence on a meeting with Roly present. Idle speculation on his motives brought her neither comprehension nor comfort. Obviously there was nothing to do but submit herself to the viscount's capricious whim or resign her claim on her legacy until or if Roly was able to redeem it.

Abigail entertained no doubts that Roly would submit himself to Lord Edgeworth's dictates for her sake. She was persuaded he was as ashamed of taking her property as she had been at making his disloyalty known to his creditor. The only question that remained was whether Percy had told the truth in claiming to know Roly's whereabouts. A sidelong glance at her silent companion's set features convinced her that it was advisable to possess her soul in patience until he elected to enlighten her on this point.

This course was rewarded when they pulled up to the side entrance to Broadlands in late afternoon. Mr. Basingstoke broke his long silence to say, "I am going to find Roly now and send him home with a flea in his ear. He can take my curricle to town tomorrow if you'd rather not ride all that distance."

"Thank you, Percy, for everything. I am very sorry I behaved so badly and made you ashamed of me today," she said humbly, swallowing a lump in her throat as she looked into his closed countenance, missing the indulgence she was used to seeing there.

"I was *afraid* for you back in that alleyway, Gail. You and Roly are like dogs with a bone when you get a notion to do something. Neither of you has the sense to stop this side of the grave, regardless of the possible consequences of your recklessness."

"I'm sorry," she said again and turned away quickly to hide the tears that were crowding behind her eyelids yet again.

It was a subdued and decorous pair who plied the shiny brass knocker now on Lord Edgeworth's door the next day. Stealing a glance at her brother's polished appearance in his high-crowned beaver and coat of blue superfine, Abigail admitted without rancor that Roly was definitely the more sartorially elegant. Last night, spurred by a passionate desire to reverse the insufferable Lord Edgeworth's low opinion of her, she had subjected her wardrobe to an intense scrutiny, the result of which was to sink her deeper into the dismals. This descent had been arrested, however, by the discovery at the back of a drawer of three lovely silk roses that had once adorned a ball dress of her mother's. These and a length of pink ribbon inspired her to retrim her serviceable straw bonnet. After an hour of sewing, she had blown out her candle and gone to sleep in an improved frame of mind.

Abigail gave a reassuring pat to the brim of her creation now as the door was opened by a soberly dressed individual of impressive girth and solemn mien. She frowned at the darned thumb of her white glove and hastily recomposed her features, hiding her hand in the folds of her skirt as she and her twin followed the servant upstairs. The smell of beeswax and lavender oil accompanying their ascent testified to the flurry of housekeeping activity her unexpected visit must have spawned yesterday. She checked a giggle at the thought of Lord Edgeworth's probable discomfort during the cleaning—men doubtless went to their clubs when confronted by household emergencies.

The Monroes were shown into the main reception room, judging by its position in the front of the house. Here too the furniture—what there was of it—smelled of polish. After a slow inventory of the room's contents, Abigail could discern nothing of a personal nature on display. The rose-colored humpbacked sofa upon which she sat and the mahogany chairs in the style known as Chinese Chippendale were handsome pieces, but, except for an elaborate pair of silver candlesticks as highly polished as the door knocker on the mantelpiece, there were no decorative objects to be seen in the room.

Her study of their surroundings was interrupted by the entrance of their host. Roly tugged nervously at his cravat, and Abigail again experienced the disagreeable sensation of being weighed and found wanting as Lord Edgeworth's assessing gaze shifted between brother and sister before he greeted them formally. When Roland went to sit beside his sister on the sofa, the viscount chose an armless chair set at right angles to it and seated himself.

"The butler will return directly with refreshments," he said. When both Monroes demurred, he directed a smile at Abigail. "You must permit me to repair yesterday's omissions, Miss Monroe."

Abigail could not prevent a blush of embarrassment from rising in her face, but she kept tight control of her tongue. "You are too kind, sir," she murmured.

"As for that, you had better reserve judgment until you have heard what I propose."

Brother and sister had a few moments to digest this enigmatic opening while the butler reentered the room, carrying a highly polished silver tray containing a gleaming pot, a glass decanter, a dish of strawberry tarts, and the receptacles necessary to partake of these offerings.

"Set it down on the table in front of the sofa, Jenkins. We'll serve ourselves."

"Very good, sir." Jenkins performed the task with deft movements, taking himself off with a soft-footed grace surprising in such a large man.

"I engaged Jenkins just yesterday. He has proved a marvelous acquisition already, unless upon longer acquaintance it turns out that he has a proclivity for nipping at the brandy."

Abigail, pouring herself a cup of coffee at her host's invitation, gritted her teeth at the mention of brandy, but went on with her careful movements, knowing herself to be under his scrutiny. She would play the lady if it killed her, she vowed, sipping the hot brew appreciatively. "If Jenkins made this delicious coffee, he is to be commended," she said lightly.

"Actually, I made the coffee," replied the viscount. At the raised eyebrows this claim produced, he explained, "Being with the army in the Peninsular was a liberal education. One acquired diverse skills there. Baking tarts was not among them, however. My batman has already discovered where to buy various delicacies in the short time we have been in London." He pressed the tarts on his guests. Roland accepted one and attacked it with every evidence of pleasure, but Abigail stuck to her refusal, not wishing to hamper her tongue with food when his lordship eventually got around to the 'proposal' he'd mentioned. Wary speculation on the nature of this had robbed her of any appetite right from the start.

She had cause to give thanks for her restraint in the next moment when Lord Edgeworth directed his basilisk stare at her twin. "No doubt your sister has told you what occurred here yesterday?" When Roland nodded, trying to chew the last mouthful of tart inconspicuously, his creditor went on in uninflected tones. "I insisted that you accompany Miss Monroe here today because any early return of her scent bottle depends on the cooperation of both of you—unless of course there is no necessity for me to detail my proposition. It may be that you are prepared to discharge the debt today?"

"N . . . no, sir."

"Very well, I shall proceed. I plan to make a short visit to my father's estate in Sussex in a sennight. I have learned that my stepmother has invited some eligible young ladies to Oakridge to dangle before my eyes during my stay. It is my intention to provide myself with a fiancée for the length of the visit in order to spare everyone embarrassment." Lord Edgeworth paused, a puzzled Roland nodded his comprehension, and Abigail set down her cup with great care as a premonition of disaster seized her.

The viscount continued in the same casual vein. "Since I have not been in England long enough to acquire a fiancée in the usual way, I propose to hire one, in a manner of speaking." In the pause that followed, Abigail's eyes clung to his.

"You must be out of your senses," she said flatly, abandoning her sworn intention to maintain a civil attitude at all cost.

"Gail," Roland remonstrated, "it is none of our affair what Lord Edgeworth chooses to do."

"I fear that is where you are mistaken, Mr. Monroe," Edgeworth said apologetically. "The blunt truth is that I plan to pass your sister off as my fiancée for the few days I am at Oakridge, after which I shall restore the scent bottle to her. Naturally, Miss Monroe cannot travel alone with me without damage to her reputation, which is where you come in. You shall both go with me as my guests. That should satisfy all requirements of propriety."

"I still say you are mad," Abigail insisted. "You said yourself that you haven't had time to acquire a fiancée in the regular way. No one is going to believe you have met and wooed a girl in less than a fortnight!"

"It will be up to us to make them believe it!" That this was uttered in a grim tone quite at variance with his previous casual manner was not lost on Abigail, but she was too intent upon convincing him of the impossibility of his scheme to dwell on this seeming contradiction.

"My father would never permit it, and if you told him we were really betrothed and then jilted me, he would kill you! Besides, I have no suitable clothes for a visit to a big country house," she finished triumphantly. "No one would believe you wished to marry such a shabby creature as I am."

"Why should your father have to know anything except that you and Mr. Monroe have been invited to the home of the Earl of Dalmore, whose son is a friend of your brother's?" he asked, continuing in the same plausible fashion. "As for clothes, there is ample time to get made up whatever you require for a few days if we begin today. At the end of a brief visit, you will have regained your scent bottle and acquired a new wardrobe into the bargain."

"It's *dishonest!*" Abigail cried. "You . . . we would be practicing a deception on your family—and on my father too!"

"This objection strikes me as rather hypocritical coming from a young woman who did not scruple to enter a man's home to remove an article illegally."

"You *know* that was only a mad impulse—the weakness of the moment, not to be compared with a deliberate hoax on the scale you propose."

"Perhaps this is merely a mad impulse on my part." He shrugged broad shoulders. "Come, Miss Monroe, let us cease this brangling. Do you wish to have your scent bottle back or not? That is all that need concern you."

"Roly," Abigail pleaded, "tell Lord Edgeworth that his scheme is ludicrous, unfeasible. We could never pull it off. It will end in humiliation and bad feeling in his family."

"Actually, it sounds rather a lark to me, and you will get your bottle back at the end, whatever happens, will she not, sir?"

"You have my word on that."

"A *lark!* It was one of your larks that landed you in the briars in the first place, and pulled me in with you," said his loving sister bitterly.

"Come, come, children, no good will be served by raking up the past," Lord Edgeworth said indulgently. "We should be off at once to find a dressmaker. There is much to be done today. Are we agreed?"

"Agreed," Roland said with a reckless laugh that brought a troubled look to his sister's face.

Surrendering to *force majeure,* Abigail nodded, but she seemed to withdraw in spirit as the mismatched trio set forth on its quest for fashion.

"Do you ride, Miss Monroe?" Lord Edgeworth asked, evidently prompted by the sight of a fashionable equestrienne overtaking them from the direction of the Park.

Roland laughed. "She was born on a horse! Our father breeds the brutes."

"There may not be time to have a habit made before we leave for Sussex," the viscount said with a frown.

"My habit is the one decent garment I own. Papa let me get a new one three years ago," Abigail replied. "It may not be in the first stare of fashion, but it is quite well tailored."

"That is a help. Now I wonder if Madame Simone still does business in Old Bond," Lord Edgeworth mused, "unless there is a dressmaker you would prefer to patronize, Miss Monroe?"

Roland hooted at that, and his sister was forced to confess that she had no previous experience of London modistes.

She was, in consequence, a trifle ill at ease when they

arrived at the premises of one of London's premier designers, and one, moreover, who was well acquainted with Lord Edgeworth. This became obvious when, having sent in his card, the viscount rose to greet a tall, dark-haired woman of uncertain age but great distinction, dressed in an elegantly simple black gown who came hurriedly out of the back room with extended hands.

"Ah, quel plaisir de vous voir encore, et de bonne santé aussi, grace à Dieu, n'est-ce pas? Votre chère maman, still so young, so *distinguée,* I miss her," the Frenchwoman said, shaking her head sadly.

"Thank you, Madame, so do I," the viscount replied, releasing her hands. "But today I bring you a new client. May I present Miss Monroe and Mr. Monroe? Can you provide Miss Monroe with a wardrobe for a country house visit—everything she will require for a few days?"

"When will she require this wardrobe?" Madame Simone asked, casting a professional eye over Abigail in her faded blue muslin. *"Un chapeau très charmant, mademoiselle,"* she said kindly, and Abigail relaxed her jaw and smiled into the shrewd black eyes.

"Merci, Madame,"

"In a sennight, I'm afraid, Madame," Lord Edgeworth said with a rueful smile.

"Oh, *mon mauvais!* When the city is full of foreigners *à ce moment*—dinners, balls—*tout le monde demande* the gowns *à l'instant, vous comprenez?*" Madame Simone said reprovingly, throwing up her hands. "But only for the affection I bore your *chère maman* I will do it—and because *cette demoiselle est si jolie.*"

By dint of biting her tongue until it hurt, Abigail remained quiescent under Lord Edgeworth's surprised glance. "Ah, yes, just so. You'll know what will make her look . . . less insignificant," he added hopefully.

"I can promise you that no *jeune fille* with eyes like mademoiselle's and wearing my gowns will go unnoticed, monsieur." The dressmaker snapped her fingers, and a young assistant appeared to lead Abigail into the rear of the premises to take her measurements.

Despite her deep reservations about the course upon which she was about to embark, Abigail enjoyed the next hour more than any within recent memory. Madame Simone returned within a few minutes to check the silent assistant's work and then had two minions parade bolt after bolt of beautiful fabrics in a virtual rainbow of colors before Abigail's bemused eyes, stopping occasionally to drape one over her shoulder at Madame's request. Sensations of pure pleasure ran along Abigail's nerves as her eyes feasted on the rich color palette and her fingers instinctively sought to caress the soft silks and smooth cottons.

The modiste kept up a stream of commentary in a bewildering mixture of French and English, sometimes directed to Abigail or one of her helpers, but just as often meant solely for her own ears. "Ah, this is the one," she cried, pulling a bolt of fabric from the arms of an assistant. She unfolded a length as she spoke and threw it across Abigail's shoulder, stepping back so the girl could see the effect in the full-length mirror on the wall,

"This is exquisite, almost the color of wood violets," Abigail enthused, "and so soft and filmy, like silk."

"It is silk and *très chère,*" Madame Simone confirmed with a chuckle, "but Lord Edgeworth was most insistent that whatever else we selected we must find a fabric to match your eyes for the evening dress." She indulged in a quintessential Gallic shrug. *"Chacun à son gout, n'est-ce pas, mais maintenant* one sees that the son of Lady Dalmore has inherited her discriminating eye, for nothing could be more enchanting for mademoiselle with those unusual eyes and your skin as fair as the *soi-disant* English rose. In fact, most clear bold colors will be flattering to your coloring."

"B . . . but are not pastel colors all the fashion at present, Madame Simone?" Abigail asked timidly, twisting her head around to follow the modiste's movements as she circled her chemise-clad client, assessing posture and figure with a critical eye.

"Yes," she replied with a dismissive wave, "and all the sheep will follow where the bold lead. You, Mlle. Monroe, although too petite for true elegance, have the perfect proportions, coloring, and carriage to stand out from the sheep, but only if you wish it here"—Madame tapped her temple with an index finger—"and here"—with a hand over her heart, *"vous comprenez?"* She gave the hesitant girl a shrewd look and added slyly, "Lord Edgeworth seems not to prefer the sheep, *n'est-ce pas?*"

Abigail's eyes flashed pure purple, but she stifled the urge to confide her utter indifference to Lord Edgeworth's opinion on females, sheep or any other subject. She mustered a smile and said casually, "Come to think of it, Madame, I don't much care for sheep either."

Madame Simone smiled. "*Bien,* then I think we shall design a carriage dress in this emerald poplin and a morning gown of sapphire cotton. Of course one evening dress must be white, *n'est-ce pas,* and is there a color *you* favor, Mlle. Monroe?"

"I have always liked yellow because it is such a happy color," Abigail offered.

"*Très bien,* but not too pale, I think. Yes, a buttercup muslin for daytime, for a garden party, *peut-être,* will be a happy choice."

"Do you think I will require so many dresses for a short visit?" Abigail asked, uneasily aware of the swiftly mounting cost, although she realized that nothing so vulgar as price would be mentioned between Madame Simone and herself.

The modiste assured her that she was merely acting on Lord Edgeworth's expressed wishes in the matter. She showed Abigail several sketches of styles that would make the most of her attractions. "Are you in your first Season, Mlle. Monroe?"

"I am of legal age, Madame, though people often think me younger because of my size." Abigail hoped her apparent candor would discourage further probing into her status in society.

"*Ça c'est bien.* Now we may cut the décolletage a trifle lower for the evening dresses. You must of course avoid the . . . the embellishments around the waist that will make you appear shorter. We shall always aim for a straight fall of color and simple lines. Any embellishment will be confined to the hem or the sleeves, *d'accord?*"

"Yes, madame," Abigail replied meekly.

When she emerged from the back premises after nearly an hour, Abigail was supplied with samples of the fabrics they had chosen for her new gowns to assist her in selecting hats and gloves to complement the outfits. The front of the shop was deserted, but before she'd had time to wonder what had become of her brother and his creditor, the men reentered the shop.

"Have you been on the toddle with the other Bond Street beaux?" she asked her brother with a mischievous smile.

"We have been engaged in research," Lord Edgeworth replied loftily. "We discovered no fewer than three milliners' shops in the immediate vicinity, but agreed, did we not, Roland, that the ladies emerging from Celeste's seemed to possess a certain *je ne sais quoi* that the others lacked, or at least their headgear did. So, if you are finished here, we will repair to Celeste's to augment that attractive straw hat you are wearing."

For a time, away from his overbearing company and dazed by the sensuous appeal of the lovely fabrics at Madame Simone's, Abigail had come close to forgetting her invidious position vis-à-vis Lord Edgeworth. By the time they left the milliner's, leaving an order for a bonnet to be made up in the emerald poplin and bearing away a villager straw with yellow ribbons, resentment at being treated like a piece of furniture to be polished and displayed for the critical evaluation of the *ton* had risen into her throat, rendering attempts at speech unwise if she was to fulfill her resolution to bear herself like a lady despite the provocation. The viscount might talk glibly of satisfying the proprieties and safeguarding her reputation, but she *knew* that behind their politeness to a valued client, Madame Simone and Celeste must be avidly speculating on her respectability and the nature of her relationship with Lord Edgeworth. Her pride was chafed raw, exacerbated by the sight of her brother, so far from appreciating her mortifying position as to be taken in by the facile good humor being expended on them by the viscount. Roly was positively enjoying himself in Edgeworth's company. She herself was immune to the viscount's brand of charm, a situation that, in the light of the role she had been cast for in his distasteful deception, was fortunate for her peace of mind.

Abigail and Roland had set off for London filled with the same apprehension that morning. By the time they arrived back at Broadlands in late afternoon, the attitudes with which they approached the immediate future had diverged so widely as to negate the natural empathy that generally existed between them. Abigail had not felt so abysmally lonely since her mother's death.

Chapter Four

What Roland Monroe in the privacy of his sister's morning room impudently termed the "Great Deception" was nearly scuttled before launching. When informed of the flattering invitation to his children to visit the seat of the Earl of Dalmore, their father's immediate response was not gratification but a flat denial of permission, at least for Abigail.

"I may not be able to control your brother's gaddings any longer, but no daughter of mine is going to truckle to a set of stiff-rumped nobs. You'll be nothing but an object of condescension to them, no matter their son has struck up an acquaintance with Roland," Lucius Monroe said bitterly. "Look at that bunch your mother came from. A gentleman's son wasn't good enough for their daughter. No, she was destined for a sprig of the nobility, although no one had ever seen the lout sober after eleven in the morning. When she stood up to them and followed her heart, they cut her off without a second thought. Not one word did she have from a single member of her so-called family from the day she married me, and the downright cruelty of it killed her in the end. She wasted away from the pain of it. You should have more pride than to wish to go among that sort."

Spurred by a vision of her precious scent bottle receding beyond her grasp, Abigail mounted a spirited argument, disingenuously pointing out that the invitation itself was proof that the viscount's family wasn't like her unknown grandparents.

This argument cut no ice with her father and the matter might have remained at a standstill had not Roland been inspired to tell his parent that Lord Edgeworth was searching for a matched pair or even a team to pull his newly commissioned phaeton. Family pride was all well and good, but the family business took precedence in the end. Mr. Monroe conceded the foolhardiness of offending a potential customer and grudgingly admitted that a few days at a country estate was not likely to corrupt his daughter or ruin her life. If she chose to expose herself to the condescension of those who falsely considered themselves her betters, it might prove a salutary experience and cure her of wishing to go among the nobility in the future.

With the biggest hurdle now surmounted, it was Abigail herself who created the next complication. As per their prior arrangement, Roland brought his sister into town in Percy's curricle for a fitting of her new clothes and another round of shopping for shoes and accessories to complete the various outfits.

The session at the dressmaker's went smoothly, and Abigail left the shop floating on a cloud of feminine contentment created by the novel experience of seeing herself dressed in beautiful clothes. Brother and sister set about the rest of their errands in harmony, but the contented haze dissipated as it was gradually borne in upon the young woman that the sums of money Roland was expending on the growing stack of packages in his arms had been provided by Lord Edgeworth. Once she had agreed to the viscount's outrageous conditions for returning her property, she'd accepted the necessity of dressing for the role assigned her, at least in theory. Seeing the actual disbursement of funds, however, gave her a nasty jolt, and she became more subdued as the number of purchases mounted.

By the time she and Roland arrived at the viscount's residence as arranged, the glow that had animated Abigail's features was long gone and she was struggling to master the resentment her unequal position with respect to Lord Edgeworth always sparked in her. She returned his friendly greeting with a stiff formality that earned her a searching look, though he made no comment.

When the threesome was settled in the drawing room and supplied with sherry, tea, and cakes by the efficient

Jenkins, Lord Edgeworth directed a smiling glance at the welter of packages reposing on a side table. "Obviously you have had a successful shopping expedition. I trust your curricle will be able to accommodate the results on your drive home."

Abigail set down the cup she was raising to her lips and stared at him in disbelief. "You cannot possibly suppose that I intend to take these things home with me!" she cried.

"Actually, I confess I did suppose it," Edgeworth admitted and waited for enlightenment.

Abigail obliged him without delay. "I beg leave to tell you, sir, that my father was extremely reluctant to grant permission for this visit to your home. I smuggled the straw bonnet into the house last time, but I have no intention of taking even one more item home with me. What do you suppose he would say if he saw his daughter with a new wardrobe he had not provided? What would he *think?* I'd rather lose my scent bottle forever than try to explain—"

"Enough!" Lord Edgeworth held up a hand, his face a frowning mask of concentration. "I do see the problem and apologize for my obtuseness, Miss Monroe. I can see that the travel arrangements I was about to propose will not do in the circumstances."

"And what is more, I have no intention of keeping any of these clothes when this charade is done," Abigail declared, spoiling for a quarrel.

The disobliging viscount refused to take up her challenge. "You are free to dispose of them any way you choose," he agreed calmly. "Have you instructed Mme. Simone and Celeste to deliver the gowns and hats to this address?"

"Yes."

"Very well. I had intended to send a post chaise to fetch you and Roland—"

"Er . . ." Roland cleared his throat and began again. "I . . . I believe my father rather expects to meet the person with whom my sister will be traveling, sir."

Lord Edgeworth's eyes swung from the apologetic mien of the young man to the young woman's half-defiant, half-haughty expression while he mentally altered his plans. "Very well then. I'll send my batman on ahead to a posting inn with your wardrobe and my horse. I'll come to Broadlands to meet your father and collect you two—you'd better stuff a couple of portmanteaux with rags or something," he said in an aside to Abigail. "When we meet up with Gibbs you can change at the inn and repack your portmanteaux. We'll bring your mounts with us, or you may take your chances on the Oakridge stable, though I cannot vouch for what is there after an absence of four years. Does this arrangement solve all our difficulties for the moment?"

Roland smiled in relief, and Abigail tried and failed to find an objection. She nodded at the viscount and sent a wordless message to her brother indicating it was time they left. As she rose from her chair, her host said casually, "By the way, my name is Max. You might try practicing it in front of your mirror so it will come readily to your lips while you are at Oakridge."

Abigail gave him a cool glance and pursed those same lips, saying nothing.

"Do you prefer that I address you as Abigail or Gail?" he persisted, his eyes on her mouth.

"Whatever you wish," she replied with a tiny shrug.

"You had better practice smiling while you are about it too, Miss Monroe, for I am serious when I say I wish everyone at Oakridge to believe in this betrothal."

"Have no fear, Lord Edgeworth. While I am at Oakridge I shall make a habit of showing all my teeth in company and I'll hang on your every word as if it were a pearl of wisdom." While Roland searched for a couple of his own purchases among all the bundles, Abigail clasped her hands in front of her breast and fluttered her long lashes, casting a look of mock adoration up at her host.

The viscount burst out laughing and took her chin between his thumb and forefinger, pinching gently before releasing her. "Do not overdo it—you want to look besotted, not simple-minded."

Abigail opened her eyes very wide. "But surely they are the same thing! One must be simple-minded to become besotted with a man," she said sweetly.

The viscount's eyes narrowed, and the smile left his mouth. "A provocative assertion, ma'am, and one that could spark an interesting discussion at a more convenient time. We must resume this little chat on the drive to Sussex."

Roland, unaware of this passage at arms, had finally succeeded in locating his belongings. Good-byes were exchanged, and the twins parted from the viscount, one animated by pleasurable anticipation, the other battling a pervasive apprehension that she could not quite define or articulate.

Three days later in one of the White Hart's best bedchambers Abigail tenderly removed the emerald green bonnet from its nest of tissue paper and placed it atop her dusky curls. By standing on tiptoe in front of the small glass hanging above the washstand she could see her head, the exquisitely pleated neck ruff of white organdie, and below it an inch or two of the bodice of her carriage dress. With Celeste's instructions replaying in her ears, she labored to tie the bonnet's broad satin ribbon the exact shade of the poplin gown in a large bow under one ear before stepping back to increase the proportion of her form visible in the inadequate mirror.

Even to her anxious and critical eye the transformation was amazing. The wide brim of the bonnet, cunningly lined in the same pleated white organdie filling in the neckline of the gown, made a flattering frame for her dark hair and complemented the simple lines of the skirt falling straight to her feet in soft folds. Abigail marveled at the artistry that could turn her small person into this passable facsimile of a fashionable female. She did not look like her everyday self any longer, a conclusion both encouraging and unnerving, and one she had no time to dwell on at present.

She didn't feel like herself either, Abigail decided as she set about packing the garments she had taken from the stack of boxes awaiting her when she'd entered this room after a drive of about two hours—two nearly silent hours on her part—in the company of her brother and the enigmatic man who had declared himself her putative fiancé for the purpose of throwing sand in his family's eyes. Come to think of it, she had begun to feel unlike herself much earlier—or perhaps outside of herself would be a more precise description—observing the events of the morning as a disengaged party.

Her father had fallen under this sharpened observation first. After wearing a face like a thundercloud all week, her parent had appeared at her bedchamber door early this morning and thrust twenty pounds into her hand, declaring gruffly that no child of his was going to find herself in the mortifying position of being unable to give vails to the servants or play at silver loo for an hour or two if such games should be offered as entertainment to the guests at Oakridge. With the pile of worn linens she had been about to stuff into her portmanteaux on view on the bed behind her, Abigail had been nearly overset by a rush of remorse as her eyes filled with tears and she threw her arms around her father's neck, murmuring incoherent thanks.

"There, there, puss, you're a good girl," the poor man had muttered, patting her awkwardly on the back. "See that you do nothing to shame your mother's training," he'd cautioned, recovering himself again as he put her away from him and strode off without another word.

All in all, it had been one of the strangest mornings of her life. She had greeted Lord Edgeworth in the main reception room, sitting stiff-backed and poker-faced, ashamed of her home's shabbiness but determined to make no apologies. The viscount had treated her with cool formality, but later when, accompanied by Roland, they arrived at the stables, he had instantly become a model of affability. She could not fault the easy manner with which he met her father and elder brother, despite harboring a disposition to do so, and the sensible terms in which he'd couched his admiration for the stable setup at Broadlands carried no undertone of condescension even to her hypersensitive ears. She'd been surprised at the depth of her relief at seeing the men deal together so easily and had been conscious of a spurt of pleasure at Lord Edgeworth's unstinting praise of her own mount.

"What a perfectly beautiful little lady," he'd said spontaneously when a groom had led Dolly and Mozart, her brother's chestnut gelding, into the yard. He patted the bay mare's glossy neck after casting a knowledgeable eye over her conformation. "Did you breed her, sir?" he'd inquired of Mr. Monroe.

"No, we breed carriage horses here at Broadlands. I traded one of ours for the thoroughbred when she was just a filly. The man who bred her found her a bit too small for his liking, but I knew she'd be perfect for Abigail, not that my daughter cannot handle a half ton of horseflesh as well as most men," her father had added with what had sounded almost like pride to his astounded daughter.

"I look forward to seeing Miss Monroe in the saddle," the viscount had said with a bow and a friendly smile in her direction.

That had been the first and last such gesture toward her so far, and of course it had been made to please her father, whose previous remark had rather invited something of that nature, Abigail mused as she removed her handkerchief, money, and a small packet of pins from her old reticule and deposited them in the green poplin pouch Madame Simone had produced from her workroom as a surprise gift. With the green kid half boots they'd had made, her outfit was now complete to a shade. Despite her strong disinclination to participate in the charade Lord Edgeworth proposed, Abigail could not in honesty deny a thrill of pure feminine satisfaction as she drew on a pair of white gloves, although she conquered the unworthy impulse to preen in front of the mirror again.

A knock sounded on the door just as she closed the straps on the second portmanteau. "Enter," she called over her shoulder, turning back to swing the bag off the bed. Abigail straightened up and met Lord Edgeworth's stare with a self-possession born of the knowledge that her appearance today would do any man credit. She willed her eyes not to importune his approval as the moment stretched beyond what was comfortable. When it came to breaking off contact, however, her eyes resisted her will, foolishly blind to the danger her intellect detected in the dark depths of his, held captive by some unfathomable message therein. Abruptly, he shifted his gaze, leaving her . . . bereft? No, not that—relieved—she assured herself quickly, forcing utter stillness on her quivering nerves. She felt touched in the wind, as though she had just run up two flights of stairs.

His scrutiny was sharp as he took in every aspect of her appearance, but his words were casual, almost careless. "Very nice. Madame Simone has not lost her flair while I was away; she has bestowed a touch of town bronze on the little country mouse."

"I trust we make a fashionable enough pair to create

the picture you desire to present, Lord Edgeworth," she responded lightly, veiling her disappointment at a compliment that was all for the modiste. Suddenly she noticed that he carried a small wooden casket as he came forward.

"This is for you, Abigail." It was the first time he had addressed her by her given name, and it sounded odd on his lips, certainly more personal than the compliment on her appearance.

"Thank you, M . . . Max," she replied, accepting the box he held out to her. "Shall I open it now?"

"Please."

She removed the lid from the box and looked inside. Abigail stood entirely still for a few seconds, her lips forming a soundless O, and then her eyes sought his. "My scent bottle," she whispered. "I . . . I did not expect . . ." Her voice died away as her eyes clung to his, overwhelmed by the generosity of the gesture.

"A girl ought to have her scent bottle with her when she goes visiting," he said, making light of the situation. "Open it." He reached for the lid of the box, freeing her right hand. She disinterred the bottle from its snug velvet nest, surprised at the weight and almost unaware that he had taken the casket into his own hands. She pulled one of the pair of dove-topped stoppers out of the bottle and inhaled deeply.

"Oh, this is heavenly! Thank you so much, Max," she cried, tears sparkling on thick black lashes as she looked up into his watchful face again, dimly conscious that the grooves in his lean cheeks had smoothed out and the dark grey eyes had lightened to pewter.

"A girl ought to have a full scent bottle with her when she goes visiting," he declared in careless accents. "Now if we are to reach Oakridge in time to dress for dinner, we had best have a nuncheon and be on our way." He turned away from her, laying the casket and lid on the washstand before walking over to pick up her portmanteaux.

Still in a daze, Abigail restored the precious bottle to its new home and replaced the casket's lid while he waited at the door, an air of faint impatience hanging over him now.

Apprehension over the first meeting between her prickly father and Lord Edgeworth had reined in Abigail's healthy appetite this morning, but suddenly she was feeling rather peckish. There was a bit of a bounce in her step as she accompanied the viscount down to the private dining parlor his man had reserved for their use.

"At last," Roland said, springing out of a Windsor chair set near the fireplace as his sister and her escort entered the room. "I've had to exert the strictest self-discipline to keep my hands off that roast chicken."

"When did you develop self-discipline around roast chicken, or any other food for that matter?" Abigail asked, opening her eyes wide. "Do I see a chunk missing below this leg?" Anticipating her twin's defense, she continued without pause, "This looks very nice indeed," passing the darned but sparkling white table cover, the pewter serving dishes, and the thick but unchipped plates under swift review. Like the bedchamber assigned to her, this room was plainly but adequately furnished and surprisingly clean. "Everything smells marvelous too," she finished with a smile at Lord Edgeworth who was waiting to seat her at the table.

"Speaking of looking and smelling good," Roland interjected, having by now had ample time to take in his sister's changed appearance, "you are certainly looking as fine as fivepence in that new rig and you smell almost as inviting as that chicken."

Abigail chuckled at the comparison but sobered immediately. "A vast multiple of fivepence, I fear," she said, turning a rueful face to the viscount. "I cannot feel comfortable about accepting this expensive wardrobe, sir. It covers me with shame."

"We have had this discussion before," Edgeworth replied impatiently. "Think of the clothes as the costumes of an actress, an essential part of the role you will be playing, and stop 'sirring' me or you will give the whole show away. *That* would cover us with shame indeed."

"*I* see! It is not shame-making to practice deception on one's family, as long as the deception is not discovered."

"Brat," the viscount said mildly. "Is she always this argumentative?" he asked Roland.

Abigail's loving brother grinned. "It has frequently been noted in the family that Gail is not timid about expressing her opinion on any topic that arises, no matter how unpopular that opinion might be expected to be."

"It had previously occurred to me that under her deceptively demure exterior lurks the soul of a gladiator," Lord Edgeworth agreed.

"Did no one ever tell you two that it is highly uncivil to discuss someone as if that person were not present?" Abigail protested indignantly.

"Thank you for pointing out our breach of civility," Edgeworth returned. "In future we shall only discuss you in your absence as per your wishes." As Abigail tilted her chin and looked down her straight little nose at him, he picked up the carving tools from the table, assuming the mien of one whose privilege and joy it was to serve others. "May I offer you some chicken?"

"Yes, please, I am famished," Abigail replied, abandoning her haughty pose as the delicious aromas coming from the dishes on the table made her mouth water.

The trio did full justice to the inn's culinary offerings over the next half hour. By the time they rose from the table, their depredations had reduced the succulent chicken to a small pile of bones and they'd made heavy inroads on the vegetables and side dishes also. Abigail so enjoyed the give and take of conversation that accompanied the meal that she did not realize until she recalled it to mind afterward that the luncheon interval at the White Hart marked the first time she and Lord Edgeworth had dealt together without restraint and resentment on her part.

As they reentered the carriage for the second part of the journey, she was still uncomfortable with the basic falsity of the situation, but she acknowledged a tiny thrill of excitement at the prospect of adventure ahead. It was at that moment that she made the deliberate decision to direct all the energy and wit at her command into playing the part of a newly betrothed girl so that her brother's creditor should have no just cause to complain of the manner in which she kept her part of their strange bargain.

From under lazy lids Max surveyed the Monroe twins seated opposite him in the carriage. The constraint that had attended the early stage of their acquaintance, understandable—indeed unavoidable—given the unpropitious circumstances of his meeting with Roland and the even stranger, almost farcical episode that had thrust Abigail Monroe through a window into his life, had gradually lessened at subsequent meetings and had entirely vanished from the moment they had entered the chaise after lunch today. He had found them entertaining companions, enjoying their reactions to the passing scene and the incidents they had related about their childhood in response to his questions. He'd noticed that often one would begin a sentence and the other would finish the thought, and he'd wondered if this mental attunement was peculiar to twins or was shared by other siblings, arising perhaps from their common experiences in a family, something he, as an only child, knew nothing of. He rather envied them their closeness in adulthood, though he could not recall wishing for brothers and sisters as a child.

Individually, the Monroes were attractive young people, well-mannered, intelligent, and conversable. Their twinship imparted an added dimension to their attractiveness. He'd seen that in close proximity they sparked interest and curiosity from those with whom they came in contact. This should work to his advantage in his scheme to foist them onto his family as the girl he planned to marry and his prospective brother-in-law.

Abigail had done herself a disservice in declaring no one would believe he'd fallen in love with someone like her, especially in such a short period of time. Dressed with exquisite taste by Mme. Simone to enhance her beautiful eyes and striking coloring, she was lovely enough today to make the appellation "pocket Venus" not altogether inapt. Given reasonably convincing performances by Abigail and himself, the houseguests at Oakridge should have no reason to doubt the evidence of their eyes. Convincing his father that he'd fallen in love in the span of a fortnight would not be so simple, however, and as for Felicity . . . Max's lips firmed as a mental picture of his lovely stepmother clinging to his arm and smiling intimately up at him flashed across his inner eye. It would be idle to expect that persuading his erstwhile fiancée that he was in love with another woman was anything other than an exercise in futility. Absent any other reason, vanity would be sufficient to keep Felicity from believing he had stopped loving her. She had not been convinced of his indifference during their encounter at Mrs. Cathcart's soirée, and he suspected her high estimation of her power to enslave would be proof against the appearance of the original Venus, let alone the "pocket" variety.

Max's gaze was fixed on the window of the carriage, but the turmoil in his head blinded him to the countryside through which they were driving. He had never intended to go down to Oakridge so close upon his return to England. For four years he'd avoided thinking about the situation there, deliberately shutting off the flow of memory and recrimination whenever they invaded his thoughts. It had been cowardly of him, of course, and he'd always known he'd have to confront his feelings sooner or later. In the deep recesses of his mind, he'd accepted that there must be a reckoning before he saw his father or Felicity again, but first he needed to take care of the practical details of starting life all over again as a civilian.

Meeting Felicity within hours of arriving in London had been akin to walking unarmed into an ambush. He'd been unable to stand his ground in the face of her offensive tactics. His grace period for reflection, adjustment, and determining his future posture vis-à-vis his father and stepmother had been as good as snatched from him, but it was unjust to lay all the blame for his present discomfort at Felicity's door when *his* only constructive action so far had been to bully a harmless young woman into becoming a human shield behind which to continue hiding. Coercing Abigail Monroe into posing as his affianced wife had been a contemptible piece of cowardice, he could see that now, but it had been an act of desperation. He could not trust Felicity to smooth his reentry into his family home—worse still, he did not know whether he could trust himself to strike the right note that would allow a minimum of future contact and still preserve an illusion of family harmony before the world. Meanwhile his ostensible role as a newly betrothed man would mandate his spending a great deal of time with Abigail, which had the advantage of reducing the amount of time he could spend in his father's or Felicity's company.

He must not allow himself to become blue-devilled, he urged his pusillanimous alter ego bracingly. Perhaps it was not absolutely inevitable that the long, unacknowledged rupture in the ties of affection that had bound him to his father in the past would become open and permanent. Assuming he could have been brought to speculate on that question four years ago, he would have said it did not signify. His presence in this carriage at this moment testified that this at least was no longer true.

At about the same time he recognized a set of elegant wrought iron gates surmounted by a pair of unicorns, Max became aware that the occasional spurts of conversation between brother and sister had ceased entirely in the last few minutes while he had been indulging his own private worries. Turning away from the window, he found both of his guests eyeing him rather tentatively.

Summoning up a smile, Max said, "We are not far from Oakridge now. Those handsome gates we just passed belong to our nearest neighbors. We shall begin to ascend shortly. Oakridge is situated on a slight rise and looks out to the South Downs."

"That must be a lovely prospect," Abigail said, her face alight with anticipation.

"It is." Conscious of relief that her misgivings about their charade were forgotten for the moment, Max tried to infuse some warmth into his voice. "The house is far enough away to appreciate a long sweeping curve of the Downs and not so near that they loom over the area. Lewes, which is a very pleasant town, is close enough to make a good destination for a ride, and Chichester is within reach if you are interested, though there is not much to see of its Roman remains."

"That sounds marvelous," Roland enthused. "Imagine standing on the spot where the Romans built their houses and temples and baths."

"If you are interested in the Roman presence in Sussx, my father has a number of works in his library that he will be delighted to have you peruse, Roland. He is something of an authority on the subject and welcomes the opportunity to converse with fellow enthusiasts."

"You have told us nothing at all about your family, Max, although Roly and I have prattled on about our childhood like bagpipes," Abigail said suddenly. "Are you much like your father? Do you have brothers and sisters? I gathered from what Mme. Simone said that you were used to escort your mother to her establishment. Has she been deceased long? What is your stepmother like? Or perhaps your father has married since you left for the Continent?" she added, as a thought occurred to her. "Perhaps you are not even acquainted with your stepmother?"

Max could feel his features freezing at the spate of questions and forced himself to smile and respond in a casual manner. "Actually, my father did remarry shortly after I left England four years ago, but I am acquainted with my stepmother. My mother died six years ago after a brief illness, and yes, I am held to resemble my father in looks." Glancing at Roland, he said, "We are now on Oakridge land. The stand of trees from which the name derives is behind the house. When we go through the gates up ahead we'll circle around the carriage drive to the south front so you may see the sweep of the Downs from the main entrance. Gibbs will be behind us to unload the rest of the baggage before taking the horses to the stables."

Max let down the window to call directions to the postilions. When he sat back again, he had his countenance under a rigid control that did not extend to his nerves, rapid pulse, or dry throat. Fortunately for his peace of mind, these involuntary functions would not be visible to the two young people he was about to introduce into his family.

The play was about to begin.

Chapter Five

Oakridge was beautiful with the late afternoon sun gilding the grey stone and bouncing off acres of windows, but it would be beautiful in any light.

The two thoughts—convictions—instantly formed in Abigail's mind upon her first glimpse of Lord Edgeworth's home from the curving carriage drive. Her eyes widened and her lips parted in a soundless sigh as she gazed upon the large Tudor structure, unsymmetrical in its present incarnation, but with the E-shaped configuration common to Elizabethan dwellings still clearly discernible in the wings at each end and the projecting central bay. The enormously tall mullioned windows on the left of the entrance must delineate the original hall, and she guessed that the smaller projections on either side most likely were stairwells. Her eyes roved over the complex roof line with its crenellation and profusion of chimneys, then lingered on the lovely oriel window over the entrance in the central projection before turning to her ostensible betrothed, who was watching her with a faint smile on his lips and a question in his eyes.

"Your home is magnificent, Max," she said.

"And yet it *is* a home," he replied, smiling at her, "or at least it was."

She had no opportunity to ponder this odd rider as the viscount turned to include her brother in a brief phrase of welcome, and by now she could feel the carriage slowing to a halt in front of the central portico.

Lord Edgeworth had the door open and had leapt down from the carriage before the postilions had time to dismount. He was about to assist his guests when his attention was drawn to a rotund figure hurrying down the steps ahead of two uniformed footmen.

"Wilkins!" he cried in what Abigail could only call a whoop, spinning around to offer his hand to the portly man whose dignity remained intact despite his haste. "It's wonderful to see you again."

"And if I may say so, sir, it is a great pleasure to welcome you home. His lordship will be so pleased."

Peeking out of the open carriage door, Abigail could see that the butler's smiling countenance—if her guess as to the identity of the neatly dressed individual wringing Max's hand was correct—echoed the delight in his voice. She'd had the curious impression that Max looked almost as young as Roly when he'd greeted Wilkins, but she must have been mistaken, for when he took her hand to help her down a moment later he looked his usual cool, slightly aloof self, although she did detect a new shade of warmth in his voice when he named Roland and herself to the butler as soon as both Monroes were out of the carriage.

Gibbs had now arrived in the second carriage. While Wilkins was deploying his underlings to unload the carriages and take the three hacks to the stables, Lord Edgeworth seized Abigail's hand and walked her briskly along the drive until they had passed the team of horses, whereupon he stopped, quirked an eyebrow at her puzzled face, and stepped back, nudging her forward.

"Look," he commanded.

Abigail tore her eyes from his, alight with excitement, and obeyed. "Oh!" she gasped and fell silent.

Before her lay a smooth green lawn widening into a park dotted here and there with mature trees, and beyond the park stretched a vista that included a stream in the middle ground with a ribbon of road on its far side traveling with it for a distance before diverging toward the curving range of hills that blended into the South Downs. The sky was an intense cloudless blue overhead with an extraordinary clarity that increased the panorama available to Abigail's rapt gaze. Lord Edgeworth was a silent presence beside her, but the utilitarian noises attending the unloading of their baggage had ceased to reach her.

The first extraneous sound to pierce Abigail's enchantment was a feminine voice, high-pitched with excitement. "Max, you're here at last! Why did you not tell us when to expect you, you inconsiderate creature?"

Reluctantly, Abigail turned from her contemplation of the soul-satisfying perfection that was the view from Oakridge to have her eyes filled with perfection of another sort in the person of the young woman who rushed past her without a glance to throw her arms around Max's neck. Conscious that she was staring at what was, after all, a private greeting, Abigail slid her eyes from the handsome couple to her brother's face, unsurprised to find Roly's gaze fixed on the blond beauty in dazed admiration. Was she Max's sister perhaps? Did Max *have* a sister? Abigail recalled asking that very question just before their arrival, but could not recall that he had answered it.

The viscount suffered the young woman's embrace briefly, putting her away from him with his hands on her upper arms. A flush appeared on his cheeks beneath the deep tan, but his voice was expressionless as he said, "Hello, Felicity. I fear my plans were not completed until yesterday, so it would have served no purpose to write. I trust I have not inconvenienced you?"

"Of course not. And you have brought guests with you. How lovely." The beautiful young woman transferred her smiling attention to the silent pair flanking the viscount.

"Yes. Felicity, may I present Miss Abigail Monroe and her brother, Mr. Roland Monroe?" The viscount's eyes met Abigail's as he added blandly, "This is my stepmother, Lady Dalmore."

Abigail's gasp was, unfortunately, quite audible to Lady Dalmore, who arched a delicate eyebrow. "Is something wrong, Miss Monroe?"

"N . . . no, ma'am. I beg your pardon," Abigail said, her cheeks burning. "M . . . Max told us his father remarried while he was in the Peninsular, but we . . . I was expecting someone . . ."

"Yes, Miss Monroe?" Lady Dalmore prompted, still smiling, though her blue eyes were cool. "You were expecting someone . . . ?"

"Someone more . . . more motherly," Abigail blurted, miserably aware of compounding her gaucherie. Despite her acute embarrassment, however, there was a tiny spark of anger igniting somewhere deep inside her at her putative fiancé, who might have spared her this scene by mentioning the interesting fact that his stepmother was younger than he was.

Lady Dalmore produced a silvery trill of laughter. "But I *am* a mother, you delightfully absurd child," she said gaily. "Did Max not tell you he has a little sister? Lady Rose is three years old. You shall meet her presently."

"I fear I have been very remiss in not supplying Roland and Abigail with Oakridge's current history," Edgeworth interjected, sounding not the least bit apologetic to a simmering Abigail. "My excuse must be that we have had subjects of a more personal nature to occupy us lately. You are mistaken, my dear Felicity, in deeming Miss Monroe a child, either delightful or absurd. She is in fact just two years your junior . . . and my affianced wife."

It did not escape Abigail's notice that her just-proclaimed fiancé was looking at his stepmother rather than at the supposed object of his affections as he made his announcement, though he had groped for her hand during the speech and she, recognizing her entrance cue, had allowed him to take it in the interest of establishing verisimilitude.

If Edgeworth had hoped to disconcert Lady Dalmore, and Abigail's intuition told her that this was indeed his object, his stepmother's reaction must have sorely disappointed him. Lady Dalmore's eyes had narrowed as she listened to her stepson's initial apology, and her lowered lashes veiled their expression for a brief moment, but by the time he pronounced himself betrothed, she was all amazed delight.

"What a lovely surprise!" she exclaimed, beaming a smile at the hand-fast pair before her. "And it must have happened so quickly too, since Max has been back in England barely a fortnight. Or perhaps," she added, addressing Abigail, "you met before Max went into the army?"

"No," Lord Edgeworth said before Abigail could open her lips. "Roland and I met on my first night back in London, and he introduced me to his sister the next day."

"Ah, so you played the role of Cupid, Mr. Monroe?" Lady Dalmore said, turning her brilliant smile on the young man who had been a mere supernumerary up to this point.

"You give me too much credit, Lady Dalmore," Roland said, returning her smile with interest. "I was no more than the occasion of their meeting."

"I am persuaded you are too modest in assessing your role, Mr. Monroe," his hostess declared before turning back to her stepson, "but however the happy event came about, you must allow me to be the first to congratulate you, Max—I am the first, I trust—on winning such a charming bride." It was now Abigail's turn to be the recipient of the countess's beaming benevolence. "And the first to offer my felicitations, Miss Monroe, except for your family, of course. You must tell me all about your family very soon, but for the moment we had best attend to your accommodations.

"I see all the baggage has been removed from the carriages and the postilions are about to depart. You'll have your old rooms, of course, Max, and Mr. Monroe may have the room across the hall from yours. As for your fiancée, most of the more popular guest chambers have already been allocated, but"—Lady Dalmore seemed to have an inspiration—"perhaps you would like to have the Queen's room? Not Elizabeth, I regret to say, but her mother, before she became Henry's consort, is believed to have visited

Oakridge, and this chamber has been referred to as the Queen's room ever since." Lady Dalmore paused to look questioningly at her unexpected guest, who dutifully murmured her pleasure at the assignment while noting with curiosity the rather wry amusement on her alleged fiancé's face.

The butler was approaching the group, doubtless seeking orders about the disposition of the baggage to pass on to the footmen. "Ah, Wilkins," said Lady Dalmore, "you may send Miss Monroe's abigail up to the Queen's—why, I don't believe I noticed your woman, Miss Monroe. Did she go inside earlier?"

"I do not have a maid, ma'am," Abigail replied quietly, meeting her hostess's questioning eyes with a composure she was far from feeling.

"No abigail? Well, no matter. Should you require assistance in dressing, the housekeeper will send one of the housemaids to you."

"Thank you, ma'am," Abigail said, but she vowed on the spot that she would die before making such a request. She kept her expression pleasant with an effort while Lady Dalmore informed Wilkins of the room assignments.

Edgeworth had apparently forgotten that he still held her hand. Abigail gave a surreptitious tug that, far from securing her release, caused him to increase the pressure of his clasp. Glancing up, she found him regarding her in a manner that somehow provided understanding and comfort, and her lips curved upward in response.

Lady Dalmore, having dispatched Wilkins to his duties, smiled brightly at the new arrivals. "The guest rooms at Oakridge are always kept in a state of readiness," she assured them, linking a slender white hand under the elbow of each man in a playfully proprietorial fashion as she started forward. Abigail, caught by surprise, was pulled along by the hand her betrothed refused to relinquish.

The countess, in her role of hostess, continued to expound as she guided her captives past the door into an entrance hall. "The men are still out riding, I believe, but our female guests have retired to their rooms to change for dinner. The maids will bring hot water to your rooms, of course, but I have had a bathing chamber installed, since your time, Max," she added unnecessarily, "for the convenience of our guests. Please feel free to refresh yourself after a weary day of traveling, Miss Monroe. Oh, here is Mrs. Howell, who will conduct you to the Queen's room. Max, you will show Mr. Monroe to his quarters, will you not?"

Lady Dalmore was forced to wait until her stepson had greeted the beaming housekeeper with a warm handshake and a prolonged inquiry into her present health and happiness. Abigail noticed that the countess's lips had tightened for an instant when Max took it upon himself to perform the introductions, naming herself as his betrothed to Mrs. Howell, whose welcoming smile grew even wider at this news.

"We shall all meet in the gold saloon at half six," Lady Dalmore informed her guests as soon as Abigail had acknowledged the housekeeper's good wishes with a soft thank-you.

"Er, do I know the gold saloon, Felicity?" the viscount asked, his brows raised.

"How foolish of me," his stepmother replied with a light laugh. "It used to be the reception room with the Chinese wallpaper and all that Queen Anne furniture. You may show Miss Monroe to her room now, Mrs. Howell."

Thus dismissed, Abigail dipped her forehead in acknowledgment and would have followed the housekeeper immediately had not the viscount taken her hand again and raised it to his lips, saying softly, "Until later, my dear." He took his time about releasing her while Abigail blushed furiously under the approving eye of Mrs. Howell, conscious that her hostess's expression was not of the same order of indulgence. She turned away and followed in Mrs. Howell's wake through a large room to a staircase, feeling for no legitimate reason rather like a foundling left on the church steps.

By the time the housekeeper, still puffing from the climb, opened the door to the bedchamber assigned to her, Abigail had lost any sense of where she was in the complex system of corridors at Oakridge. They had met no living soul on the journey, nor had any sounds of human occupation reached their ears. The sense of strangeness and isolation was not dissipated by her first glimpse of the Queen's room when Mrs. Howell stepped back and waved her inside.

"It is a beautiful room," she said dutifully, smiling at the complacent housekeeper, who nodded.

"Yes, all the ladies who visit Oakridge wish to see where the poor queen slept, not that the furnishings date that far back, except for the tapestries. Over the years a number of guests have asked to have this room during their stay, although there is no bell rope here. Their maids usually sleep in the small room next this. As you do not have your maid with you, I'll send one of the housemaids up to wait on you. Mavis is a good willing girl, though a bit of a chatterbox, and she has aspirations to become a dresser. I'll say this for her, she does have a knack for dressing hair—she is forever practicing on the other maids. She will be thrilled to do your hair, Miss Monroe, so thick and glossy as it is," Mrs. Howell added, watching as Abigail, having removed her gloves, now took off the green bonnet and ran her fingers through her flattened curls.

"Thank you very much, Mrs. Howell. I shall be glad to have Mavis help me, especially since I doubt I could ever find my way to the gold saloon, or anywhere else, without a guide."

Mrs. Howell waved away this confession. "You'll soon learn your way around, Miss Monroe, though the place is a bit of a warren, I grant you, what with this wing being older than some other sections and the whole place added to and changed over the years. I'll send hot water right up, unless you would like to have a real bath in the new bathing room her ladyship put in?"

"Perhaps tomorrow, Mrs. Howell, thank you."

"Very good, miss. I'll send Mavis up directly to unpack for you."

When the housekeeper had whisked herself out the door, Abigail took stock of her temporary quarters. It *was* a beautiful room, she assured herself, having conquered her initial dismay at the vast, high-ceilinged space with its scant but massive appointments. The canopied bed looked big enough for an entire family, but its hangings and coverlet were exquisite, a pattern of jewel-toned crewel work designs of fanciful flowers and vines on a creamy wool background. Against one wall stood an enormous walnut cupboard, as heavily carved as the bedposts, that would swallow up her new wardrobe with no difficulty; for that matter it could no doubt accommodate every stitch she owned with space to spare. Standing beside it was an out-sized carved and contorted object that might be a chair but could as easily be a throne or an instrument of torture. No upholstery or loose cushion softened its uncompromising oak surfaces.

She wandered over to the bed wall to examine the series of faded but still lovely tapestries that covered most of the long wall. It took her several minutes to discover that the scenes represented the story of the Garden of Eden. The fireplace, in the middle of the wall opposite the bed, had a wooden surround that was strewn with extraordinary animals, fish, and fowl carved in high relief chasing each other all over the surface. There was a single painting on either side of the fireplace, ancestral portraits by the look of them, a man and a woman equally richly garbed in Elizabethan dress. Both were staring haughtily out at her from heavy gold frames. She could see no resemblance to Max, something for which to be thankful. The present scion of the Waring family did not possess a bulbous forehead or ears that stuck out from his head at right angles.

Abigail continued her tour of the room, busily working out dates in her head. This wing of the house must be almost three hundred years old if Anne Boleyn could have visited here. She thought there wasn't much real furniture in those days, but the large oak chest standing at the foot of the bed looked very old. The top was plain and flat, but the long sides were divided into three panels that were carved somewhat crudely. She ran her fingers over the age-roughened wood, wondering if it might be a dower chest that had contained the dowry an earlier Waring bride brought to her marriage. This was idle speculation, of course; she did not know whether Oakridge has been built by one or more of Max's ancesters, had come to the family through a later marriage, or had been purchased quite recently. She had best guard her tongue in company, she realized uneasily, lest she reveal her abysmal ignorance of the family of her intended bridegroom. She writhed in remembered embarrassment at her maladroit reaction to the introduction to Lady Dalmore earlier, though she held

Lord Edgeworth—she must think of him as Max—greatly at fault for not foreseeing the consequences of keeping her in the dark. Her annoyance at his failure to prepare her for his extremely young stepmother still rankled despite the subsequent tide of impressions she had received of her surroundings. He had not divulged the existence of a young half sister to her, nor did she as yet know whether he possessed other siblings. He had left her ill-prepared for the role he expected her to play, and anxious with it. She would be afraid to open her mouth when meeting the earl this evening after making a fool of herself in front of the beautiful countess already. Perhaps it was merely a case of exacerbated sensibilities that had her thinking she'd detected mockery in Lady Dalmore's playful reaction to her own *bêtise,* but that she'd been at a severe disadvantage in that scene was not in question.

Abigail was gnawing on her lip, shrinking inwardly from a picture of the unknown earl as a harsher, haughtier, and more formidible version of his son that had planted itself in her imagination when a knock on the door heralded the entrance of a small redheaded sprite with a snub nose, freckles, and a gap between her front teeth. The girl's first words confirmed that she was the maid chosen by Mrs. Howell to wait on her.

"I'm Mavis, miss," she said with barely contained glee as she set down a large can of hot water in order to bob an awkward curtsy. "I'm to be your dresser while you are here and do your hair and take care of your clothes. She says to assure you I'll be ever so careful wi' the irons, and that I will—it was only the oncet that I burned a sheet, and it was an old one. I learned how to use the irons right quick after that, and Mrs. Howell will tell you that not even Miss Forbes, her la'ship's dresser, can get out the creases in the seat of gowns as good," she finished triumphantly.

The broad grin that accompanied this proud claim changed to an expression of comical disbelief when the aspiring dresser, who could not have been more than sixteen, took possession of the water can again and glanced around the historic chamber. "Well, if this don't beat all!" she exclaimed in disgust. "Look at all the scratched old stuff in here, and just two thin little carpets on these uneven old boards. It's a mercy it's not winter or you'd freeze your feet for sure. Not even a proper dressing table neither—just that narrow table like a shelf, and a dinky little stool—and you the young master's promised wife!"

Abigail could not help chuckling at the maid's indignation on her behalf as she said soothingly, "It is really an honor to have this bedchamber, Mavis. It was slept in by Anne Boleyn about three hundred years ago."

"Well, I hope it looked better when she had it," Mavis replied, pouring the hot water into the basin standing on the table against the tapestry wall after she'd placed the towels that had been on top of the can on the scorned stool. "Will I help you get out of your gown now, miss?"

"If you'll finish unpacking for me, Mavis, I'll take off my gown and wash my hands and face," Abigail said, putting the towels on the table and settling herself on the stool as she spoke. "I'll wear the white dress this evening."

Abigail's spirits rebounded over the next half hour in the company of the ebullient Mavis, who kept up a running commentary as she unpacked and disposed of her temporary mistress's clothes in the huge cupboard. Cries of pleasure and approval of the luxurious fabrics and rich colors were interspersed between comments on the other guests enjoying the earl's hospitality at the present. Visitors obviously meant considerable extra work for the resident staff even when the guests brought their own personal attendants, but Mavis seemed to revel in the increased sociability in the servants' hall, and she took a vicarious pleasure in the activities of the family and guests, most of whom she would not even catch a distant glimpse of during their stay at Oakridge.

Abigail found herself enjoying the eager ministrations of the housemaid, willingly consigning her unruly tresses to Mavis's clever hands. "I have no skill at devising arrangements for hair," she confessed when the girl asked how she would like to wear her hair that evening. "Generally, I merely sweep it all up in one hand and tie a ribbon around as much as I can capture. I should get it cropped, I suppose, it is so unmanageable."

"No, no, it is beautiful hair," Mavis crooned almost reverently, sweeping a brush through the curly mass, "thick and silky and black as midnight. I'm agoing to pin fat curls on top of your head and weave a white ribbon in and out—if you will trust me?"

Abigail, relaxing under the strong brush strokes that made her scalp tingle, gladly gave permission to her handmaiden to exercise her talents while she sat on the stool in front of a small square of glass that was even less adequate than the one at the inn. Mavis had condemned it in no uncertain terms on sight. "I brought a message up to her la'ship's dressing room oncet and had a good look round when Miss Forbes went into the next room to fetch a pen," she said, continuing her brushing. "All blue and silver it was, with satin hangings and one of those long chairs you can put your feet on, in blue velvet that was. There was a shiny big dressing table wi' a mirror as big as one o' these wall hangings, and there must have been a hunnert bottles and jars on top of it, full of sweet-smelling creams and perfumes. Heaven couldn't be no richer nor that." She sighed in remembered rapture, her busy fingers continuing to form curls all the while

"There," she announced a few minutes later, deploying a single long curl along the side of Abigail's neck, "you can look now, miss."

Abigail's extravagant praise for the beaming maid's efforts was only slightly exaggerated, for she could see, even in the pitiful little mirror, that her difficult hair had never been so attractively arranged before. Her self-confidence, which had plunged after the initial meeting with the lovely countess, resurfaced and she concluded with no false modesty that her appearance tonight would set off her mother's pearl necklace and earrings. She ventured to hope that she looked like no one's poor relation at the moment, even in this stately home.

"Thank you, Mavis, you have done a marvelous job in getting me ready. Is it time to go down to dinner, do you think? I have heard no dressing bells, and there is no clock in this room."

"Mrs. Howell gave me her watch to make sure I had you ready on time, miss," the maid said, pulling the timepiece out of the pocket of her apron. "We have ten minutes to get to the spot where Lord Edgeworth's man said his master would join you so you would not have to go in alone, you not knowing anybody yet."

"Oh, how thoughtful of him," Abigail said, smiling suddenly as one nagging concern was removed.

"Will you take that pretty shawl I unpacked earlier?" Mavis suggested. "It would add what Mrs. Howell calls a touch of elegance."

Abigail laughed. "Yes, thank you. I begin to think I need you to tell me what to wear, Mavis. My mind was wandering, I fear. Oh, yes, that looks lovely," she added a moment later when the maid had draped over her arms the beautiful Norwich silk shawl that her mother had brought from her home to her marriage. She slipped a small white reticule over her wrist and followed the girl out of the Queen's bedchamber, her head held high.

Max closed the door to the room Roland Monroe would be occupying and crossed the hall to his old bedchamber, stopping just inside. His ears picked up the sounds of his batman unpacking in the next room as he cast a swift look around the room that had been his ever since he'd come out of the nursery. It looked exactly as it had when he'd last seen it, but there was no sense of homecoming, only familiarity.

What was unfamiliar—jarring—had been the sight of Felicity rushing up to welcome him to his ancestral home. Once he'd expected to be the one welcoming and introducing her to Oakridge. They'd met in London during the Season when he'd been staying at the family's town house. His father had gone back to Oakridge to supervise the planting. When he'd returned in June, Max had presented the girl who had just agreed to marry him. When the smoke cleared, his father had been the one to introduce Felicity to Oakridge. And now she was graciously playing lady-of-the-manor to the heir, which was, he concluded grimly, her right. And here he was, furiously resenting the situation, which was *not* his right. Max railed at his stupidity. He was acting as if he'd never accepted his father's marriage to Felicity. He had no business being here in this house in this frame of mind, but he had come, however ill-judged the decision, and he'd damned well better carry it off with no one the wiser. Except Felicity, of course, he acknowledged bitterly. That was beyond repair, but he still had the chance to keep his father in the dark as to the state of his feelings. It was a matter of concealment on the one hand, and acting in a convincing manner toward Abigail Monroe.

If only his father had not been off riding when they arrived. The idea of meeting him in a room full of gawking strangers was abhorrent, but it looked inescapable.

The faint sounds of horses' hooves brought Max over to the window that overlooked the stable block. His eyes picked out his father's straight back riding his favorite hack among the party heading for the stables, and he frowned in consideration. If his father went straight to his room to change, there would be no chance of seeing him before the house party gathered for dinner. Until his mother's final illness dictated otherwise, his parents had shared a bedchamber, an arrangement that was not common in their circle. There was no way of discovering before dinner whether this still applied with his second wife. He'd slit his throat before knocking on the door to any room shared by his father and Felicity, not that he had any idea what rooms they were using at present.

As the riders dismounted and began making their way back to the house, Max made a quick decision and headed soft-footed toward the staircase that was closest to his father's library on the off chance that the earl might stop there before going upstairs.

Ten minutes later Max was back in his own room, his hopes of seeing his father alone having come to nothing. The earl must have gone upstairs directly.

Max was short and uncommunicative with his batman during the interval before dinner. It wasn't until the name of Abigail Monroe reached his ears that he looked away from his image in the glass and paused in the process of tying his cravat. "What did you say about Miss Monroe, Gibbs?"

"Merely that Wilkins suggested that you might wish to escort Miss Monroe into the gold saloon to spare her having to run the gauntlet, as it were, of persons completely unknown to her. He introduced me to the young maid who will act as Miss Monroe's abigail, and I told her you would meet Miss Monroe at the top landing leading down to the gold saloon."

"That was well done of Wilkins. How did you know where I should meet her—Wilkins again?"

"Yes, sir. He kindly explained the layout of the house to me. He seemed most pleased about your betrothal."

"News travels fast," Max said with a grimace. "I told no one save Mrs. Howell, the housekeeper—and Lady Dalmore, of course."

"A country house is like a village in that respect, I should imagine."

Max grunted and returned his gaze to his task in the mirror. No one could tell from his cool manner, but Gibbs must be seething with curiosity over this betrothal that he had learned about only this afternoon when he met the Monroes at the inn. At least he could trust the fiercely loyal batman not to discuss his employer's affairs in the servants' hall. Obviously all his father's servants already knew the situation. Odd that his father would probably be the last person at Oakridge to hear of the betrothal, either from his wife or his valet.

He spared a thought for Abigail Monroe who would be the cynosure of all eyes tonight. Despite her somewhat feisty nature, she was essentially a tender lamb about to be tossed to the wolves. It would be his task to pull the teeth of as many of these lupine creatures as possible. He was guiltily aware that he should have begun by warning her about Felicity, who would not willingly share the center stage with another lovely female. He'd not been impervious to the condescension in her manner toward Abigail earlier, nor, despite her good manners, had Abigail. Naturally she could not have known that the Queen's chamber was as far away from his own apartment as it was possible to get at Oakridge. Did Felicity fear he would be unable to control his ardor if his betrothed was quartered less than a day's march away?

This sour reflection coincided with a fatal mistake in his precise movements and resulted in the abandonment of the neckcloth he'd been laboring over for ten minutes. After uttering a few choice oaths that failed to relieve his feelings, he began the painstaking chore again with a new neckcloth that Gibbs handed him with the wooden mien of the perfect valet.

Chapter Six

As he neared the staircase closest to what his stepmother had referred to as the gold saloon, Max was experiencing none of the happy anticipation of a young man returning to hearth and family after a long absence. However, the first sight of the petite brunette standing in conversation with a young housemaid in an ugly mobcap considerably lightened his spirits. In the simplicity of virginal white and pearls setting off her shining crown of near-black hair, Abigail Monroe was adorable. If she never opened her mouth she would epitomize the romantic ideal of young maidenhood on the brink of blossoming into a desirable woman. He could visualize her as the pet of sentimental dowagers and aging beaux who would gaze upon her freshness and recall their salad days with nostalgia.

His brief but intense acquaintance with her had taught him how very deceptive appearances were in Abigail's case. The image of ethereal fragility that her fair countenance and slight build conjured up would disintegrate quickly enough if the little shrew gave rein to her hasty temper or decided to favor the assembled company with her opinions of their manners and morals. From his own experience of her he would not rule out either course, given the apposite combination of circumstances. Her nature was transparently honest and uncompromising, and she was too inexperienced to have learned as yet to deal diplomatically with the widespread hypocrisy that characterized social intercourse among the top tier of society. If Abigail's tolerance became strained, Max suspected they could be in for some exciting scenes in the future. Given that everyone believed her to be his intended bride, he should be a lot more anxious about that challenging prospect than he was. The part of his internal makeup that found some, no doubt unworthy, amusement in observing the foibles of human nature play themselves out actually welcomed the opportunity for entertainment. He could almost feel the beginning of anticipation of a sort.

He'd found the young women he'd met in Spain and Portugal during the winter lulls in the fighting to be as near interchangeable as made no difference, with their stiff manners, downcast eyes, and ever-vigilant duennas. Some had been lovely to look at, but even these diamonds had failed to kindle enough interest in him to try to penetrate their vapid demeanor to discover the person behind the lovely face. There was nothing vapid about Abigail Monroe; her ardent soul was visible behind those incredible eyes. He'd never seen their like for sheer beauty and expressiveness. An unwary man could drown in their depths. He was not an unwary man and thus in no danger, but he did not mind owning to an unfamiliar spurt of excitement as he increased his pace toward the waiting girl.

"Sorry to keep you waiting, my dear," he said, sending his voice ahead of him. His lips twitched at the look of expectation in luminous violet eyes when she turned to him. "I do not believe I have ever seen you look lovelier," he murmured, bending over her hand, perfectly willing to gratify her innocent vanity, especially in the presence of the maid, who would no doubt rush back to the servants' hall to broadcast this intelligence. Being the bearer of fresh gossip, particularly of the sentimental variety, would convey a momentary importance on her that would thrill someone as far down in the strict hierarchy as this child must be.

"Thank you, Max. I owe the transformation entirely to the skill with which Mavis has dressed my hair." Abigail smiled at the girl, who swelled with pleasure at the praise.

"Yes, you have really done justice to Miss Monroe's beautiful hair, Mavis," he agreed, adding his mite. "I'll take her down now," he said in smiling dismissal.

As the maid scurried away, Max offered his arm to his supposed fiancée, and she placed her fingers on his black sleeve, subjecting him to a thorough assessment as she did so. "You look superb in evening dress," she remarked with a total absence of shyness as they started down the stairs.

"You will have me blushing," he said, only half facetiously. In truth, he *was* a bit startled at her casual candor.

"No, why?" She looked surprised. "Is a female not permitted to notice a man's appearance or pay him a compliment?"

He hesitated before replying. "It is not that precisely, but in general a young female does not notice a man's appearance, at least she does not acknowledge that she does, certainly not when the man is not very well known to her."

"Well, I am supposed to be marrying you, which presupposes some slight degree of acquaintance," she pointed out dryly, "but I do take your point and shall try to remember to be blind to masculine appearance in future lest I disgrace you, which brings me to a sore point. Why did you not tell me that your stepmother is so young?" she demanded in remembered indignation.

"My dear girl, it never occurred to me that it was of the least significance," he replied dampingly.

"Liar," she retorted without heat, but there was speculation in the look she cast up at him, and he tried to increase their pace that had slowed during this exchange.

Abigail was having none of it. "I refuse to go a step farther until you answer one question," she said, stopping dead. He was a step ahead of her, and their eyes were nearly on a level when he glanced back. He scowled, but she was wearing her stubborn look.

"What is it?" he asked, feeling his face freeze.

"Do you have any other brothers and sisters beside Lady Rose?"

"What?" The unexpectedness of the question confounded him, and he stared at her blankly.

"Is your hearing impaired?" she inquired with a spurious sweetness that made him long to put her over his knee.

"You are the most impertinent snip—"

"What is impertinent about wishing to know whether you have other siblings so I do not make as much of a fool of myself in front of your father as I did this afternoon with Lady Dalmore?"

Max laughed in sheer relief. "But your face was such a picture when you told Felicity you had expected she would be more motherly," he said, enjoying the pout that rounded her lips.

Abigail, refusing to be disarmed, expelled a breath,

pursed her lips, and tapped on the step with an impatient toe. "You still have not answered my question."

"No, you little goose, I have no brothers nor—I thank the good Lord for small mercies—any sisters either."

The fervor with which he denied having sisters succeeded where attempts to charm her or snub her had failed. She burst out laughing and allowed him to pull her down the rest of the stairs. They were still smiling at each other when they entered the gold saloon hand in hand.

Of one accord they came to a stop just inside the arched entrance. Max's eyes sought and found his father standing near the fireplace, talking with a young man and woman.

The earl must have had one eye on the doorway, however, because their glances locked immediately, and he excused himself, coming forward with a smile of welcome.

Max glanced briefly at Abigail, who was taking in the room's decor with wide eyes. He pulled her forward with him just before meeting the earl's outthrust hand, struck by the thought that his father looked very much the same as the last time he'd seen him. He wondered why this should surprise him—four years was not so very long.

"It's good to have you home, son."

"It's good to be here, sir." Max broke contact and moved Abigail in front of him to face his father. "May I present Miss Abigail Monroe, who has done me the honor of consenting to be my wife." He released her lingeringly, and Abigail sank into a curtsy.

"How do you do, Lord Dalmore?"

The earl reached for her hands and raised her to her feet. "This is indeed a pleasure, Miss Monroe," he said, smiling at her with warmth. "Max is to be commended for his good taste and congratulated on his great good fortune in winning your affections."

"Th . . . thank you, sir, but I also have been smiled on by fortune," she replied, transferring her own smile from the father to the son and back.

"Will you think me a doting parent if I agree there is some small degree of mutuality in the bestowal of fortune's favors?"

"No, sir. I would think that you are naturally grateful and happy to have your son returned safe from the war."

The earl's probable agreement with this sentiment was

destined to remain unspoken, for Lady Dalmore glided up to the absorbed trio with Roland Monroe in tow just then. Several other persons entered the saloon at that point also, and the next few minutes were given over to general introductions.

Max concentrated on mastering the identity of the guests gathered under his father's roof, glad not to be wondering about the hungry—or hopeful—expression in his father's eyes when he'd looked on his son and the girl he pretended to love. The only people he knew were Lord and Lady Grafton, neighbors and longtime friends of his parents, accompanied by their daughter, Marjorie, who had been a gawky adolescent when Max had last been in England. Evidently the sweet-faced girl had been presented this past spring.

Two of the male guests had been present at Mrs. Cathcart's soirée a fortnight ago, members of Felicity's adoring court. Sir Archie Rhodes, some few years Max's senior, he knew by reputation, and that not a good one, from his pre-army days in London. The other, Mr. Douglas Talant, was about his own age and was accompanied by his sister, who, though not in the first blush of youth, was probably several years younger.

Max found himself being surveyed in a frankly approving manner by Lady Winter, a fashionably dressed and bejeweled woman in her late twenties. There did not seem to be a Lord Winter in attendance, which increased his natural wariness, though she was rather young to be widowed. The last to be presented to the newcomers were Mr. and Mrs. Carmichael, who adopted a matching air of polite detachment as they greeted the son of the house and the Monroes.

His father played the role of host with ease and authority, but it was obvious as those present drifted and shifted into smaller conversational groups that the guests were all Felicity's friends and contemporaries with the exception of the Graftons. Max wondered idly if young Marjorie had been provided to pique his interest. She was too much younger to have come very much in his path in the old days, still in the schoolroom when he went off to the army. Miss Talant was tall and spare of figure, wearing an unbecoming gown of a drab color among the pastels of the other women and exuding a faint air of disapproval that he suspected was chronic. Except for Felicity, whose stunning beauty would always cast other women into the shade, Abigail was easily the most attractive female in the room.

Sir Archie, true to his philandering nature, had hemmed Abigail into a corner and was keeping her well entertained, if her laughing face was to be believed. Even as the thought crossed Max's mind that he'd have to rescue her before she was betrayed by her inexperience into any lapse in the decorum expected of very young ladies, Abigail made a tiny gesture to her passing brother, who changed course and joined the twosome. Inexperienced she might be in society, but his putative fiancée was apparently not nearly so impressionable as to be easy game for practiced seducers like Rhodes. The next time he looked away from Lord Grafton, who was welcoming him home with gruff sincerity, Abigail was engaged with Lady Grafton and Marjorie, encouraging the latter with an air of smiling interest in her chatter.

Despite conscious discipline, Max's eyes strayed to Felicity, who was listening to Mr. Carmichael and looking absolutely radiant in a gown of tissue silk embroidered all over with gold thread. Obviously the saloon had been decorated to serve as the perfect background for her golden beauty. The only thing he recognized was the pale Aubusson carpet. Gone were the highly polished mahogany chairs and tables with their gracefully curving legs. Gone too was the wallpaper imprinted with colorful scenes from a Chinese garden that had fascinated him as a boy. He had no quarrel with the gold-and-white striped paper that had replaced it, but there did seem to be a great profusion of mirrors and chairs with straight fluted legs gilded in the French style. A swift survey revealed that everything in the room appeared to be gold or white—curtains, pillows, upholstery, even the tables. There were no pictures on the walls anymore, just the portrait of his mother over the fireplace.

Max froze in disbelief, his eyes glued to the full-length painting of Felicity in the identical gown the flesh-and-blood edition was wearing at the moment. It was occupying the place where his mother's portrait had always stood. How could he have failed to spot the substitution immediately? he demanded of himself, feeling like a traitor to his mother. Granted that when he'd first entered the room, he'd been too preoccupied with the initial meeting with his father to notice anything else, but he'd been here for upwards of fifteen minutes by now. Max tugged at his shirt collar that felt too tight as he tore his gaze from the painted face of his stepmother and headed toward the corner where the earl was now speaking with the Monroe twins.

"Where is Mother's portrait?" he asked without ceremony, striving to keep all feeling from face and voice as he looked at his parent.

The earl's hesitation was barely perceptible before he said, "The painting of Felicity was completed just recently. We thought to ask you if you would prefer to have your mother's portrait hung in your rooms before putting it in the gallery."

"I would be happy to hang it in Grandfather's house in town."

"Margaret was my wife for three-and-twenty years. While I live, the portrait remains at Oakridge," the earl said with soft finality.

"I would very much like to see your mother's portrait before I leave Oakridge, Max," Abigail said, fixing her eyes on his face in a compelling fashion.

"Yes, of course," Max managed, willing his fingers to unclench.

"Max's mother was a lovely and much beloved person," the earl said, smiling faintly at the Monroe twins. "She always said, funning of course, that she could not have had anything to do with Max's birth because he was my image. I am persuaded when you study her portrait, you will agree with me that he has his mother's mouth, and he is like her in ways that don't show in paintings."

"Where is the portrait now?" Max asked again.

"In the library. Perhaps you would like to take Miss Monroe to see it after dinner?"

"Yes."

"Thank you, sir, I should like that," Abigail said into the little silence following Max's short agreement.

The entrance of Lady Rose Waring and her nurse into the saloon provided a welcome interruption. Max saw his father's face transformed by the light of adoration and turned to look for the source. He could feel his own features melting into a smile at the sight of the golden-haired cherub in the doorway.

For a moment the child clutched her nurse's hand and drew nearer her skirts. Then, spotting her father, she abandoned this support and ran to him. "Papa! You did not come to sit with me while I ate my supper," she scolded, casting herself into the arms reaching down to receive her.

"I'm sorry, sweetheart, but Mama needed to talk with me and there was no time to go to the nursery. But I have a wonderful surprise for you," the earl said, turning the little girl in his arms to face his son. "This is your brother, Max, who has come home from far away. What do you think of him?"

Max stared in fascination as Rose's round blue eyes considered him with the unself-conscious intensity of childhood before she looked up at her father again. "I think he looks almost like you, Papa," she replied solemnly.

"And you look almost like your mama," Max replied, equally solemn.

"Do you think so, Max? I vow I was never so . . . so sturdily built as Rose." Lady Dalmore had slipped unnoticed into the group around her daughter. She laughed lightly, her eyes flicking around the captivated circle of adults.

"She is quite exquisite, Lady Dalmore." Abigail smiled at her hostess.

"And in grave danger of being spoiled by her doting father, I fear, Miss Monroe." The countess threw her husband an arch look. "Wilkins has announced dinner, my lord. Nurse"—glancing around and raising her voice—"it is time Lady Rose returned to the nursery. Come, my sweet, give Mama a kiss and go with Nurse."

Lady Rose responded to this request by tightening her rosebud mouth and her grip around her father's neck. The earl nuzzled her delicate jawline until she squealed and giggled, displaying pearly teeth. "I shall come to the nursery at breakfast time," he promised, detaching the child's arms and extending her toward the countess. "Now give Mama a kiss and say good night to our guests like a good girl."

The cherub leaned forward and kissed her mother's cheek obediently before the earl set her down. When her hand was safely tucked into her nurse's, she smiled shyly up at Max, aiming her farewells in his direction.

"Good night, little sister."

This appellation seemed to please the child, who paused and considered it. "I have never been a sister before," she said, her smile widening to display twin dimples in her cheeks. "Good night, big brother."

This drew a chorus of chuckles from the adults whose eyes lingered on the small figure as she skipped merrily away with her attendant.

"Little imp," said her father, unable to disguise his pride.

Max had never seen that expression on his father's face before—complete adoration about summed it up. Did he look at Felicity that way? He rejected the errant thought forcefully, but not quickly enough to avoid the sensation of being stabbed. Wrenching his glance from the earl, he caught the secret little smile on Felicity's lips as she turned her eyes from him to his father, who was offering his arm to Abigail, indicating that they were about to proceed into the dining room.

Felicity's awareness of his discomposure steadied Max's swirling impressions better than a pail of water in his face. Perforce, he offered her his arm, but pulled Roland Monroe along with them as they gathered in the rest of the guests.

His control reestablished, Max went into the dining room, which, he saw immediately, had also been the beneficiary of Felicity's penchant for gilded magnificence. There he gave, by his own estimation, a flawless performance as a man deliriously happy with his lot in life. He exerted himself to be attentive and encouraging to his dinner partners, Lady Grafton and Mrs. Carmichael, and remembered to send intimate glances and smiles down the table to his alleged fiancée at periodic intervals, once even lifting his glass to her in a silent salute that, he was delighted to see, brought a blush to her fair cheeks.

Infinitely more difficult, he managed to prevent Felicity from catching his eye even once during the leisurely course of a lavish meal that was probably delectable, except that he could not seem to recall or even register the flavors of the few foods he actually put into his mouth, though he was certainly aware that favorable comments flew around the table as various delicacies appeared.

Max watched the parade of ladies dutifully withdrawing at the end of the meal with mixed feelings. It was definitely a relief that for the next half hour he need not censor his eyes from feasting on Felicity's beautiful face after four long years of deprivation. He could not be surprised into revealing the closeness of their former relationship. Their betrothal had been of such short duration that it had never been announced in the papers, but his single-minded pursuit of the incomparable Miss Stanton had been noted in his own circle at the time, and her popularity was such that all her actions were continually under the intense scrutiny of those participants and observers of the annual scramble to establish the progeny of the upper classes in suitable marriages.

He had effected his escape into the army and out of the country before Felicity's betrothal to his father had become generally known, but he would not dare wager anything of real value that no one among the men helping themselves to his father's port on this summer evening knew that the earl's son had once desired to marry his stepmother. The only course available to him in the event that the truth became common knowledge was to steadily maintain that it was ancient history, forgotten by all in the happiness of present attachments. Meanwhile, he prayed that pride and determination would keep the upper hand over base human emotions for the next few days. He did not delude himself that it would be easy; he'd already experienced hot flashes of fury or resentment that demanded the relief of expression. He would need to maintain a constant guard over his too-ready tongue.

Max found that his status as a soldier newly returned from the war eased his way into the masculine gathering as everyone professed interest in his opinions on the chances of achieving a lasting peace. Thankfully, there was no opportunity for private conversation with his parent, and, in any case, he felt an obligation to assist young Roland Monroe in becoming more comfortable in strange company. The lad's natural deference in the presence of older men did him no disservice. He spoke only when directly addressed, but expressed himself clearly then, even if mostly to deny holding an informed opinion. He was probably wishing himself elsewhere, Max realized with belated sympathy, but his manners did credit to his upbringing.

He recognized that he had been undeservedly fortunate in his accomplices, given the rash nature of this undertaking. Abigail possessed a natural ease of manner combined with an air of eager interest in what was taking place around her that was sweetly engaging. It was unexpected also when he considered that their acquaintance had begun when she broke into his house, and had rapidly advanced to quarreling and contention as she volubly opposed his plan to foist her off onto his family as his betrothed.

Though obviously of gentle birth, Lucius Monroe had just as obviously come down in the world. He inhabited a decaying hulk of a house and bred horses for a living. There had been no London Season for Abigail. On the occasion when she had defended her title to the scent bottle she'd climbed through a window to retrieve, he recalled her saying her mother had been deceased for eight years. How would a motherless girl make her bow to society, even a limited local society, without a respectable female relative or friend to sponsor her?

His thoughts trooped on as he considered Abigail's actions from the moment they had descended from the chaise this afternoon. However it had come about, she had gained the poise and assurance to take this odd assortment of houseguests in her stride so far. Much too late, Max was suddenly alive to the enormity of the deception he had embarked on and his reckless disregard of consequences if it should be discovered. A chill coursed down his spine, and the hand that raised the glass of port to his mouth was not quite steady. Roland's discreet tug on his elbow didn't help, but it did bring him back to the moment. Best to admit his dereliction.

"I beg pardon," he said to the table at large, having no idea who had spoken to him. "I fear I was woolgathering."

"Where had your thoughts wandered?" Lord Grafton asked with a tolerant smile.

"To Abigail—Miss Monroe," he replied, surprised into telling the truth. He looked around, still surprised, at the laughter that greeted this admission.

"I believe my son's very understandable lapse of attention tells us it is time to rejoin the ladies," the earl said, rising to his feet.

Amid good-natured laughter the men pushed back from the table and headed for the gold saloon.

Max was the first to enter, his eyes flashing around the room, seeking Abigail, his mood apologetic.

She was sitting on a settee covered in gold brocade, in animated conversation with Lady Grafton, and she gave him a natural smile that calmed his nerves somewhat.

"Would you think me utterly high-handed if I stole Miss Monroe away for a few moments, Lady Grafton? I want to show her my mother's portrait," Max said in a confiding tone accompanied by a wheedling smile directed at his mother's old friend.

"Not at all, dear boy," Lady Grafton replied with a chuckle, "but I would definitely conclude that you have as good an eye as your father for feminine pulchritude."

"One might even say the same eye." Max reached out his hand to Abigail, furious with himself for having indulged in bitter humor as he sensed Lady Grafton's piqued interest.

He was also conscious that Felicity was watching them as a blushing Abigail made her excuses to the older woman and allowed him to lead her out of the room. In point of fact, they were undoubtedly the cynosure of most, if not all eyes at this moment, and he would do well to keep their little expedition under ten minutes to safeguard Abigail's reputation, even though they had his father's blessing and notwithstanding that betrothed couples were granted somewhat more leeway to seek exclusivity from time to time.

"Should we perhaps wait until the morning?" Abigail suggested softly, her thoughts mirroring his as they stepped into the corridor. "I feel as if everyone is holding a stopwatch on us."

"You are overly anxious," he assured her soothingly. "It was my father's suggestion, after all. Who would dare disapprove of what he has endorsed?"

She subsided and accompanied him without another word.

Except when he indicated the turns in their route neither ventured any remarks until they entered the earl's library.

"Oh, my, isn't this wonderful!" Abigail turned shining eyes on him after a comprehensive look around the long room with its linenfold paneling and tall rows of shelves coming from one long wall at right angles.

"At least it seems to have been spared the decorator's ministrations," Max noted.

Abigail ignored this dry comment. "There must be thousands of volumes," she said, sounding rather breathless as she eyed the movable stairs designed to assist in retrieving books from the highest shelves.

"Yes," Max murmured vaguely. He left her without another word when his searching glance did not discover the portrait on the short wall where candles burned in sconces. He looked in the shadowed spaces between the rows of shelves, moving rapidly, his heels ringing on the wooden floor. "Here it is," he called a moment later, then, hearing her footsteps, "I am going to bring it down where the light is better."

The footsteps stopped. Max hoisted the heavy frame away from the wall where it rested and carried it across to the huge old walnut desk, where a many-branched candelabrum reposed. Its lights flickered when he placed the frame on the floor, leaning it against the desk, and stepped back.

"Mother was about eight-and-twenty when this likeness was painted," he said, joining Abigail where she stood studying the half-length portrait of a brown-haired woman seated behind a desk. She appeared to have paused in the act of writing a letter to gaze out at them from luminous hazel eyes thickly fringed with dark lashes. "She was forty-one when she died six years ago."

"I think I have never seen a more gentle face. She was lovely, Max. You must miss her a great deal." Abigail's voice was soft, and her eyes remained on the painting.

"I do," the man at her side said tersely.

"I was only thirteen when my mother died."

"I was more fortunate than you," he said, responding to the mournful note in her voice. "I had my mother until I was one-and-twenty."

Their eyes met then, hers shimmering with unshed tears. "It cannot be easy, seeing another in her place."

"No," he agreed, turning away abruptly. "We had best return to the gold saloon before everyone begins to wonder what we've got up to sans chaperone."

She recoiled a little, no doubt from the harshness he

could hear in his own voice, and began to walk rapidly toward the door.

Taken unawares, Max had to hurry to catch up with her. He mumbled an apology to which she nodded, but she did not look at him again as they walked back to the saloon in a silence that he regretted but could not bring himself to breach, not even to acknowledge her unspoken sympathy. It must seem as though he had rejected her sympathy, but he had no right to accept what she would never have offered had she known the shameful truth—that, much as he had loved his mother, his resentment of his father's second marriage had more to do with masculine jealousy than with filial devotion. If she knew the truth, she would despise him.

Not that a low opinion of his character held by a rigid little moralist like Abigail Monroe would trouble him greatly, but it would be bound to affect her ability to portray herself as a girl in love with her betrothed. He felt they had made a good beginning, and he was not going to jeopardize the success of his mission. It was too vital.

Consequently, Max rearranged his features into a coaxing smile and seized Abigail's hands as they neared the arched entrance to the saloon. "Come, Gail, let us not sink into the mopes, brooding over the past. Let us try to enjoy the evening. It shouldn't be too difficult—you have made a great hit with everyone already." Which was true, he told himself with satisfaction, with one notable exception. He'd seen no indication that Felicity had formed a good opinion of his temporary fiancée, but perhaps it was asking too much to expect Felicity to welcome a female who might siphon off some small portion of the masculine attention and admiration that she was used to regarding as exclusively hers.

"Everyone has been most kind and welcoming," Abigail replied, giving him a serious look, "but you must know that I am out of my depth in such a gathering as this. I have no experience of society, no acquaintances in common with anyone here. The best you can hope for is that I will be considered a . . . a pleasant nonentity and tolerated for your sake."

"Do you really believe that?" He searched her countenance for signs of false modesty and found none.

"Of course," she replied, surprised. "I have seen none of the plays and operas, read none of the books these people discuss, heard none of the current *on dits* circulating among the *ton*, or visited any of the places they frequent. Small talk about the weather and the food and decor of Oakridge can only take me so far, you must be aware."

"Unless things have changed drastically since I was last among the *ton,* I am persuaded you will soon discover that most people will not *discuss* a book or play but rather *mention* having read or witnessed it so as to show themselves *au courant* with the latest rages. If I were you, I would not hope to become educated on any of these topics that receive a passing mention, my dear girl."

Max had bent closer to Abigail to keep his words between the two of them as they reentered the saloon. His head swung around when Felicity, popping out of nowhere, said gaily, "Now, Max, it really won't do for you to monopolize Miss Monroe all evening. Mr. and Miss Talant were just saying that they have exchanged no more than two words with her as yet. I promised I would bring her to them to remedy that, and, Max, I believe Lady Winter wished to ask if you were acquainted with a friend, or perhaps it was a relative, who was also fighting in Spain," she added over her shoulder, taking Abigail's arm to lead her away.

For the rest of the evening Max did not get within speaking range of Abigail again. It was not until he had closed his bedroom door behind him with leisure to replay the last two or three hours in his mind that he began to suspect that this had not been entirely due to the random ebbing and flowing tides of social interchange that occurred in fair-sized gatherings. Mayhap it was conceited of him to suppose that Felicity, busily playing concerned hostess, had arranged that he and Abigail were always separated by the length of the room, but essentially that was what had happened.

Abigail had been deposited near the Talant brother and sister by her hostess while he had obeyed Lady Winter's beckoning finger. By the time he had maneuvered himself into position to have a clear sight line to the corner where Abigail sat, Mr. Talant had left the two women to join a group of which Felicity was the center. His father, no devotee of whist, had sacrificed himself for the enjoyment of the Graftons and Mr. Carmichael at a whist table, removing himself from the changing patterns of conversation among the others.

To do Felicity justice, she had not encouraged the other men to surround her and ignore the rest of the company, but none of the subsequent shuffles had moved Abigail into his orbit. When he'd tried to take a seat near her as the tea tray was brought in, Felicity had pressed him into service to help distribute the cups. By the time he'd completed that little task, Sir Archie was settled in the chair next to Abigail. Max's later offer to guide Abigail to her quarters after tea had been greeted with broad grins and Felicity's sweet refusal to countenance this blatant attack on propriety.

"I would not dream of letting Miss Monroe go off without my seeing that she is comfortably settled," she said as the ladies were preparing to retire. "It will give me a chance to tell her something of our schedule for the next day or two."

So Max had joined the other men in presenting the ladies with candles to light their way to their bedchambers. Fast footwork had enabled him to snatch a quick moment to thank Abigail for her assistance and wish her pleasant dreams with an air of devotion as he gave her a candle. His reward was a smile tinged with wistfulness as she went off in company with her waiting hostess.

Felicity's smile as she bade him good night was somewhat akin to that of a cat at the cream pot.

Chapter Seven

To Abigail's relief, Lady Dalmore released her arm when they separated from the other women, who seemed to be lodged in a different wing from that containing the Queen's room. They headed down a dark corridor toward a flickering light that was the only source of illumination apart from the candles they carried. Neither spoke for a few moments until they turned to the right at the end of the hall, where the precious beacon stood on a table placed where two corridors met at a T intersection. At the end a door led to a short flight of stairs descending.

"Do you find the darkness and the distance disconcerting, Miss Monroe?" the countess inquired, seemingly more as a matter of interest than concern.

"No, but I am trying to memorize the route so I shan't have to trouble anyone to guide me in future."

"The trick is to remember to turn right before these stairs and left after them on the way to the Queen's bedchamber. On the way to the main house you turn left at that marble-topped table after climbing the stairs into the other wing. See, this is your corridor now."

"Thank you, I'll remember that. Are the stairs there to compensate for a difference in the ground level of this old wing?"

"I suppose so." Lady Dalmore shrugged. "Are you settling in comfortably?"

"Quite, thank you. It is a beautiful old room. It feels very historical." When her polite comments drew no response from her hostess, Abigail cast about for something else to say. "Are the lovely wall tapestries original to the Queen's room?"

Having turned her head toward the countess, Abigail saw that her slim shoulders hunched slightly once more. "I really couldn't say. You will have to ask my husband about this old wing. I rarely come here. It is mostly used for storage these days, I believe."

"Are . . . are there no other bedchambers still in use then?"

"Oh, yes, I believe one or two of the men may be quartered here this time. Here we are." Lady Dalmore stopped outside the Queen's room while Abigail digested this information. In the uncertain light of their candles, her eyes, turned now on her guest, seemed to have narrowed. "Odd that we should not have met during the Season, Miss Monroe. I was frequently at Almack's balls this spring. I thought I had seen all the eligible young ladies at one time or another."

"Not odd at all, ma'am. My mother died when I was but thirteen. I have never had a London Season."

"Never? Then how on earth did you manage to meet Max?"

Lady Dalmore's assumption of artless curiosity rang falsely with Abigail, but she hung on to her manners. "I believe Max mentioned earlier that my brother, Roland, introduced us," she said, scrupulously avoiding an outright lie.

"Then he called at your home, I take it? Where is your home, by the way?"

"I live in Richmond, and no, Max did not call there, not initially, I mean. He bumped into us, almost literally, in London, where I was shopping with my brother." In the face of this determined interrogation, Abigail jettisoned her scruples about lying, keeping a polite little smile on her lips as she did so.

"And this happened shortly after he met your brother? They do say that life is replete with such happy little coincidences, do they not, Miss Monroe? And here you are, betrothed, after a whirlwind courtship. Such a romantic story."

"It is rather." Abigail returned smile for insincere smile until the countess reached out and opened the door.

"I'll say good night then, Miss Monroe. Sleep well."

"Lady Dalmore," Abigail began, and her hostess, who had already turned away, looked back over her shoulder. "You mentioned telling me something about the routines at Oakridge."

"Yes, of course. Breakfast is served anytime after eight, but most of the ladies prefer to eat in their rooms. The maid who brings up your morning chocolate will show you to the breakfast room if you wish. I believe some of the men and one or two of the ladies plan to ride tomorrow morning if you are interested. Luncheon is generally at one. Tomorrow we dine *en famille,* but plan to have people come for a small ball the day after tomorrow. Will that do for now?"

"Yes, thank you. Good night, and thank you again for escorting me to my room. It was most kind of you."

"Not at all. Good night."

The light grew dimmer as Lady Dalmore set off to retrace the route back to the main house. After a second or two, Abigail gave a little shake of her head and prepared to enter her bedchamber, though not without some misgivings concerning her accommodation in an isolated wing of this great house, her hostess's scarcely disguised curiosity about her betrothal, and, above all, her own unwisdom in allowing Max Waring to dragoon her into this distasteful deception.

Concerns about her location vanished as soon as Abigail stepped into the Queen's room, blinking in the unexpected light of a branched candelabrum on the long table on the bed wall and another on a tall stand to the right of the fireplace. Surely that had not been there earlier?

"Mrs. Howell had one of the footmen bring that up for you during your stay, miss, and this chair too," said Mavis, bouncing out of an appealing bergère with a big smile splitting her face. "She agreed it wasn't fitting for the young master's promised bride not to have a comfortable chair and enough light to see by."

Abigail laughed, absurdly pleased at this evidence of concern for her well-being on the part of the staff at Oakridge. "Please thank Mrs. Howell for me, Mavis."

The maid was already relieving her of her shawl, which she proceeded to fold neatly. Before Abigail had taken off the second shoe, Mavis was at her side, eager to be of assistance. It was easier to submit to this earnest desire to be of service than to argue for independence at this hour, she decided, and settled back to enjoy a rare session of pampering.

Almost as soothing as the rhythmic strokes of the brush through her hair was the girl's chirping voice describing the excitement in the servants' hall at having the heir back home after four years. Abigail gathered that the longtime staff members who had the privilege of knowing the viscount from childhood were rather lording it over the newcomers. Mavis, having had the great good fortune to receive a compliment on her talent for arranging hair from Lord Edgeworth within hours of his return, had vaulted to the forefront of this group and was still all aglow as she tenderly readied her mistress for sleep. Abigail was warmed by the good will flowing out of her from this segment of the Oakridge population on the strength of her supposed connection with the son of the house.

As she slid between sweet-smelling sheets of fine linen, watching Mavis leave the darkened room with her candle, Abigail was suddenly suffused with well-being, physical and mental. It was a delightful sensation and almost compensated for the antipathy that emanated from her hostess. But she was not going to dwell on that now, she vowed, snuggling deeper into the smooth pillows; tonight she was simply going to abandon her pleasantly fatigued body to dreamless sleep.

Which, rather surprisingly, she discovered to be the case when she awoke to milky sunshine, feeling totally refreshed and full of energy.

This mindless contentment stayed with her as she drank the chocolate Mavis brought, and listened to her recital of Wilkins's pronouncement that the mist would burn off before nine. It was not until she was being helped into her dark blue riding dress that thoughts of the undercurrents she'd sensed at Oakridge surfaced again, gobbling up her complacency. She tried telling herself they were the products of an overactive imagination, but she was not naive enough to accept this simple explanation.

She had not imagined that Max had been less than forthcoming about his family before tossing her into their midst. The constraint between father and son was not a product of her imagination; it was palpable, as was the thinly masked resentment in Max's attitude toward his stepmother. For reasons known only to himself he had lied to the countess about not being able to let her know when he would arrive at Oakridge or that he was bringing guests of his own. For her part, Lady Dalmore treated Max as if he were an old friend, refusing to recognize his boorishness toward her. And the surface civility she displayed toward her stepson's betrothed would not bear close scrutiny. Suspicion rather than welcome looked out of her eyes, although Abigail was not fool enough to try to convince any male of this. All was done behind an airy, casual manner that falsely proclaimed her innocent of any intent to wound.

Now, having examined and solidified her initial impressions of her hosts into loose beliefs, Abigail acknowledged another unpalatable truth: it was not simply that she felt unwelcome—an understandable reaction in the circumstances—no, she returned Lady Dalmore's antipathy in full measure. She *hoped* it was not entirely due to a despicable jealousy of a beautiful woman—she *knew* it was not merely that—but she was ashamed of herself for whatever portion of her own dislike arose from such a base motive. Having taken herself severely to task, she firmly resolved to conceal her feelings and act on her father's command not to shame her mother's teachings.

Thus Abigail, full of good intentions, sallied forth to engage her hosts and the company in social congress. Again Mavis escorted her to the area of the main communal rooms, but Abigail now felt confident that she could find her own way back to the Queen's chamber. She thanked the maid and entered the breakfast room with the skirts of her habit swept over her left arm. She carried hat, gloves, and crop in her right hand so that she need not hold up the riding party by returning to her room or calling the maid away from her normal duties to fetch them for her.

Abigail stopped just inside the bright room, surprised to find it empty except for her host, seated at a large round table set in the enclosure formed by an oriel window bay.

"Good morning, Miss Monroe."

Abigail's momentary embarrassment faded at the earl's smiling greeting, and she came forward to the chair he pulled out next to his own, but she was still puzzled. "Am I disgracefully late, sir?" she asked, dropping down onto the chair and putting her belongings on the next one for want of a better place as Wilkins entered the room through another door.

The earl laughed, looking so like his son that she lost her initial shyness. "No, you and I are the vanguard this morning. May I say it is delightful to see a female prepared to eat a proper breakfast," he added as Abigail helped herself to some of the food on the tray the butler presented.

"I generally wake up ravenous," she admitted, "and this looks and smells wonderful." She added a fragrant muffin to her plate and accepted the cup of coffee Wilkins poured for her with a smile of thanks.

It was after she had taken her first bite of ham that Abigail glanced up to see her host looking at her with disconcerting intensity. She blinked, then plunged in. "Do I have mustard on my chin?" she asked, raising her serviette from her lap.

"No, no, Miss Monroe, I beg your pardon for staring so rudely," the earl apologized, "but I have had the strangest feeling ever since last night that your face is familiar. We have never met before?"

"No, sir, never."

"It must be your eyes. Only once before have I ever come across eyes of so deep a blue, more violet than blue, in fact. Many years ago in my youth I was used to spend some part of each summer with cousins in Herefordshire. There was a young girl, a child really, on an estate nearby with eyes such as yours. Extraordinary, is it not, how something—someone—can be forgotten for years, decades even, and then suddenly be recalled to mind in precise detail."

It was obvious that Lord Dalmore was lost in reminiscence, his remark not a question, but Abigail, thinking to hold up her end, said idly, "My mother was from Herefordshire, near Leominster."

"What was her name?"

"Katharine Fellowes."

The earl set down the cup he'd been raising to his lips. "Little Kitty Fellowes!" he cried, a look of pleasure overspreading his countenance as he examined Abigail with doubled interest. "May I say that you strongly favor your mother, my dear? My cousins were particular friends of Tom Fellowes, your Uncle Thomas, and we ran tame at Brentwood in those days. I was older than your mother, five or six years at least, but I remember her with great fondness to this day. She was a sweet child and quite lovely, even at the awkward age of thirteen or fourteen when I saw her last. I stopped going to Herefordshire after I started university and lost track of her completely. I wish you will relay my kindest regards to her."

"I'm sorry, sir, but my mother died eight years ago." The flare of elation at hearing her mother praised by someone who had known her as a girl expired as quickly as it arose, and Abigail was miserably conscious of a stinging behind her eyelids. She looked down at her plate and swallowed painfully, unable to bear the sympathy she saw in his lordship's eyes with composure.

"I am so sorry, my dear child. Recollection of such a loss remains painful, I know." The earl cleared his throat, but went on slowly after a moment, "I never learned what became of Kitty beyond a passing reference to a marriage that did no have her family's blessing."

Abigail lifted her head proudly and met the earl's sympathetic gaze directly. "My paternal grandfather was a gentleman who nearly wasted his entire inheritance before he died. My father was his only child. He turned to breeding horses to save his land and home. He met my mother when she was just seventeen. He was seven-and-twenty and still struggling to survive as a gentleman and landowner. My mother's family refused his request to marry her, and when they eloped, cut all contact with their daughter. She never heard from any of her family again to the day of her death."

"It is a sad fact of life that more pain can be inflicted on people by those close to them then by their enemies. Sir Charles Fellowes was a proud, even a haughty man, as I recall. Kitty was his only daughter and the apple of his eye. I would wager that he suffered as much from the estrangement as did your mother," the earl said, shaking his head at the tragedy of it.

"Except that Sir Charles always had the remedy in his hands, sir." Abigail's words were quietly spoken, but she met her host's eyes unflinchingly, a challenge in her own.

"Yes. Apart from losing his daughter, he robbed himself of the joy of knowing his grandchildren, thus doubly impoverishing himself. Are you and Roland the only issue of the marriage?"

"No, we have an elder brother, Albert, who is six-and-twenty."

The earl was prevented from continuing the conversation by the arrival of several persons into the breakfast parlor close on each other's heels. Max and Roland strolled in together to join the chorus of greetings while the others were still milling about, and Roland came over to Abigail in response to a beckoning finger.

"Roly, the most marvelous coincidence! Lord Dalmore knew Mama when she was a girl!"

"Really? In Herefordshire?"

The twins' voices had been pitched low, but Max, coming around the table in Roland's wake, caught the gist of the quick explanation Abigail gave her brother and smiled into her shining eyes. "You see, my sweet, more proof that we were destined to meet."

"What a romantic thing to say!"

This impulsive remark emanated from Miss Grafton seated next to the earl, who, finding all eyes fixed on her in amusement, blushed rosily.

"Take heart, puss, your time will come," her father said with a chuckle, helping himself to the meats on the tray being circulated by Wilkins.

The indulgent laughter provoked by Miss Grafton's youthful confusion gave Abigail time to master her own unguarded reaction to Max's declaration. She scolded herself for being so startled by his fervent voice. Naturally he would look for opportunities to make pretty speeches and send melting glances in her direction. It was his intention that everyone at Oakridge should believe him to have contracted a love match. She must not forget that she too was playing a role, but for the moment she was more concerned with helping Marjorie Grafton to recover her countenance. To that end she smiled across the earl and said, "I am looking forward to exploring this lovely country, Miss Grafton. Do you know the area well?"

Abigail kept her interested expression as Miss Grafton launched into a breathless description of the scenic beauties of the countryside, aware on one level of the poor child's gratitude at getting her embarrassment behind her. On another level, she was conscious of Max at her side, removing the chair with her belongings to the wall, then substituting another for it and seating himself, while Roland took the place next to him.

The conversation in the breakfast room was quite lively. Eventually all the male guests put in an appearance, although not everyone intended to go riding. Abigail and Miss Grafton remained the only females at the table and neither took part in the discussion of the direction of the proposed ride. At one point Lord Dalmore, with an apology to Abigail, leaned toward his son, suggesting in a soft voice that if Max would act as host he might skip the ride in favor of putting in a couple of hours dealing with estate matters in his office.

"I do not plan to ride very far with Roland and Abigail

this morning, sir, since our mounts spent most of yesterday traveling," Max replied smoothly.

Abigail opened her lips, prepared to offer to ride anything in the stables, but the sudden pressure of Max's hand on her wrist beneath the table kept her silent. She swept a look under her lashes from the son's noncommittal expression to the father, whose eyes flickered before he said in quick apology, "Of course, stupid of me to have forgotten. The work can wait."

A moment later, after a comprehensive glance around the table to assure that his guests had all eaten to their satisfaction, the earl proposed that they adjourn to the stables.

"Wilkins was right, the mist is all gone by nine o'clock," Abigail remarked, glancing out the windows as everyone got to their feet.

"Ah, you have already learned that Wilkins is our weather prophet," Lord Dalmore said, falling into step with Abigail. "He has lived near the South Downs all his life and knows all nature's secrets in this area."

As the riders headed for the stables, the earl pointed out various features of Oakridge to Abigail, who sniffed appreciatively as her steps released the scent of thyme plants between the flagstones that formed the pathway. "Oohh, delicious," she said, smiling up at her host, who smiled back, his dark grey eyes lightening in the same way that his son's did.

"When I visited my daughter in the nursery this morning, she was eager to talk about her 'new brother'—after she had rung a peal over me for my nonappearance yesterday, of course," the earl confided at the entrance to the stable yard. "She also wished to know the identity of the 'pretty lady' who had come with Max. She was very pleased when she understood that you were to become her new sister."

Confusion hindered Abigail as she stammered her appreciation of the compliment. Dropping her eyes, she only hoped it would be attributed to maidenly modesty and not the guilt that assailed her for lending herself to the deception Max was practicing on his family. Lord Dalmore appeared to be a genuinely kind man, which added to her burden of shame.

Abigail recovered her composure in the bustle that attended the mounting of a considerable number of people. Max, who had fallen back with Roland and Miss Grafton when they all left the house, came forward to toss her into the saddle. Dolly, as if to refute his earlier implications of travel fatigue, pawed and skittered at first while Abigail calmly proceeded to adjust her skirts and make herself comfortable.

"That is a spirited little beauty you have there, Miss Monroe," Lord Grafton commented from the back of a rangy grey.

"Dolly is certainly frisky but there is not an ounce of harm in her, sir," Abigail replied in quick defense of her darling as she brought the bay under control with hands and voice. "She's not used to being among so many riders. I rarely have company on our rides," she explained.

"Well, it is evident that you manage her beautifully," the earl said, swinging himself onto the back of a black stallion.

The riding party split in two shortly thereafter, with Miss Grafton joining the Monroes and Max at Abigail's invitation, while the earl, Lord Grafton, and Mr. Carmichael headed east toward Ditchling Beacon, one of the highest hills in Sussex. Sir Archie and Mr. Talant evidently had decided against riding.

The young people agreed to ride westward along the foot of the downs. They paired off spontaneously as Max set a quick initial pace that Abigail delighted in matching. He said nothing to his companion for a few minutes, but Abigail was aware that he was assessing her capabilities as a rider. Since riding was as natural to her as breathing, her mind was free to enjoy the sunshine and contemplate the folded shapes of the distant hills that blended smoothly each one into the next. They did not appear to be a true green from a distance, she decided, but were rather yellowish green in some places and brownish in others. Their outlines were soft but clean in the clear air, the tops barren of any structures as far as she could tell, though no doubt there were shelters for the shepherds who tended the sheep that grazed the slopes and flatish summits.

When Max finally broke the silence that had scarcely impinged on her consciousness, her fascination with the approaching hills was only partially overcome. "I . . . I beg your pardon, Max, what did you say?" she asked, bringing her eyes around to her escort.

"I asked what you and my father were talking about on the way to the stables that made you color up like a Bath miss."

She gazed at him blankly, her mood of deep contentment suddenly shattered. Her wits remained scattered for a few more seconds before she was able to address his question. "Why, nothing, nothing of any significance; we talked the merest commonplaces."

"The merest commonplaces would not bring a blush to your cheeks," he persisted, and she saw that his mouth was set in a straight line.

"I did not blush," she denied, more from annoyance at having her blissful mood ruined than any desire for concealment.

"Do not toy with me, Miss Monroe. You are a poor liar—your face gives you away every time. Why are you trying to protect my father? Were his comments so out of place that you are afraid to repeat them?"

"If you must know, your father was telling me your little sister was pleased to hear that I would become *her* sister," she declared in exasperation. "What ails you anyway? One would think you were jealous of your own father, but," she went on rapidly out of pure contrariness, "since you seem to admire the ability to tell convincing lies, I promise I shall cultivate the skill assiduously for your future benefit, my lord."

Abigail was glaring at Max during this childish fit of temper, but she was unprepared for the shout of laughter that capped a parade of emotions she could only guess at that crossed his face.

"There is one skill you need not practice, my dear Abigail. You have brought being vixenish to the height of perfection. I vow I have never met a girl with such a shrewish tongue, but better that than lying," he said, his teasing inflection turning serious. "You are wrong there. I do not admire dishonesty and deceitfulness in a woman, or the kind of pretense in which females cloak their real nature when they are on the catch for a husband."

"You are very severe on females, my lord, but I do not

believe my sex is inherently more culpable than yours in this area."

"You are very young and inexperienced in worldly dealings with worldly people, Abigail."

"And you dismiss my opinions on this basis? I find that a specious argument. We have human nature in Richmond too, you know, and one comes across it in history and literature as well. I believe virtues and faults are fairly evenly distributed between the sexes."

"Then heaven forbid that I should try to convince you otherwise," Max declared. "It is certainly a more comfortable belief, that is if you as a female do not object to losing your preeminence in the softer virtues such as tenderness and sympathy."

"Truth has nothing to do with comfort, and I can certainly cite instances of tenderness and sympathy on the part of men," Abigail replied, ready to defend her position. "From the little I have seen of him, I would venture to suggest that your father embodies both of those 'feminine' virtues to a considerable extent."

Something fierce flared in Max's eyes for a second, and his lips parted, but he clamped them shut and swung around to greet Roland and Miss Grafton who had caught up with them while they dawdled over their argument.

"Aren't the hills magnificent?" Miss Grafton enthused, smiling at Abigail. "Not majestic like real mountains perhaps, but more friendly."

"Yes," Abigail agreed, "although I might not think so if I lived right underneath them in that village we just passed snugged up against the slopes."

"The hills can seem brooding to some, I expect," Max said, "but not if you've always had them in your back yard, so to speak."

"How high are they?" Roland asked.

"Ditchling Beacon is over eight hundred feet high, but Littleton Down, farther to the west, is the tallest of the South Downs. They lose height as they go eastward to Beachy Head."

"I was wondering earlier if there are any structures or villages on the tops of any of the hills—some seem flat enough," Abigail observed.

"Yes, but there is no water to support settlement. The

chalk has swallowed it up down through the ages," Max explained. "There aren't even many trees in the western end except those on Chanctonbury Ring."

"The downs have been left to the sheep mostly," Miss Grafton added. "Shall we ride toward Chanctonbury Ring? I am persuaded Mr. and Miss Monroe would like to see its crown of beeches."

"Good idea," Max said with approval.

As the riders continued on their southwesterly course, Max told them about Sir Charles Goring who had planted the barren top of Chanctonbury Ring with a grove of beech trees while still a boy and watered them in his youth over fifty years ago.

Roland and Abigail were suitably impressed. "Look at the height and steepness of that slope," Roland cried. "However did he manage to get enough water to those trees to establish them?'

"Painstaking dedication, perhaps even fanaticism," Max said. "Also a lot of labor."

"They do look like a crown as you mentioned before, Miss Grafton," Abigail said, "a dark crown for a regal hill."

The closer they came to the dome-shaped mound the more excited Abigail became. "Oh, I would dearly love to climb it!" she cried when they were in the shadow of the hill.

"We can come back another day," Max promised, "when the horses are more rested. You can see how steep the paths are."

"I did not mean on horseback. I'd like to *climb* it!" she repeated. "Have you ever walked to the top?" she asked Max.

"Yes, frequently when I was a boy. You start out walking but in the end it may be a scramble on hands and knees. The turf can get really slick and slippery, and the winds arise without warning, almost strong enough to tear you off the slopes sometimes."

"I'd still like to try it," Abigail said. "The view from the top must be heavenly."

"It is that. You can see into Surrey on the north, and past the Devil's Dyke hill on the east, Cissbury Ring, the shoreline and the sea to the south, and on a clear day the spire of Chichester Cathedral is visible to the west."

Abigail was enchanted, trying to picture the scene from an eight-hundred-foot eminence. Oakridge would no doubt look like a toy set in its parkland. What would the sea look like? She had never seen a body of water larger than a small lake. She'd not seen much of anything, she realized. Perhaps they might ride to the shores of the Channel one day during her stay in Sussex. How far would that be? She turned impulsively toward Max but, finding him chatting with Miss Grafton and Roland, held her tongue.

Abigail's contributions to the sporadic conversation among the riders on the return to Oakridge dried up, and she grew thoughtful. The countryside was lovely, and she had welcomed the exercise, but the morning had not been one of unalloyed delight by any means. Her private exchanges with Max had been unexpectedly sharp, arising out of the blue, or so it had seemed. She had been snappish at first, even briefly childish in indulging her quick temper, but Max had been patronizing, an attitude that never failed to arouse her resentment.

He had called her young and inexperienced, which was true. She who had been nowhere and seen nothing beyond her local community had challenged his philosophical opinions. For a moment she was humbled, nay abashed, at her daring, or foolhardiness, but she rallied as the familiar rhythms of Dolly's gait soothed her spirits. It was unarguable that worldly people had more experience to draw upon, but their reactions were still largely determined by the sort of people they were *au fond,* and human nature did not alter greatly. Selfishness could be masked by pleasant manners and personal charm, but the actions of such people revealed their natures if one delved deeply enough. An inability to accept people at their own valuation was, for better or worse, a part of her own nature. As a disinterested observer, she was willing to delve beneath the surface of the sophisticated cast of characters interacting on the stage of Oakridge at present. Certainly there was ample scope for observation.

The younger group of riders returned from their morning exercise first. Roland and Max stayed to see to the horses, and the young ladies headed for the house after a short detour through the kitchen garden to admire the bounty therein. Abigail bent over a lavender plant and pulled its bushy stems through her gloved fingers, inhaling deeply. "I simply love the clean scent of lavender," she confessed, laughing up at her companion.

"So do I," the younger girl said, imitating the action. "Do you know when you smile like that you look very like your brother, Miss Monroe?"

"Well, we are twins, after all, so that is not surprising."

"Oh, I did not realize. It must be delightful to have a brother or sister one's own age. My sisters have been married for years and are so much older that we never played together as children. They were out of the schoolroom before I came out of the nursery."

Abigail rose, brushing a few leaves from her skirts, which she slung over her arm as they resumed walking. "Let me tell you it is not always delightful. Roly and I squabbled and played together all our lives and formed an alliance against our brother, who is five years our senior and always held us in contempt. He bullied us unmercifully."

Miss Grafton laughed at this frankness. "My sisters treated me like a pet when they remembered my existence, which I daresay is much to be preferred, and they have me to stay with them frequently, which is very agreeable. I have five nephews and nieces, who are spirited but quite sweet. You and Mr. Monroe seem so attached I am persuaded he will miss you very much when you and Max are married."

"Er . . . yes," Abigail said.

"Will you marry soon?" Marjorie asked as they stepped into the house from the terrace.

"Oh, no . . . that is, we have not had time to discuss the matter yet . . . everything happened so quickly," Abigail finished weakly, blinking in the sudden dimness of the interior.

"Mr. Monroe said you and Max have known each other less than a fortnight," Marjorie continued, sweetly impervious. "It must be utterly thrilling to know right away that someone is the person you wish to spend your life with. Several times this Season I have thought I might be in love, but the feeling never lasted for longer than a sennight, so Mama said I must not even think about marriage until I felt I loved the same man for at least a month!"

"'Your mama is quite right," Abigail said, hoping they

would reach the parting of their ways before this delightful but indiscreet child posed any more personal questions that had her scrambling for answers. However, beyond confessing that she too would wish to be swept off her feet by the man she would marry, Miss Grafton caused Abigail no more qualms by the time they separated to change out of their habits for lunch.

Chapter Eight

Having appeased her initial hunger at her hosts' excellent table, Abigail took advantage of her tablemates' concentration on conversation or cuisine to absorb the details of the dining room. Last night she had been too intent on avoiding any behavior that might bring her to the notice of the sophisticated company into which she'd been plunged to spare attention for her surroundings.

They were certainly impressive—sumptuous was the word that sprang to mind—as she noted the ornate silvergilt appointments gracing the table for a family luncheon. Three massive floral arrangements dominated the center line of the wide rectangular surface covered in snowy linen. The cutting garden at Oakridge must be enormous if this display was a sample of the lavish use of blooms indoors.

The room boasted noble proportions and a high ceiling that was ornamented with a surprisingly delicate tracery of white plasterwork. Surprising only because the walls were papered in a bold blue-and-gold striped pattern, and the deep red background of the huge turkey carpet was richly strewn with gold and blue among many other colors. The curtains at the long windows were made of the same gold brocaded fabric as the chair seats and were tied back with deep blue velvet draperies under heavy valences of the same. There was no denying it was a handsome room, but

Abigail found herself wishing the sunny breakfast room was the venue for lunch. Fourteen people were a great many to accommodate, of course, she hastily amended. No doubt Lady Dalmore wished to avoid any sense of crowding her guests into an inadequate space.

Actually there were only thirteen at table today, the earl having been called to a distant corner of the estate to deal with some problem that had arisen while he was out riding. When Lord Grafton had commiserated that his host was missing a capital luncheon, Lady Dalmore had laughingly assured him that wherever he was on the estate there would be some farmer's wife eager to stuff the earl with food, all of it the sort that added unwanted pounds to a man's frame.

"I have been threatening to put him on a diet of broth and vegetables if he cannot learn to refuse these offerings," she added brightly, smiling around the table at large.

Max did not join in the general murmur of laughter that greeted this wifely pronouncement. Abigail, noting the little muscle that twitched in his cheek, wondered with a stab of sympathy if the countess's remark reminded him of something his mother might have said in a similar situation. This first visit to his home where another woman now presided in his mother's place must be enormously difficult for him. She made a comment on the scenery through which they had ridden that morning, thankful to see the conversation take a new direction.

Although there was never a dearth of conversation at table that afternoon, Max's participation was scant, but not so minimal as to be obvious, at least Abigail hoped it was not obvious to anyone other than herself. She suspected that his attention, though covert, was fixed almost wholly on his stepmother, whose bright charm was being expended chiefly for the benefit of Mr. Talant, sitting beside his hostess.

Abigail's eyes shifted to Mr. Douglas Talant and lingered. *Goodness,* why had she not realized last night that this was quite the handsomest man she had ever beheld, even better looking than Max in the strict aesthetic sense. On meeting him she had registered the well-shaped head of wavy golden hair and finely chiseled features, but there had been a want of animation in his bearing and expression that had rendered him rather insipid. That could not be said of him at this moment as he gazed at Lady Dalmore. He was positively rapt, almost mesmerized. Abigail's thoughtful eyes briefly considered Miss Agnes Talant seated next to her brother. What a pity the beauty could not have been more evenly divided in the Talant family. The fair coloring in the man was an unhealthy sallow in the woman; both had blue eyes, but the sister's were smaller in size and lighter in color. Her thin hair was a faded beige, worn scraped back from a high forehead. Her figure was gaunt, and her expression varied from warily attentive to faintly disapproving. A quality of alertness about her betokened intelligence, but Abigail had yet to hear her offer an unsolicited observation. It was difficult to accept Miss Talant as a friend of the vivacious Lady Dalmore. Abigail's glance drew even more thoughtful as it returned to her hostess.

Lady Dalmore's eye caught hers and continued on around the table, making a swift assessment of the progress of her guests. "Max," she said gaily, "you must let me show you all the improvements we've made at Oakridge after lunch."

"Another time perhaps, Felicity," Max responded. "I promised to show Abigail and Roland the armament room directly after lunch. Have you improved that too?"

"That musty horror?" Lady Dalmore gave an exaggerated shudder. "One visit when I first came to Oakridge was quite sufficient for a lifetime."

Lord Grafton's genial laugh bridged any slight awkwardness that might have arisen as the guests began to discuss ways to spend the afternoon hours before tea would be served in the garden room. Abigail's vagrant speculations now included her supposed fiancé, for his excuse for refusing his stepmother's invitation had been a pure fabrication. She could recall no mention of any tour after lunch, certainly not of the armament room.

There was a twinkle in her eyes a few moments later when she glanced up at Max as she and Roland accompanied him out of the dining room. "I don't share Lady Dalmore's horror at the prospect of a visit to the armament room, Max, but I confess I had rather hoped to see the rest of Oakridge too."

"All in good time," he promised with an intimate smile

that sent a little warning frisson along her nerve ends as he tucked her hand under his arm against his rib cage.

From the corner of her eye Abigail saw that Lady Dalmore was marking their progress down the hall. After they turned the first corner, she tried to pull her hand free but subsided obediently when Max's grip tightened. She remained quiescent while the viscount answered Roland's eager questions about the collection of weapons the Waring family had amassed down through the centuries.

The armament room was not musty-smelling at all, but Abigail could comprehend that it would not appeal to the delicate sensibilities of many females. Long, narrow, low-ceilinged, and inadequately lighted, the very setting contributed to the ghoulish effect of dozens of instruments designed to inflict pain on the human body. Lances, halberds, broadswords, even a crossbow hung on the oak-paneled walls, along with shields painted with fading and flaking coats of arms. Tall glassed-in cases near the door held hunting guns and rifles that she dismissed as having no antique interest as the trio gravitated to the other end of the room, where three suits of full armor were assembled on stands. Max kindled a light and brought a lamp with them so they might better appreciate the workmanship that went into the various parts.

After a few minutes Abigail left the men to their discussion and wandered back to the center of the room, where a glass case displayed a half-dozen beautifully chased and jeweled daggers that still looked extremely functional despite the lovely decorations that turned them into works of art. The sheaths were even more intricately embellished and must be very valuable indeed, assuming the stones were not glass.

"That one is Spanish," said Max at her side, "about two hundred years old. The hilt and sheath are made of gold and the stones are all real, although only the rubies are of top quality, I believe."

"It's gorgeous and, I daresay, just as deadly as the most utilitarian version." Abigail had started a little at finding him so close, but her voice was admirably cool as she slanted a glance at his face, where the fine-grained skin stretched tightly over high cheekbones burned dark by an Iberian sun. Mr. Talant might have the advantage if one considered sheer symmetry alone, but he possessed little of the masculine vitality that radiated from Max in waves even when he was standing still as now. She was relieved when Roland's voice asking something about the dueling pistols in the next case provided her with an excuse to move away from the man whose changeable humors could annoy her exceedingly but whose physical presence was beginning to have a disturbing effect on her breathing apparatus among other things.

"The ivory-handled pistols belonged to my grandfather, who was notoriously hotheaded and is known to have twice killed his man in duels," Max said, taking the pistols out of their case to let Roland test their weight and balance.

Abigail drifted away during the ensuing discussion of the finer points of gun crafting between the men, her eyes drawn to a pair of fencing foils on the wall.

Seized by an impulse, she pulled one of them from its hooks and brandished it aloft. "Oh, Roly, would we not have loved to have laid our hands on a real épée or sword during those marathon war games we used to play with Percy!" In the grip of childhood memories, she assumed a fencer's stance and saluted. *"En garde!"* she cried, and proceeded to execute an original version of a lunge. "I would dearly love to learn how to fence," she said wistfully, straightening up again.

Roland shook his head, laughing. "You were ever a blood-thirsty little creature. It was fortunate for Percy and me that we had to make do with broken branches for weapons."

"I will be delighted to teach you to fence," Max said, smiling at his assumed betrothed.

"How very brave—or rash—of you, Lord Edgeworth, to contemplate putting a weapon into a female's hands," said a voice from the doorway.

The trio in the armament room turned as one to see Lady Winter strolling forward, displaying a look of amusement.

"A perfect gentleman would beg to differ with you," Max said, keeping a straight face, "but I have a sinking feeling that you have spoken no more than the truth, Lady Winter."

"Max," Abigail said, casting him a look of the deepest

reproach, "are you attempting to rescind an offer made before witnesses?"

"Nothing of the sort, my sweet. Since meeting you, I have discovered in myself a singular taste for martyrdom in the cause of fulfilling your every whim and wish. You shall certainly have your fencing lessons."

"You would appear to be fortunate indeed in your choice of suitors, Miss Monroe," Lady Winter said to a blushing Abigail. "Now is the time to secure concessions, for the vast majority of men are not nearly so indulgent after they have put the ring on your finger." These sentiments were couched in a playful fashion, but there was something in the widow's expression that contradicted the lightness.

"I shall take your wise counsel to heart, ma'am," Abigail replied with a smile. "Is this your first visit to the armament room?"

"Yes, as you have no doubt gathered, it is not on Lady Dalmore's tour, but I like old houses." Lady Winter turned from Abigail to Max, asking as she slid her hand under his arm and cast a glance up at him from under her lashes, "What is the oldest item in the collection?"

In the next fifteen minutes Abigail received a lesson in the genteel art of flirtation from a master as Lady Winter proceeded to command Max's full attention, employing a lively blend of flattery, wittiness, and wide-eyed interest that begged the question of sincerity but was certainly entertaining. In the interest of furthering her education in the social graces, Abigail hung on the widow's every word. Max also played the game well, responding promptly to Lady Winter's overtures with an abundance of smiling charm that displayed more of his strong white teeth than Abigail had yet been treated to, but it was done with an air of granting indulgence as toward a child that struck a familiar chord. In one sense it was rather a relief to see that this condescension was not reserved for herself as an inferior or infantile being, but it was disconcerting, nonetheless, to think it might be the common currency of exchange between the sexes at this rarefied level of society.

Abigail's ruminations were brought to an end when Max leaned over and took the fencing foil she'd all but forgotten from her hand. "If we are all agreed that we've exhausted the entertainment possibilities of the armory for the present, I move that we proceed to a tour of the rest of the house, if that will not bore you, Lady Winter?" he added politely as he replaced the foil on the wall.

"I believe I shall take a turn in the shrubbery to soak up some sunshine," Lady Winter returned. "Thank you for interrupting your tour for my benefit, Lord Edgeworth. I'll see you all at tea presumably." With a graceful wave of one beringed white hand, the widow made her exit.

Lady Winter's actions upon leaving the armament room gave the lie to her expressed intentions. It was not sunshine but her hostess that she sought out, discovering Lady Dalmore outside her morning room in conversation with Mrs. Carmichael. The women were on the point of parting as she approached them and Mrs. Carmichael lifted a hand in acknowledgement of her presence as she headed for a door that led to the kitchen and cutting gardens.

"Where did you disappear to so quickly?" Lady Dalmore asked her friend.

"To the armament room, and it was not quick. I had to enlist the assistance of a footman to find it."

"So it was not entirely a lie."

"Did you suspect your stepson of trying to avoid your society, Felicity?" Lady Winter asked with an assumption of innocence while her light brown eyes noted the brief compressing of the other woman's lips that was the only indication of her annoyance at having betrayed herself by the half question. She went on smoothly, "I have been furthering my acquaintance with your future daughter-in-law."

Lady Dalmore had herself well in hand now as she raised arched brown brows. "I shall be exceedingly surprised if it ever comes to marriage. Being newly returned from the wars, Max was no doubt ripe for the plucking, but that wide-eyed innocence the Monroe girl projects will bore him to death before the banns are read." Voice and smile expressed cool amusement. "Besides, the chit is totally ineligible; she has never even had a Season, which tells you that the family is beneath consideration. A few days floundering among the guests here will cast her rustic manners into unflattering relief and bring Max to his senses."

"Do you think so?" Lady Winter appeared to consider this argument. "When I entered the armament room Miss Monroe was attempting to execute a fencing maneuver, which some might deem reflective of an unladylike taste for singularity, but Lord Edgeworth seemed enchanted by the exhibition. I must admit that I have not noticed anything amiss with her manners, accent, or general deportment that would render her ineligible. Her clothes too are in the best of taste and the first stare of fashion with an added fillip of seeming perfect for her alone. Also, Lord Grafton was singing the praises of her horse at lunch, a pure thoroughbred, I gather, all of which indicates that there is no lack of money in the family."

"Money and eligibility are not invariably paired, you will agree, Moira."

Lady Winter, the well-born relict of a manufacturer of woolen goods whose generosity to the government during the war years had been rewarded with a baronetcy in his old age, took this in her stride. "Of course, Felicity, and we both comprehend the difficulty of the well-bred but dowerless female in remaining at the level of society into which she was born. There you have succeeded better than I, though if you will forgive me for pointing it out, all this"—with a gesture encompassing their surroundings—"would have come to you eventually if you'd taken the son instead."

This extraordinary frankness did not offend her hostess, but irritation colored the voice in which she replied, "You know I had little choice in the matter once Dalmore came on the scene. My father's debts were so pressing we could not afford to gamble on waiting until I was safely married to Edgeworth to seek relief from the earl, which might not have been forthcoming in the circumstances. Besides, Dalmore is a very satisfactory husband."

"Then let me urge you in all sincerity to content yourself with your satisfactory marriage, Felicity. You must know Dalmore would be furious if your association with Mrs. Cathcart came to his ears as it might well. He might tolerate Archie Rhodes as a cicisbeo because he plays the game openly. He scatters his favors and will let the woman set the pace. I suppose his devotion gives a woman a certain cachet if that is what you desire, but Douglas Talant is not a safe person to encourage. He's madly in love with you, and I would not put it past him to do something egregious that would plunge you into scandal. You cannot expect anyone to believe that you and that prune-faced sister of his are bosom bows. She is more likely to blacken your name to save her precious brother than provide you with a cover for a dalliance."

Lady Dalmore had been growing restless during this unexpected jobation from her old friend and now she snapped, "That is enough, Moira. Dalmore is well aware that men pay court to me. For a middle-aged man that is part of the appeal of taking an Incomparable for a wife. He likes to see me admired. It reflects credit on his manhood perhaps, or at least on his taste and ability to support the best. I am perfectly capable of handling Douglas Talant. I will see that he keeps the line, have no fear."

"Very well." Lady Winter shrugged. "Never let it be said in future that I failed in friendship by not warning you to watch your step. Edgeworth was watching you and Douglas Talant closely at luncheon. I do not know whether he is the sort to put a flea in his father's ear or not, but—"

"If Max is jealous, it is on his own behalf, not his father's," Felicity retorted with a toss of her head.

Lady Winter stared into the supremely confident countenance of her beautiful friend and shook her head wonderingly. "Then he is giving a masterful performance as a man besotted with a very pretty fiancée."

"That is precisely what it is—a performance," Felicity said, and hers was the last word on the subject as a footman came toward the women still standing outside the morning room at that moment with a message for his mistress. The two women went their separate ways and did not meet again until the members of the household, permanent and temporary, gathered in the garden room in late afternoon.

After an enjoyable tour of the house with Max as an informative guide, followed by a pleasant ramble through the grounds to the stream that left her windblown of hair and leaf-stained of fingers, Abigail headed to the Queen's room to freshen her appearance before tea. Mavis, who was returning a gown she had ironed, regarded her mistress in undisguised horror when Abigail proposed to dismiss her, saying she just planned to wash her hands and run a brush through her hair.

"Look at you, no hat, no gloves, face all flushed. You

look like you've been pulled through a bush backward. Is that a smear of dirt on your gown? *No,* don't touch it, you'll set the stain in," she scolded as Abigail began a guilty search for the mark on her skirt. "Here, sit down while I work on it. I'd be shamed to send you out looking like no one took care of you. I'd never be able to hold my head up in front of Miss Forbes and the other ladies' dressers."

Abigail sat meekly in the chair indicated, glancing with amused affection at the scrawny young girl with the highly developed sense of responsibility, scrubbing at the small mark with a towel dipped in water. The tight red curls escaping from the ugly mobcap seemed to have the same coiled energy as the girl herself.

"There," Mavis said with deep satisfaction a moment later, scrambling to her feet, "it all came out. On a warm day like this I think mebbe the wet spot will be all dry afore you get to the garden room. This cloth is as fine as a cobweb almost and such a pretty green. What do they call it?"

"The fabric is jaconet muslin, the color of the deepest jade stones."

"I never seen anything half so pretty, I'm athinking. Now, let's get to that hair."

Watching Mavis's nimble fingers restore order to her unruly tresses, Abigail reflected that the maid embodied an odd combination of traits, an intensely practical nature allied to a soul that craved and responded to beauty in all forms. Her attitude toward the enameled gold scent bottle was one of awe and reverence. Her eyes were drawn to it repeatedly, but she was reluctant to touch it, fearful of damaging something so beautiful and fragile.

If it were not for Mavis and her funny little ways, she would be rather lonely off in the oldest wing of Oakridge, Abigail realized as she retraced her steps to the main house a few minutes later. So far she had found none of the guests to be nearly so interesting as an uneducated young girl working as a domestic. What did that say about her own tastes and inclinations, she wondered uneasily. The only person she felt at all drawn to was the earl, and that was partly because he remembered her mother with fondness.

Abigail's steps lagged a little as she neared the garden room. It had been a marvelous day for the most part, riding in this lovely country and spending the afternoon exploring with Roly and Max. Now she must join the other guests and prepare to make small talk, or rather, pretend to take an interest as the others made small talk about persons and places unknown to her. She lifted her chin, pulled her shoulders back, and stepped into the garden room, nudging her lips into a curve.

Pleasure lighted Abigail's eyes as she glanced around, just as it had earlier when Max had showed them the room his mother had preferred above the rest. Part conservatory, part sitting room, it was on the ground level with access to terraced gardens through sets of French doors. Exterior doors and windows of an existing room had been removed years ago and replaced by open arches giving onto a three-sided addition with a slate floor and walls that were predominantly made of glass. Light now flooded the original room, offering enhanced views along with the comforts of a conventional sitting room. Green plants and flowers in abundance graced the addition and gave one the sense of being outdoors. She liked the informal atmosphere achieved by simple furnishings. Chairs with caned backs and seats mingled with stuffed pieces upholstered in cheerful chintz fabrics in an appealing array of comfortable-looking furniture.

A number of the chairs were occupied when Abigail arrived. A few people were clustered about Lady Dalmore, who was dispensing tea from a couple of large silver pots with the assistance of Wilkins. Beyond the arches she could see Lady Grafton and Marjorie examining a small potted lemon tree that she had admired when Max had brought them here earlier.

A swift glance located Max in conversation with Sir Archie and Mr. Carmichael. He spotted her in the doorway and excused himself, coming up to her with a smile. "I wondered what was keeping you, but it was worth the wait. You look as if you have just stepped out of a bandbox."

"The credit goes entirely to Mavis," Abigail said with a grin. "I fear she regards me as a slightly dim-witted child who must be coached and guided lest I disgrace myself in company."

"Mavis can relax; you'll do. How do you like your tea?" Max inquired, leading her to a chair.

Abigail was conscious of a warmth spreading through her at the careless approval, but she offered a mild protest. "I don't like to interrupt your conversation, Max. You must not feel you have to dance attendance on me at all times. I can get my own tea."

"Of course you can, but the whole point of the exercise is to convince everyone that it is my utmost delight to dance attendance on you," he explained in the patient tones people reserve for those unfortunates of limited understanding.

"A little sugar, no milk," she said smartly, seating herself in the chair he indicated. She must curb this tendency to forget that she was "on stage" at Oakridge, Abigail resolved, and stop pouting like a child who has been unjustly corrected. The fault was hers for permitting the carefree hours spent in Max's company to take her out of her role. She pasted what she hoped was an adoring expression on her face as she watched Max approach Lady Dalmore, who treated him to her brilliant smile as she poured and fixed the tea he requested. He remained to chat with her and Miss Talant, seated beside her, for a bit.

Abigail's eyes wandered lazily about the room, noting the relaxed air that prevailed as snatches of thought and disjointed phrases rose out of the indistinguishable murmur of social intercourse. A man's rich chuckle briefly registered, then a woman's playful protest. Marjorie Grafton, cup in hand, plopped herself down in the chair on her left. Abigail was attending to the young woman's enthusiastic comments on the greenery in the conservatory when trousered legs and pale green skirts impinged on her side vision. She turned to accept the teacup Max was holding out to her as her hostess sank gracefully onto the cane-backed chair on her other side.

"I understand that your horse has been much admired today, Miss Monroe. A thoroughbred?"

"Yes, ma'am, a four-year-old bay mare."

"I would adore to try her paces sometime, if you will permit?"

"Of . . . of course, anytime," Abigail said, hiding her surprise. "I am persuaded you would find Dolly a wonderful ride. She is small, but possesses surprising speed and stamina, apart from being beautifully mannered."

"I gather you are an accomplished rider?"

"I can attest to that," Max put in while Abigail wondered what she was supposed to reply to such an inquiry.

"I too," said Miss Grafton. "Miss Monroe and Dolly almost seemed like one creature—of one mind, I mean, when we were galloping this morning."

"You were well tutored then?" Lady Dalmore said, her eyes shifting back to Abigail, who chuckled.

"Not really tutored at all. My brother likes to say we were all born on a horse. It is not surprising we ride well when our father breeds horses."

Lady Dalmore lifted one brow as she studied the young woman next to her. "As an avocation?"

"No, to keep a roof over our heads," Abigail said calmly, returning the look as she took a sip of her tea.

"I see. I have been looking to purchase another hack. Since breeding horses is your business, you might be willing to sell Dolly if she suits me?"

"I am so sorry, Lady Dalmore, but we raise carriage horses, not riding horses, and I could never bear to part with Dolly."

A short throbbing silence was thankfully shattered by a piping little voice that drew all heads toward the doorway.

"Mama, Mama, look what I found in the garden after my nap!"

Lady Rose Waring, her angelic face alight with excitement, left her nurse behind and ran across to her mother's chair. Under the indulgent eyes of those in the immediate vicinity, the little girl dug her hand into the lace-edged pocket of her apron and pulled out a greenish brown object, which she thrust at her mother, who recoiled violently.

"*Rose,* drop that disgusting thing immediately! *Nurse!*"

As the child stared at her parent in consternation, her rosebud mouth puckering, Max hunkered down on his haunches and put out his hand, saying cheerfully, "May I see your treasure, Rose? Brothers don't find frogs as disgusting as mamas do."

It was touch and go for a second while the little girl blinked rapidly, looking at her mother's angry face. When she turned, solemn-eyed, and opened her hand over Max's, Abigail let out the breath she'd been holding.

"Well, isn't he a beauty. Where did you find him?"

"Near the little-boy fountain, under a bush."

Abigail was aware that Lady Dalmore was berating the hapless nurse, who pleaded ignorance of her charge's forbidden pet, but her eyes were on Max's dark head bent over the little girl's curly golden one as they examined the tiny frog cowering in his palm. "May I see him too, Lady Rose?" she begged, bending forward with a smile.

The child obligingly pulled Max's arm nearer to Abigail. "He tried to hop away from me, but I catched him," she confided to her pet's new admirer.

"So I see, and you did not hurt him at all, but he is not very happy indoors, you know, and I expect that his mama is looking for him near the fountain. She will be very unhappy if he is lost."

Since Lady Dalmore was ordering the nurse to remove frog and child from the room, Abigail's suggestion was very timely. It found favor with Lady Rose, who was persuaded to take her frog back to his home.

Thanks to the opportune arrival of the earl at that moment and his subsequent offer, upon being acquainted with the situation, to accompany his daughter on this errand of mercy, the desired exit was accomplished without any lamentations on the part of the child.

A collective sigh of relief was exhaled by those who had witnessed the incident, Lady Dalmore recovered her composure, and the afternoon wound to a close with good manners and good cheer reigning unchallenged.

Chapter Nine

"Max, I must talk to you."

Max froze in the act of opening the door to his bedchamber. After deliberately suppressing the frown that had knitted his forehead on hearing the low voice, he pulled his hand back and turned to face his former love.

"Where did you spring from, Felicity?"

"I was in there," she replied, gesturing to a room across the hall. "I saw you and Mr. Monroe walk by."

He nodded. "Through a crack. What did you wish to say to me?"

"Not here," she said, glancing at the door Roland Monroe had entered less than a minute before. "Let's go inside," motioning toward his room with her head.

"Not on your life." He stood with his back against his door regarding her with a little smile on his lips.

"I do not wish Mr. Monroe to hear what I have to say."

"Then I would advise you to speak very softly." His own voice did not drop below a normal conversational pitch.

She sent him an annoyed look that failed to move him, then shrugged and sighed. "Very well. Since you have been avoiding me, I had to try to catch you as best I could in order to speak privately."

"Well, you have succeeded. What is on your mind that demands such . . . unusual precautions?"

"Max," she began softly, taking a step closer and looking up at him in an attitude of melting concern, "you must know this proposed marriage is quite impossible. You—"

"And just why is it impossible, Felicity?" He interrupted her without qualm, not troubling to mask his anger.

Lady Dalmore backtracked hastily. "Oh, I grant that she is an appealing child and quite pretty in her way, but you must see that she is totally out of her element here at Oakridge among our friends."

"None of my friends are present at Oakridge, so that is not an issue."

"Do not be so difficult, Max. You know perfectly well what I mean. Not to put too fine a point on it, Miss Monroe is completely ineligible. Your father would never condone a connection with a family of horse breeders!"

"Did my father send you to me with this message?"

She hesitated for a second, probably debating whether she could get away with the lie, he decided with the cynicism his earlier dealings with her had engendered. He preserved a bland expression and waited.

"With a houseful of guests, Dalmore and I haven't had an opportunity to really discuss the matter yet," she said, "but you cannot be so naive as to believe he will welcome such a low connection."

"I will deal with my father if and when he raises any objections to my marriage. You need not concern yourself in the matter any longer; in fact, I am amazed that you of all people would venture to raise arguments to a person contemplating matrimony, knowing from personal experience how unlikely it is that even valid arguments will have the desired effect."

The countess flinched under the biting words, but she continued to regard him with large blue eyes full of appeal as she erased the distance between them. "Max, I know how much I must have hurt you, but you should understand that I really had no choice. My father's debts—"

"Must I remind you that your father had already given his consent to *our* marriage?" he interjected. "You were not coerced into marrying my father. Tell the truth for once in your life, Felicity."

"The *truth* is that you are not in love with Abigail Monroe!" she hissed at him defiantly. "Admit it—you have contracted this betrothal to revenge yourself on me."

"I say, Max—oh, I beg your pardon, Lady Dalmore . . . I did not realize . . . I only heard Max's voice," Roland Monroe stammered.

At the first sound of the door latch, Max had put Felicity away from him forcibly enough that she was obliged to right her balance. Now he said easily to the embarrassed youth, "That is all right, Roland. Lady Dalmore had already delivered my father's message. Tell him I'll speak to him after dinner, Felicity," he added, looking at her briefly.

"Yes, of course," the countess murmured. "If you will excuse me, I shall see you in the gold saloon presently." The words were directed at both men, but her smile was exclusively for Roland Monroe as she turned and walked away.

"You wanted to speak to me, Roland?" Max prompted as the young man's eyes followed the countess's progress down the hallway.

"What? Oh, yes." Roland's glance fell on the magazine he carried, and he held it out to his friend. "I thought you might be interested in an article on Scott. I found it in this old issue of *The Gentleman's Quarterly* that was on the desk in my room."

"Thank you, I would like to read it." Max accepted the

magazine with a smile and turned back to enter his room with a valedictory wave.

He closed the door behind him a second later, grateful for the blessing of privacy in which to try to make sense of the impressions colliding in his mind after the wild scene with Felicity. He glanced at the magazine in his hand and tossed it on a chair, heading over to the window, where he gazed out, seeing nothing.

It was not surprise he was experiencing, he admitted, trying to bring a painful honesty to the exercise. At their first meeting at Mrs. Cathcart's soirée he had realized that Felicity was not about to ease his recovery by setting herself at the distance her married status would indicate and ignoring what had been between them. Why else had he seized on the plan of providing himself with a fiancée for this first visit to his home under radically changed circumstances? Still being honest, he acknowledged that he'd never really expected to gull her into believing he was in love with another woman, but it was in her own interest to play along with the charade and maintain the appearance of amity and civility that would spare everyone embarrassment. And here she was barely concealing her antagonism for Abigail Monroe in front of her guests.

It was unlike Felicity to act so contrary to her own interest, and it made him very nervous indeed. The gloves had certainly been off in that charming little bout just now. After circling around mouthing platitudes, she'd responded to his goading challenge by slinging what she believed to be the truth of his actions in his face. Roland's interruption had saved him from having to make a lying denial of her accusations, because of course he was not in love with Abigail Monroe, and on some level at least he was enjoying the element of retaliation that was part of the engagement farce, though revenge was not his object. Honesty forbade denying that he could not help wondering if, had Roland not intervened, her next words would have been an accusation that he still loved *her.* And would his instinctive denial have also been a lie?

He was not evading an answer, he told himself, nor denying that he'd been aware of her lovely features and beautiful body during their argument. When she'd all but cast herself upon his chest, his heart rate had accelerated and the familiar fire had started in his loins. It had taken a real effort to keep his hands off her when she cast appealing looks up at him from limpid blue eyes. But even while his muscles had ached to take her in his arms, his brain had been judging her. She was vain, calculating, inconsiderate, and, he suspected, beyond the influence of morality when her own selfish interests were at stake. Surely love could not exist in tandem with such harsh opinions? At most it was simple animal lust he was battling.

Max's teeth and fists were tightly clenched as he stood rigidly by the window, forcing stillness on his body. He was furious enough with his own weakness to put his fist through the glass, but anger and self-disgust were actually the less important components of his feelings at the moment. He was growing increasingly uneasy in the face of his observations of Felicity's behavior in the twenty-four hours he'd been at Oakridge. His experience of her four years ago had taught him how clever and calculating she'd been in the furtherance of her ambitions while presenting and preserving a public image of maidenly perfection. Her machinations had been cloaked by a vivacious charm that made her universally appealing while her radiant beauty made her similarly desirable.

The charm had been less universal in her own home since his arrival. She had attained her goals of wealth and position, but gratitude to the man who had made them possible evidently did not inspire a pretense of devotion. No, that was not fair. His thinking was colored by the way she had looked at him and touched him unnecessarily, both at Mrs. Cathcart's and in the hall just now. He'd not observed enough interaction between Felicity and his father to judge their conjugal relationship lacking in any respect. It might be precisely what both parties desired.

He'd not noticed any strong maternal affection for her adorable daughter in Felicity either, but again, fairness demanded that he reserve judgment at present. What he *had* noticed was her encouragement of the pathetic devotion of that tailor's dummy Talant in front of her guests at luncheon today, but at least his father had not been forced to witness the impropriety.

What concerned him most at this moment was Felicity's thinly veiled antipathy toward the girl he claimed as his betrothed, who was entitled to be treated with respect and consideration on that count alone. This dog-in-the-manger attitude, while comprehensible in the abstract, was unpardonable if reflected in the demeanor of a hostess. He might not be in love with Abigail Monroe, but she was an innocent party coerced into playing a role that would be distasteful enough to any young woman of sensibility under the best of circumstances. She was playing her part with grace and good humor and, contrary to Felicity's scornful gibes, fitting in rather well in a quiet way. He might consider her nature too hot-tempered and deplorably frank for his personal taste, but she was no less a lady for that, and he'd be damned if he would allow Felicity to indulge her spite by making the poor girl uncomfortable in this house where she was a guest.

Spite. The word brought him up short. His opinion of Felicity's character after she'd thrown him over for his father had been far from charitable, but he would not have ascribed spitefulness to her had he not witnessed several subtle attempts to embarrass or denegrate Abigail. Well, she would have him to deal with if she continued in this vein, he vowed grimly.

Max's expression must have reflected his thoughts because his batman, appearing in the dressing-room doorway at that moment to assist him in changing for dinner, gave him a long hard stare before announcing that there was hot water in the basin. He disappeared back into the dressing room without further comment.

With a concerted effort Max slammed a mental door on his bitter musings and strolled into the dressing room. "Have our people been treating you well, Gibbs?" he asked with a smile, not realizing for a moment that he had spoken as though he still belonged at Oakridge. His smile faded.

"Yes, Captain. Wilkins seems a good sort and so does Mrs. Howell. They've set me up real comfortable. Sure beats any of our billets in Spain or Portugal."

Max laughed in genuine amusement, accustomed to Gibbs's reluctance to admit to being impressed by anything they had run into in their four years together. "My father's head groom is a downy old bird well worth cultivating, but I'd advise you to avoid his valet. The earl is not high in the instep, but Collins is toplofty enough for both—that is if he still has the same man I remember. A wizened, dried-up creature with neat, fluttering little hands and a perpetually pursed mouth?"

"That's the one, all right, Captain. Not too happy to see the likes o' me at the same end of the table, he wasn't, but you being the heir and all, Wilkins and Mrs. Howell insisted on putting me near the top."

"I believe the servants' hall is always more strict about protocol than the house," Max replied with a grin. "I wonder what they've settled about the redheaded child who is only a housemaid but is waiting on Miss Monroe while we are here?"

"I hear that her la'ship's dresser, Miss Forbes, near had hysterics at the idea of associating with her, but Mavis, that's the girl's name, begged to stay with the other maids, so all's bowman there." Gibbs slanted a look at his master, who seemed to have overcome whatever had bedeviled him earlier as he washed and prepared to shave again before dressing for the evening.

"Could have knocked me over with a feather when I found out the lady who came running out to greet us yesterday was the countess," Gibbs said, keeping his eyes on the neckclothes he was taking from a dresser. "She didn't seem any older than Miss Monroe, but o'course I didn't get a real close look, what with having my hands full attending to Allegro and the other horses."

"My stepmother is considerably younger than my father." Max's words were careless, dismissive, and his eyes remained on his image in the mirror as he stroked a razor down his cheek.

All ensuing verbal communication between master and batman before Max went down to dinner pertained strictly to sartorial matters or Allegro's accommodation in the earl's stable.

As on the previous day, Max's interim destination was the stairwell nearest the old wing. This time he arrived before Abigail, but spotted her hurrying toward him a moment later, an unclouded smile on her lips. As he took in the shining dark ringlets cascading from a topknot, the pale clear skin touched with rose on high cheekbones, and the perfect proportions of her delicate frame garbed in a diaphanous creation in a deep rose color that echoed the vibrancy of her spirit, Felicity's words "quite pretty in her way" surfaced in his mind. Now there was a classic example of understatement. Wasp-tongued she might be, but his pseudo-fiancée was delectable to gaze upon, he concluded with an internal smile as he took her hand to descend.

The predinner interval was a near repeat of the previous evening except that his little sister did not put in an appearance. Max found himself experiencing a surprising pang of disappointment. A picture of the child regarding him with somber eyes and trembling lip when he had tried to mitigate her mother's dramatic reaction to the presence of a frog in her drawing room had reappeared several times in his mind during the intervening period. Hopefully, their father had been able to ease Rose's distress and restore the happy anticipation that had propelled her into the garden room initially. Seven-and-twenty was an advanced age at which to learn how to be a brother, but the idea had a distinct appeal. Abigail must have been thinking along similar lines, for as they headed into the dining room, she whispered that she hoped Lady Rose had not been too upset to find her new pet unwelcome indoors. Max squeezed her hand in approval before they took their places, recalling how sweet she had been with the little girl. She shot him a surprised glance before her lips curved in response and her lashes swept down, affording him an excellent view of their dark length and luxuriant thickness.

Abigail was seated between Mr. Carmichael and Lord Grafton tonight. Over the course of an elaborate and well-prepared dinner, Max made it a point to observe her dealings with her neighbors. Judging from the free flow of conversation and the animation and frequent smiles on all three faces, his betrothed was having no difficulty in consorting with those Felicity considered her betters. Mrs. Carmichael, on Lord Grafton's other side, also joined in the discussion from time to time. From his position between the dour Miss Talant and Lady Grafton, whose arthritis was acting up and coloring her view of the world at present, Max could only gaze with envy at the merry party across the table.

At her end of the table Felicity gave equal encouragement to Douglas Talant and Sir Archie, who were vying for her favors. Max trusted that her refusal to acknowledge the presence of the son of the house was not apparent to any one else. His father's customary urbanity and ease were in evidence at the other end of the table as he included Roland Monroe and Marjorie Grafton in his conversation with the determined Lady Winter.

He was not the only person interested in observing the interplay among the dramatis personae, Max realized when he had to speak twice to gain Miss Talant's ear. The difference was that Miss Talant's interest was focused exclusively on her brother's attentions to his hostess. The silent malevolence with which she regarded Felicity gave Max a momentary twinge of unease before his eyes were drawn once again to Abigail's laughing face as she responded to something Lord Grafton said.

After a rather short session of port and politics among the males in the dining room, the earl led his guests back to rejoin the ladies. Max parried his father's attempts to introduce a private note as they walked side by side by expressing concern for his small sister's reaction to her temporary banishment from the company during tea.

The earl laughed. "At this age children are volatile creatures. Within two minutes Rose was happily engaged in conducting a search for the frog's parent. Apparently, Miss Monroe saved the day, or at least a tantrum, with her suggestion that the mother frog was mourning the loss of her offspring, and Rose was bent on effecting a reunion."

Max grinned. "It was certainly an inspired idea," he agreed. "I am not at all sure what it should feel like to be a brother to an infant, but Rose is a sheer delight."

Lord Dalmore looked closely at his son, and some of the tension eased from his countenance. "Yes, she is the great joy of my old age," he said quietly.

"You are not old," Max protested instinctively. "You could probably go ten rounds with me right this minute."

"Heaven forbid. You may believe me when I say the idea holds no appeal at all, but I thank you for the flattering thought."

They entered the saloon shoulder to shoulder at that moment, and Max caught Felicity's quick glance and the subsequent narrowing of her eyes before she resumed directing two footmen who were rearranging chairs. It seemed that music was to be the order of the evening.

Without warning memories shafted through Max, images of a younger Felicity looking ethereally beautiful—almost angelic—as she sang on numerous occasions during the weeks he had courted her. She had been singing at a musical evening on a much grander scale than tonight's gathering the very first time he set eyes on her, and the sight had been electrifying. He had been a man struck by lightning. He'd combed through the appreciative audience after her performance until he'd found an acquaintance to perform the introduction to this enchantress. Elements of awe, reverence, obsession had driven his single-minded pursuit of the girl who eclipsed every other female he'd ever seen in beauty, grace, and accomplishments. In his youthful passion he'd invested her with every feminine virtue, thus setting himself up for inevitable disillusionment, he now saw with the clarity of hindsight. It was a permanent source of humiliation to be forced to acknowledge the romantic idiot he'd been at three-and-twenty. Nothing could have been more effective in teaching him to distrust appearances, especially the appearance of virtue in young women, than Felicity's subsequent actions. There were times in the past few years when he'd been accused by his comrades of being overly critical of the fair sex, but a hard lesson once learned was not to be lightly disregarded. At this point he was grateful for the education.

Max shook off his disagreeable memories as he located Abigail seated next to Miss Talant. She was making a valiant effort to sustain a conversation, but he interpreted the quick sideways look she shot him as one of appeal and reacted accordingly, crossing over to stand near the settee the two women occupied in uneasy alliance.

"Are you fond of music, Miss Talant?" Max asked, producing what he hoped was a winning smile.

It won nothing but a steely look as the lady replied, "Not at all, Lord Edgeworth, at least not of amateur performances."

"But just think, it might have been charades," he pointed out with a gravity that had Abigail catching her underlip between her teeth as she studied her clasped hands in her lap.

Miss Talant paused to consider and conceded, "I daresay that would have been even worse."

Seeing that the furniture arrangements seemed to be completed, Max offered an arm to each lady and escorted them over to the grouping in front of the pianoforte, ushering them into the second row and seating himself between them. Recalling Abigail's earlier concern about her lack of shared experiences with the rest of the guests, Max subjected her delightful profile to a swift scrutiny, but she appeared serene as a summer sea. He had a feeling—conviction really—that Felicity, well aware of his betrothed's nonexposure to societal gatherings, would seize the opportunity to set Abigail at a disadvantage in front of everyone. He was determined to foil any such move if it meant swearing that Abigail was the victim of a putrid sore throat that had attacked her in the interim since dinner. The lazy gaze he swept around the company was belied by a mental version of a battlefield alert going on inside his head.

In the event, it was Miss Talant whom Lady Dalmore first invited to perform for the company, an invitation that was summarily declined by that lady with the bald statement that she neither played nor sang. Mrs. Carmichael graciously agreed to play for them, selecting a Beethoven sonata that was competently executed and well received. Lady Winter next sang a couple of rollicking songs with sly, amusing lyrics in a breathy contralto. At this point Lady Dalmore acquiesced to the repeated entreaties of Sir Archie and Mr. Talant, seating herself at the pianoforte. She was a picture of elegance and grace, her high-dressed hair gleaming gold in the dancing light from a multibranched candelabrum placed near the instrument.

Her silken soprano was still as lovely as he remembered, and she employed it with well-trained skill on some difficult arias from Mozart operas. The severest critic would be forced to allow that she looked supremely beautiful throughout the polished performance as she accompanied herself on the japanned instrument that had belonged to the first Lady Dalmore.

At the finish Max's applause was long and enthusiastic. His stepmother's smile as she glanced at him would have lost a shade of its complacence, however, had she known that some of his fervor sprang from relief at the welcome realization that, beautiful though she had looked while singing, he had experienced no inclination to liken her to an angel or a goddess on this occasion. His spine stiffened when Felicity glided away from the pianoforte, her eyes on the girl by his side.

"Your speaking voice is so musical that I am persuaded you number singing among your accomplishments, Miss Monroe," she purred. "Would you give us all the pleasure of hearing you perform?"

Max's lips parted when Abigail hesitated, but before he could step in, she said, "I am unused to performing before so many people, ma'am, but if my brother will assist me, I'll do my best to oblige."

As his eyes ran over her face, Max saw that Abigail's color was a trifle heightened, but she was quite composed when she rose from her chair and joined Roland at the pianoforte.

And well she might be composed, a dazed Max concluded a moment later when the Monroe twins launched into a duet. Who would have expected that so powerful a voice could issue forth from such a petite instrument? The composition was unfamiliar to him, some sort of paean to spring, but its fast tempo demanded a virtuosity in phrasing and an extensive vocal range that Abigail summoned seemingly without effort. Her voice blended marvelously with Roland's light tenor during the combined parts and soared in the solos.

Max's lungs deflated when the song ended, and he realized that he'd been listening so passionately he'd been holding his breath. There was an instant of complete silence in the large room before the guests exploded into applause. Abigail blushed and held up her hand. "Thank you all so much. I would like to explain that the music we just performed is an original composition by my brother." Pride radiated from her face as she smiled at her twin.

It was Roland's turn to look self-conscious at the complimentary remarks flowing about them, but his deep blue eyes glowed with the pleasure of having his work appreciated. He began to rise from the bench, and Max, seeing Felicity about to make a move to go forward with the program, forestalled her, raising his voice in a request. "Please sing something else, Gail. A love song perhaps?"

"Please do, Miss Monroe," Lady Dalmore added, doing her duty when the girl glanced to her hostess for guidance.

A chorus of approval rang out from the audience, settling the matter. After a low-voiced exchange between brother and sister, Roland began to play and Abigail stood near his shoulder, facing the company.

For the next few short moments Max sat spellbound, his eyes never leaving Abigail's face as she sang Bononcini's lyrical "Per la Gloria d'adoravi," her tones as clear and perfect as bells. She stood unmoving, her hands clasped loosely together at her waist, and the sheer artistry and emotion in her rendition of the ageless love song sent chills chasing up his spine. It was nothing like his reaction to Felicity's singing in the past, he assured himself. That had been Cupid's dart, a *coup de foudre,* love at first sight—whatever one chose to call the idiocy that prompts a previously sane individual to surrender his heart into the care of a complete stranger. He already knew Abigail Monroe, and while he was prepared to agree that she was a good companion, despite a few irksome idiosyncracies, and was, thankfully, devoid of missish traits, he was not in the least in love with her. It was pure admiration—even awe—in the presence of her musical gift that had him wallowing in a pool of sensual pleasure.

All too soon the song ended and the applause began, but any afterglow Max might have enjoyed was curtailed by the sight of Agnes Talant bringing her hands together in a perfunctory fashion while her habitual expression of discontent remained fixed. He wondered fleetingly just what it would take to please or excite the creature before returning his attention to Abigail, who was coming back to her place beside him, her eyes bright and her cheeks flushed from the heady praise that had been heaped on her.

They should have saved Abigail until last, Max reflected as the remainder of the musical program suffered by comparison with her performance. He did his duty, simulating enthusiasm for several lackluster renditions, wishing all the time that he could spirit Abigail and Roland off to a room with a pianoforte where he could prevail upon them for a private concert.

When the company was enjoying refreshments at the end of the musical portion, the second memorable event of the evening occurred. He was happily engaged in a lively discussion of their favorite composers with Roland and Abigail when his father came up to them. Taking Abigail's hand in his, the earl raised it to his lips and smiled down at the bemused girl.

"I'd like to thank you for the great pleasure you have given me tonight, my dear Abigail. When you were singing, I could close my eyes and see your mother again as she was that last summer. You have inherited her musical gift as well as her eyes."

"Thank you, sir, for the kind words. Roly and I certainly owe our musical abilities to our mother, who trained us from the time we were scarcely out of leading strings. She thought it a great shame that Papa and Bertie are not at all musical, and she was determined to share her gift with us."

"Why did you never mention that you were acquainted with Miss Monroe's mother, Dalmore?"

Unaware that Lady Dalmore had come within hearing distance of the small group, Abigail started in surprise at the sharp question.

The earl turned to his wife and smiled. "Hello, my love. Until this morning I was unaware that Roland and Abigail are the children of an old friend from my youth."

Max, watching Felicity's face as his father explained the circumstances that had led to the happy discovery, had no difficulty in discerning the chagrin beneath the careful pose of interest she'd assumed. He'd have wagered his entire fortune at that moment that his former fiancée was recalling the earlier scene in the corridor outside his bedchamber when she had confidently asserted that the earl would dislike his son's proposed match. He was enjoying himself mightily as he observed her summoning up her social adroitness to make the appropriate comments on her husband's disclosure. The fact that she carefully avoided any eye contact with her stepson during the ensuing conversation was convincing proof that his assumptions were right on the mark.

Later, as he bade his betrothed a smiling good night when she retired with the other ladies, Max mused that, all in all, it had been quite a satisfying day. If Felicity had the good sense to abandon her underground campaign to get rid of the girl he had ostensibly chosen to become his wife, they might manage to muddle through this visit without incident. It had never been his intention to embarrass his family when he appeared at Oakridge with a prospective bride in tow, but he had the grace to be grateful to the Monroe twins for possessing the quality and character to rescue what he could now see had been a half-baked scheme, fraught with previously unconsidered perils.

They were over the hump now, he decided with an optimism too long in abeyance, and he could turn his mind to the pleasant pursuit of acquainting Abigail with all the secret nooks and crannies inside Oakridge, as well as his favorite haunts in the locality. Seeing his home through her eyes was proving unexpectedly enjoyable. The word "renewal" unaccountably floated into his mind, but he dismissed it as fanciful as he softly whistled a few bars of the song Abigail had sung so enchantingly earlier in the evening.

Chapter Ten

Abigail floated off to the Queen's room in a contented daze when the gathering broke up. Singing was always a joyful activity, something she did every day of her life, but tonight had been a revelation. The wave of admiration and approval surging from her audience had engulfed her, lifting her to a thrilling state that was part excitement, part gratification, leavened by awe. Never before had she experienced the heady power of holding an audience in the palm of her hand, and she relished it above anything, she acknowledged privately, casting a half-guilty glance around the empty corridor as she made her unaccompanied way to her quarters. She was ever mindful of her mother's gentle strictures against unmaidenly pride in personal accomplishments, but nothing could take the shine out of her pleasure as she relived those few moments of triumph earlier this evening when all ears, with the possible exception of Miss Talant's, had been tuned into her voice.

Mavis's running narrative of the goings-on in the servants' hall while she prepared her mistress for bed that evening went in one of Abigail's ears and out the other despite her smiles and nods. She emerged from her waking dream long enough to respond to the maid's cheerful good night, then promptly resumed her blissful train of thought, sinking gradually into a sleeping version of the same.

Some of the glow remained when Abigail awoke the next morning, and her mood was sunny as she donned her riding habit. Max had proposed riding to the town of Steyning, and she was eager to see more of the delightful Sussex scenery.

The spring in her step gradually lessened, however, as Abigail decreased the distance to the breakfast room, and eventually she was forced to face her foolish reluctance to launch herself into a day that would end with a dance. There was no comfort to be had from tonight's entertainment being not a public ball but merely a gathering of friends and neighbors whose socializing would include an informal dance. If dancing lessons had never formed a part of one's education, there was not a penny to choose between private and public humiliation, one of which was scheduled to be her lot tonight. To be relegated to the ranks of the elderly, decrepit, or disinclined spectators would be hard enough to bear for her own sake, but Abigail had sensed Max's pride in her musical performance last night, and she really dreaded the thought of disappointing him this evening. And, she admitted with difficult honesty, it was a stinging blow to her own pride not to be able to exceed Max's expectations in all areas. She'd have had to be stupid indeed not to realize that it was the peculiar circumstances under which they had met, not any battery of feminine charms, that had propelled her into her present position as ostensible fiancée of the heir to one of England's premier earldoms. Innate resentment at his complete indifference to her as a person had made her as prickly as a nettlebush initially, over and above her revulsion from the deception he demanded from her. Actually, the prickles had dulled a bit after the boost to her self-confidence provided by her beautiful new wardrobe. Yesterday had been unexpectedly enjoyable. Max had been companionable during their morning ride, and later in the armament room had shown himself to be good-natured and intent on his guests' pleasure.

None of this made it any easier to fail him now, Abigail concluded gloomily, squaring her shoulders and forcing a smile to her lips as she marched into the breakfast parlor to begin her trial.

The unexpected sight—and sound—of Lady Dalmore merrily entertaining her guests struck a blow to Abigail's purpose and resolution. The sinking sensation in the pit of her stomach gave the lie to her automatic denial of a reluctance to meet her hostess when she was feeling so unsure of herself. She retrieved her slipping smile as she slid into a place between Marjorie Grafton and Mr. Carmichael, but Lady Dalmore must have read her thoughts.

"Surprised to see me, Miss Monroe?" she inquired gaily, turning her high-powered smile on the girl, who had murmured a general greeting to those at table. "I was just explaining that, with an upcoming interview with our cantankerous chef this morning, I felt the need of more internal fortification than chocolate and cold toast could supply." In a pale blue gown of sheer voile, Lady Dalmore was the personification of appealing femininity as she gave an exaggerated little shudder of resignation or dread at the prospect that awaited her in the kitchens.

In the wake of the appreciative little ripple of sympathy and amusement that went around the table, sparing her a reply, Abigail noted that her hostess was toying with an omelet as she spoke, though not actually consuming it.

For Abigail the next half hour was a lesson in the art of charming and holding an audience without a single note of music. Granted that the audience was predominantly masculine and predisposed in favor of beauty and animation, honesty demanded an acknowledgment that there was something for everyone in the countess's performance. In marked contrast to the previous day's luncheon, she gracefully discouraged Mr. Talant's attempts to monopolize her attention this morning, offering occasional semi-flirtatious remarks to her lord on the other side of the table as part of the ubiquitous charm she dispensed impartially. She told one or two self-deprecating stories of her initial efforts as a bride of nineteen to take over the reins of a large country house, among interspersed inquiries about her guests' plans for the morning. Upon being informed by her stepson that the four youngest members of the party planned a visit to Steyning, Lady Dalmore leaned toward Abigail with a bright smile, assuring her that she would find this a delightful destination and expressing disappointment that household duties would prevent her from joining her guests' excursion.

Abigail said all that was proper to the occasion, masking her relief. Lady Dalmore's presence would have made it impossible to alert Max that his supposed betrothed was about to become a social liability. The awareness of a painful duty to be performed acted like a nagging itch during the interminable meal, one that she must resist the urge to scratch as she imposed a stillness on her muscles and tried to project a serenity she was a long way from feeling.

When the party started to break up, Abigail seized the opportunity to lean across the chair Marjorie Grafton had just vacated and whisper an urgent request to speak privately to Max before their ride. She then strolled out of the room in what she fondly hoped was a casual manner and lingered a few feet from the door until Max caught up with her. He was relaxed and smiling, and knowing she was about to destroy this mood added desperation to the shaky voice in which she blurted, "Max, I have something terrible to confess!"

Concern wiped out his smile. "What is it, Gail? What is wrong?"

"Max, there is to be a ball tonight and I cannot dance!"

Abigail had not known what Max's reaction would be to this crucial social lack, but as she stood anxiously before him, her fingers laced together, her eyes searching his face, she realized she had *not* expected the blankness with which he stared back at her, and certainly not the crack of laughter that erupted from him a second later.

"Nonsense," he said soothingly, smothering his amusement, perhaps in response to her patent anxiety. "Of course you can dance. Females are born knowing how to dance."

"What an idiotish thing to say when I have just told you I *cannot* dance!" she snapped, her sense of inferiority transformed into unbecoming temper. "I have never danced in my life." Infuriated with his obtuseness, she enunciated each word clearly, as for the benefit of the deaf or mentally deficient.

"Quarreling, children? Before the banns are even read?"

The patronizing amusement in Lady Dalmore's voice coming from the breakfast room doorway interrupted Abigail in full spate, no bad thing, she had the wit to realize as she flashed Max a glance of appeal.

"No quarrel, Felicity, just Abigail giving me a well-deserved trimming in true wifely fashion," he explained with unimpaired cheerfulness. "If you'll excuse us, I am about to make my humble apologies to her. We'll see you at luncheon," he added, taking Abigail's elbow and propelling her around the corner.

"Humble apologies? That I would enjoy," Abigail said, her composure restored by the sheer ludicrousness of the situation. "Seriously though, I really cannot dance, Max. I am sorry. Perhaps we could say my family are Dissenters and hold dancing to be a cardinal sin," she suggested, half in earnest.

"I have a better idea. I'll teach you to dance this afternoon," he countered, grinning down at her in a manner that had her pulses quick-stepping.

"Max, do be serious," she begged, ignoring her pulse rate. "No one could learn to dance in one afternoon. Perhaps I should develop a migraine after dinner, then I—"

"You would not miss a meal," he finished, still grinning.

"There is that consideration, of course," she admitted, unable to prevent her lips from curving in response to his nonsense, "but you must see that it would save a deal of awkwardness for you if I were simply not present this evening."

"Trust me, there will be no awkwardness if you abstain from dancing, but you are innately so musical and graceful in your carriage and movements that I am persuaded we shall have you dancing by this evening."

"We?" she squeaked in alarm.

"Just trust me, Gail," he repeated, giving her a little push. "Go and put your hat on now or the others will be wondering what is keeping us."

Abigail hurried off to her quarters, smiling and surprised. It would have taken an Agnes Talant to remain unmoved by Max's sunny and infectious confidence, but the element of surprise was equally prominent in her reaction. Could this ebullient man with the impish charm be the cold-eyed, tight-lipped individual who had commandeered her services by employing tactics she did not hesitate to stigmatize as moral blackmail?

Puzzlement joined Abigail's other emotions as she considered the Max Waring she had encountered less than a fortnight ago and the man who had just lightheartedly proposed to instruct her in the art of social dancing. The aloof, sardonic London Max had not exuded any noticeable warmth or charm of manner on arriving at Oakridge—quite the opposite, in fact. The impersonal affability he displayed toward his stepmother was oddly chilling to witness. From the very first moment Abigail had detected a disconcerting aura of antipathy or antagonism beneath his smiling courtesy when addressing Lady Dalmore, and his attitude toward his father had been no warmer, a punctilious respect that did not quite conceal an unfilial avoidance of any private conversation with the parent he had not seen in four years. Though his conduct remained essentially unchanged two days later, Max seemed to have cast off a burden of some sort that had weighted his spirits. Today he appeared as one released from a long sojourn in prison. Abigail had no idea what had wrought the transformation, but her own spirits soared in response, and her step was light as she made her way to the stables, where the others were chatting in a desultory fashion while the grooms readied the horses.

The day was as fine as the previous one with the addition of a little breeze to mitigate the effect of the sun's rays beating down on the riders an hour later as they viewed the remains of Bramber Castle above the narrow Adur River. The fortification was alleged to have been built after the Conquest by Robert deBraose, one of the Conqueror's followers. The seventy-five-foot-high wall of the keep—all that was still standing—testified to its former prominence. Abigail considered it quite intimidating even in its ruined state. Max explained that in all probability the site had formerly contained a Saxon castle on its mound. The four rivers of Sussex running south to the Channel had always been vital to the defenses of the island just as they had been the means over the ages of cutting paths through the otherwise solid line of hills that buttressed the south coast.

The village of Bramber lay downhill from the castle past St. Nicholas's church with its squat Norman tower and nave dating from deBraose. Max pointed out the fifteenth-century oak-framed building near the bridge that local legend said had served as a refuge for Charles II on his last night in England.

It was only a short ride toward the northwest to Steyning from Bramber. The noble bulk of Chanctonbury formed a backdrop to the pretty old town that, like Bramber, had been more prominent when both were ports in the days before the river had silted up. Buildings dating from the Middle Ages amiably rubbed shoulders with jettied Tudor dwellings and Georgian inns, all having grown together naturally over the centuries. The visitors exclaimed over the steeply thatched Saxon cottage in Church Street and admired the odd mixture of styles, sometimes in the same building, that coexisted in visual harmony. Everything about Steyning was clean, neat, and attractive including those of its citizens the riding party had encountered thus far.

"It feels . . . friendly," Roland said suddenly as they sat their mounts, looking over a garden wall at the end of one of the little streets ending at the feet of Chanctonbury.

"Yes," Marjorie Grafton said eagerly, "I never see Steyning without thinking it must be a very pleasant place in which to live."

Abigail, who had been gazing dreamy-eyed past the gardens to the slopes of Chanctonbury, patted Dolly's neck absently. "It is indeed a delightful town," she agreed, "but I would still like to climb Chanctonbury Ring—on foot."

Max laughed. "I promise you shall have that dubious pleasure before we leave Oakridge, but we must be getting back now if we are to teach you to dance this afternoon."

"Teach her to *dance*!" Marjorie Grafton's startled gaze swung from Max to Abigail. "Surely you . . . I mean . . . that is, everyone . . ." Her voice trailed off into embarrassed silence as Abigail shook her head.

"I am afraid not, not a step," she admitted with a wry twist to her lips.

"Can *you* dance, Mr. Monroe?"

"Why, yes, a little." Roland's admission was even more reluctant as he warily eyed the now-indignant Miss Grafton.

"Then why have you never taught your sister, your own *twin*?"

"She never asked me to teach her."

"I did not know you could dance, Roly."

"You can remedy that omission today, Roland," Max said smoothly, ignoring Abigail's surprised interjection. "May we count on your assistance too, Miss Grafton? The four of us can make up a set that will simplify matters considerably."

"Of course, sir. And I am persuaded Mama would be delighted to play for us if you wish."

"A capital idea. Thank you, Miss Grafton. You see, my love, I told you the situation was easily rectified."

"Yes. Thank you, all of you." Abigail mustered a weak smile, but she mistrusted the gleam in her fiancé's dark eyes. She strongly suspected that he was laughing at her ignorance despite these zealous efforts on her behalf. No one enjoys being found wanting, but the inability to dance was not, after all, a moral failing, the sensible Abigail sternly reminded her foolish and prideful alter ego. She must conquer this missish sensitivity and make a real effort to relax and enjoy whatever the day brought—or at least bear it with good grace.

Abigail found it was surprisingly easy to follow her own sage advice that afternoon as the riding party gathered in the music room with the addition of Lady Grafton, whose matter-of-fact practicality put the novice dancer at ease from the start.

"Marjorie tells me you have never danced at all, Miss Monroe?"

"No, ma'am."

"Have you ever seen other people dancing, your parents' guests during your childhood perhaps?"

Abigail's face broke into a wide grin as she turned impulsively to her brother. "Oh, Roly, do you remember that occasion before Mama became ill when they gave a dinner party, and we sneaked downstairs later when we heard the music? The ladies looked so elegant and graceful in their finery as they circled the gentlemen. I was completely enchanted and would have stayed shivering in the hall forever had not Papa caught sight of us and banished us to our rooms," she added, her smile becoming wistful as she turned back to Lady Grafton.

"Then you know how country dances look at least, which is a help," that lady remarked, seating herself at the pianoforte. "Now, if you will all take your places, we'll run through some of the basic movements for Miss Monroe's edification. You try to go along with them, my dear."

As Abigail applied herself diligently to learning the steps, the mood in the music room was one of merriment. The other young people alternately guided, pushed, and pulled her through the unfamiliar movements. Having grown up with two brothers, whose practice had never been to spare her sensibilities, she took their lighthearted criticisms in good part.

At one point her brother yelped in pain and grabbed the instep she had trodden on.

"I am so sorry, Roly, really I am. It is just that I keep forgetting which way to turn," Abigail confessed. "Did I hurt you badly?"

"No, no, think nothing of it, I pray you, sister dear. My foot should be as good as new in a month or two," he responded with great politeness.

"For shame, Mr. Monroe," said Lady Grafton, laughing. "Your sister is too light on her feet to do you permanent damage. The turns are a bit confusing at first, but it will soon become automatic. You are doing very well indeed, my dear child."

"Now, *I* have no complaint at all to make if you turn the wrong way occasionally," Max said a few moments later when Abigail's misstep brought her up against his chest. "There are certain secondary benefits," he added, his voice sinking to a murmur as he put his arms around her to steady her balance.

Abigail blushed and stammered out an apology as she stepped quickly back. Something in his teasing expression, an underlying question or invitation, sent her eyes skittering away in alarm. Her wits scattered too, and for the next few seconds she could not think which was her right foot and which the left. Nor was she confident that her suddenly wobbly legs would obey any commands her brain might issue.

Lady Grafton's brisk, "Shall we begin again?" broke the

spell, and the lesson resumed with Abigail concentrating fiercely on learning the sequence of movements, her serene countenance belying heightened inner excitement.

After about two hours Lady Grafton settled back in her chair with her hands quiet in her lap and beamed a satisfied smile at the four flushed and triumphant dancers, who had just executed a flawless performance of a lively country dance.

"Excellently done, everyone," she stated. Then turning to Abigail, she went on, "With your natural sprightliness and graceful carriage, I am persuaded you should have no difficulty in participating fully tonight, for you have seen that there are great similarities in all the dances. If you cannot recall a specific movement, you need simply copy the other ladies. If there were to be a cotillion, I might perhaps caution you, but it is danced infrequently these days."

"But there might well be a waltz these days, might there not, ma'am?" Max inquired with an air of assumed innocence. "Abigail should really learn to waltz, do you not agree?"

Lady Grafton could not suppress a smile at his audacity, but she protested, "Miss Monroe is not yet out, Max. It might be thought unseemly if she were to waltz. The dance is far from universally sanctioned in any case, especially in the country."

"Oh, but Mama, Miss Monroe is an engaged woman, not at all the position I held at the beginning of the Season this year," Marjorie interjected. "And if Lady Dalmore offers her guests the opportunity to waltz, surely that must constitute sanction enough?"

Max hid a smile as he watched Lady Grafton wrestle with the problem of seeming to criticize her hostess if she spoke her mind on that subject to her innocent daughter. "There can be no objection to Miss Monroe's learning the steps among friends in the privacy of my home, can there, ma'am?" he asked in wheedling tones.

"If you are fatigued, Mama, I shall be happy to play the music," Marjorie offered, holding out a hand to her mother who, seeing herself outmaneuvered, laughed and gave way to their exhortations. Miss Grafton took her mother's place at the pianoforte and launched immediately into a popular waltz tune.

Abigail had heard of the German dance that was all the rage among the *ton.* Roland had brought home waltz music for her to learn, but she had no idea what the dance looked like being performed. As the music with its strong initial beat drummed in her ears, she stood stock still, her eyes clinging to Max's. He was smiling, but for an instant Abigail saw herself as a rabbit in a snare, watching the approach of the trapper. She blinked twice to rid herself of the unbidden vision.

"This is the approved stance for the waltz, my love," Max began. "I place my right hand on your waist, like so, and take your right hand in my left." Abigail felt the warmth of his hand through the thin cotton of her gown, and her muscles tensed in response. She tried to ignore the sensation and concentrated on breathing as inconspicuously as possible, though the thought crossed her mind that it was hard to conceal anything from someone standing so close. "And your left hand goes to my waist," Max continued in the voice of one explaining a diagram in a textbook. "That is fine for the moment, but you'll want to apply a little more pressure for safety's sake when we really begin to circle around the room." Abigail had broken eye contact to watch with dull surprise as her left arm, performing like an automaton, had obeyed his instructions.

"Now I begin by stepping forward on my left foot while you go back on your right," Max continued. "Let's walk through the motions first."

Within a very few minutes Abigail had learned the simple footwork and experienced the exhilaration of moving smoothly around the room to the lilting music. Every pulse in her body had quickened from the moment Max had guided her first halting steps. Sheer elation had lent wings to her heels as they circled the room's perimeter, swooping and turning as one fluid entity. Unlike the mannered movements of the country dances, waltzing seemed to demand no mental concentration on her part. Her feet seemed to know what to do instinctively, and her body responded instantly to the pressure of Max's hand on her waist.

When the music ceased, Abigail's lips formed an involuntary protest that, to her credit, she managed to stifle before voicing. Max's dancing dark eyes told her this laudatory effort had been wasted on him as he laughed and pulled her more closely into his arms, compounding this egregious breach of decorum by whirling her off her feet into a dizzying spiral.

"Why is Max spinning my new sister around when the music has stopped and why is everybody laughing?"

All heads turned to the doorway through which Lady Rose Waring had entered, carrying a doll nearly half her own size.

Max released Abigail and strode toward the small figure. "Shall I spin you too, Sister Rosebud?" he demanded.

"Yes!"

He scooped up child and doll as one, nodding to Marjorie Grafton who, still seated at the instrument, began to play another waltz tune.

Abigail, grateful to see everyone's attention shift away from herself, sank onto a chair pushed against the wall and seized the moment to catch her breath literally and emotionally. Her head was still reeling and her pulses thrumming following what she realized had been an enchanted interval, a moment out of time to be savored and brought out of the memory bank on gloomy days back at Broadlands when she was embroiled in the thankless task of trying to combat and disguise the ongoing decay of her family home.

Like the others in the room, Abigail followed the progress of the incongruous pair—trio if one included the child's doll—circling the room to a more moderate waltz tempo than that to which she and Max had just danced. Their cheeks were pressed together, the little girl's golden ringlets mingled with Max's wavy dark hair as he cradled her in his right arm. His left hand extended the child's right in a parody of the waltz position while two chubby legs dangled several feet off the ground. Lady Rose's dimpled fingers clutched at the back of her brother's collar for support, but pearly teeth gleamed and she laughed with delight as they whirled by the smiling onlookers.

This is another scene I shan't forget, Abigail promised herself, noting the tenderness of the man's expression as he gazed at his newfound sister. *How good he is, and why does this surprise me?* The thought flitted through her mind and was gone with all the others that had crowded in during the session in the music room.

In due course the dance ended as did the lessons. The men unrolled the carpet back into the center of the room, and the ladies repositioned the chairs and music stands in their usual places. The sense of something magic dissolved in these commonplace actions, and the arrival of Lady Rose's nurse seeking out her wandering charge signaled a realignment of forces.

Max took Roland off to play billiards, and Lady Grafton declared her intention of resting before dressing for the earlier dinner hour demanded by the scheduled evening party. Marjorie confided to Abigail that she was going to try to snare Lady Dalmore's vaunted bathing chamber before Lady Winter took up lengthy residence there as was her wont.

Abigail, succumbing to Lady Rose's pleas, accompanied nurse and child upstairs for a tour of the nursery quarters. The little girl's happy chatter and the nurse's approving looks during the half hour she remained there were compensation enough for the sacrifice of her restful privacy.

Chapter Eleven

This was the moment he'd been anticipating since that day in Mme. Simone's shop, Max realized as Abigail floated into the saloon before dinner, arrayed in a gossamer-light gown that matched her extraordinary violet blue eyes to a shade. She stood out like a rare jewel against the white-and-gold background of the redecorated saloon, or perhaps—taking in the ranks of pastel-clad females present—she was more like a rare tropical fish among a school of herring. Amused by this uncharacteristic flight of fancy, Max headed for the door in order to get a closer look at eyes and dress, a satisfied smile playing about his lips.

The satisfaction and the smile were destined to be short-lived, however, replaced by growing frustration over the next hour as Max's attempts to snatch a few moments with Abigail all came to nought. While he was extricating himself from a conversation with the Carmichaels and Lord Grafton, Felicity whisked Abigail into the corner where she had been exchanging banter with Sir Archie Rhodes and Mr. Talant. The countess then set off to find her butler, who promptly announced dinner.

"You'll be taking Miss Talant into dinner tonight, Max," Lady Dalmore announced brightly, stepping across the path he was treading toward Abigail. Since she had Miss Talant in tow by then, civility demanded that he offer the woman his arm. Any faint hope that he might find Abigail on his other side at dinner was squelched when he saw her take her place between Douglas Talant and Sir Archie. To make matters worse, she was seated on the same side of the table as he so that he was denied even the meager consolation of watching the parade of emotions cross her mobile countenance as she listened to her partners and responded to their witty sallies or flirtatious overtures.

Max was seated at his stepmother's left during dinner. When their eyes met, she made no effort to hide her gratification at the success of her machinations, but Max had been prepared for this and was careful to show her smile for smile while he privately conceded her petty triumph. It crossed his mind that "petty" was the *mot juste* for many of Felicity's actions during this house party, and he marveled that he had never seen this side of her during the memorable weeks of their courtship. Had it always existed? Had he been blinded by love—or infatuation—or had four years of a loveless marriage wrought a change in the nature of the girl who had once seemed to epitomize feminine perfection? One day soon he would pursue this fascinating train of thought, he promised himself, but he'd best keep his wits about him at present if he was to remain alert to any further attempts on Felicity's part to discomfort the girl he'd introduced into Oakridge as his future bride.

Under the circumstances there was no enjoyment to be had during dinner, but Max could claim one small triumph, albeit one extraneous to his personal problem of seeing the visit through without incident. He discovered quite by accident that the dour Miss Talant did have one interest in life apart from keeping her susceptible brother out of her hostess's clutches. It seemed that she was a passionate gardener, and the discovery was in the nature of a godsend in view of his suspicion that he would be sentenced to partner the charmless female on every possible occasion Felicity could contrive. Dredging up snippets of memory about his mother's gardening practices at Oakridge, he sustained a discussion that took them through two courses. At times he was barely treading water regarding techniques and soil treatments, but Miss Talant was for once too involved to be critical. His reward was the growing irritation he sensed in his hostess as her share of his attention was increasingly poached on by the suddenly loquacious Miss Talant.

In turn Max presented an attentive face to the countess, his expression cool and contained as he listened. Felicity's attraction for him had never been solely her beautiful face and desirable body. He'd admired the lively intellect that manifested itself in a quick grasp of the essentials of a question and the nuances of a situation. She had been articulate and entertaining as a very young woman, and four years of marriage had not changed this. His smiles were unforced as he listened to her amusing account of the foibles of some of the neighbors who would be attending her evening party, though he was moved to issue a mild protest at one point.

"Are you not being a trifle harsh in your judgment of the Reddings, Felicity? I grant you they are not *au courant* with the *on dits* of the Polite World, but you do them less than justice to assume from this that they are in any degree deficient in understanding. The squire is as shrewd as he can stare in farming matters and county affairs, and he is a good neighbor into the bargain. As for Mrs. Redding, she will never be a fashion plate, but she has a heart as big as all outdoors," he concluded, recalling the warm welcome he had always received at Harvest Hall and his mother's abiding affection for its kindly mistress.

Felicity's light laugh rang out. "I would not dream of dissenting; in fact, I'll go further and point out that *everything* about Mrs. Redding is as big as all outdoors, especially voice and derrière, but if there is any truth in you,

Max, you must concede that one would not dare to look to either Redding for scintillating conversation!"

"It might depend on the subject under discussion," Max said, responding to the gay challenge in her voice, "but in general I would not disagree. Is that so very important to you, Felicity, the ability to make scintillating conversation?" he inquired, looking more closely at her than he had hitherto permitted himself to do during this visit.

"That depends on the company . . . and the circumstances," she said softly, meeting his glance squarely, the laughter fading from her face.

All Max's defenses rushed to the fore at the abandonment of what he had come to think of as her party manner. He deliberately relaxed his jaw and summoned up a social smile. "I agree that generalizations are dangerous," he said as if her remark had been a question. "One must not expect the circumstances this evening to breed a high degree of scintillation, your guests and your neighbors having so little in common. Do not despair though. Music is a great uniting force, and most will enjoy the dancing."

Into the silence that greeted this pomposity, Mr. Carmichael on Felicity's right spoke to attract her attention. As she turned with palpable reluctance, Max glanced down the table and saw that his father's eyes were focused on them. The distance was too great to discern his expression, which meant, thankfully, that his own was equally unreadable. He did not lower his gaze until the earl redirected his attention.

Without warning, impotent rage and sorrow welled up in Max, leaving him shaken. How had such an appalling state of affairs ever come about in the first place? How could she have done what she did? How could *he* have betrayed his own flesh and blood? Other men might, but not *his* father. Was his present misery his own fault? Would other sons have ranted, shrugged, and moved on? Forgiven and forgotten? He wished he understood everything that had happened four years ago, but his blind flight from the people who had betrayed him had prevented any dialogue or explanations being offered by his father or Felicity at the time.

Max's unhappy soul-searching was brought to an end by Miss Talant's voice in his ear. It was with something akin to gratitude that he turned to the prim spinster and willed his wayward wits to follow the sense of her remarks on horticulture for the remainder of the meal while he toyed with a veal collop and took two bites of a sauté of mushrooms.

The first of the earl's guests arrived just as the men were leaving the dining room to seek out the ladies. The venue for the party was to be the great hall, whose vast proportions rendered it most suitable for a dancing party.

Felicity's penchant for decorating had wrought a transformation in the austerity of the great hall for her party, Max allowed, sweeping a glance around the long room. She'd had trellises brought in from the gardens or, more probably, built for the occasion, judging by the sheer numbers of them. Plants, vines, and flowers were inserted in these structures, creating an initial effect of a stone-walled garden. The musicians she'd hired were positioned in a veritable bower at one end, tuning up their instruments as the men entered the hall.

The earl joined his wife near the entrance to greet their guests. Max spotted Abigail and headed toward her, ignoring Felicity's soft call. He raised his fiancée's small hand to his lips, turning her to present their backs to the nearest spectators, of which there seemed to be an inordinate number.

"At last! I've had to wait an age to tell you that you are looking especially lovely tonight." He enjoyed the view of her thicket of black lashes as confusion drove them down and pinked her cheeks.

"Please, Max," she whispered, but he was enjoying her confusion too much to desist, gallantry and propriety alike thrown to the winds.

"Please, Max, what?" he inquired teasingly, but at that moment rescue came from another quarter. He'd ignored Felicity's summons, but there was no ignoring his father's cheerful bellow.

"Max, come and greet our neighbors after four years in foreign climes."

Max retained Abigail's hand and drew her along beside him as he obeyed the parental command. The polite smile on his lips became real when he spotted the Reddings at the head of a straggling line of entering guests. He and Abigail arrived at the scene just as greetings were being exchanged with their hosts. Max seized the squire's hand and wrung it heartily.

"It's very good to see you again, sir," he said to the tall, broad-shouldered, grey-haired man with the highly colored, weatherbeaten countenance of a person whose days were spent primarily out of doors. He released Abigail's hand to sweep Mrs. Redding into an enthusiastic bear hug, kissing her on both cheeks. "A trip to Sussex wouldn't be official without seeing you, ma'am." He stepped back and directed an amiable leer at the plump matron fighting to get her breath back. "*And* looking in high bloom too in your purple finery. I vow you've grown younger in the last four years!"

A deep chuckle rolled out of Mrs. Redding, setting her double chin quivering. "And you, my young rogue, have grown into even more of an unprincipled flatterer on foreign soil, but I own I am thrilled to see you returned safe and sound of wind and limb, wicked smile and all. You were always in my prayers while you were off fighting in that godforsaken place," she added, serious now.

"Thank you, ma'am, I think I knew that and took comfort in the knowledge. How is Tom and where is he? Won't he be here tonight?" Max cleared his throat of emotion and glanced quickly back to the entrance hall, where more people were arriving.

"Tom sends his compliments and regrets that they will be unable to attend," the squire said.

"They? Oh, yes, I believe my father wrote that Tom had married. One of the Fowler girls, I understand?"

"Yes, Meg, the third daughter," Mrs. Redding said, nodding her purple-plumed headband. "A dear girl and expecting to be confined any day now with their first child."

"So you are soon to become grandparents? It is difficult to think of Tom as a married man. It seems like yesterday that we were schoolboys together, forever getting into scrapes."

"You need not remind your father and me of that. Lord, we counted ourselves fortunate time and again to discover that you had not broken your necks after some of the stunts you got up to," Squire Redding said, gripping Max's shoulder with a huge hand. Do I apprehend that you are about to enter parson's mousetrap yourself, lad?"

"Is this your young lady?" asked Mrs. Redding, who had

been eyeing Abigail standing quietly at Max's side watching the reunion.

"Yes. Forgive me, my love, for neglecting you. I plead my excitement at meeting dear friends after many years." Max smiled at Abigail and took her hand before presenting her to the Reddings, retaining it as she sank into a curtsy. Both greeted Abigail with every evidence of good will, and she responded with shy pleasure to their warm wishes for her future happiness in the married state.

"You must take what Mr. Redding said earlier with a grain of salt, my dear," said Mrs. Redding, directing an earnest look to Abigail. "Our Tom and Max were a high-spirited pair as adolescents, but they're both good lads at heart." She embarked on a description of one of their youthful peccadilloes, but the squire reminded her that there were others eager to welcome the prodigal son and meet his beautiful betrothed. This last was uttered with a gallant bow in Abigail's direction.

She dimpled at him and said to his rib, "I hope you will tell me the rest of that story later, Mrs. Redding," before she and Max found themselves surrounded by well-wishers.

Max had no complaint to make about the reception accorded him and his betrothed by his old neighbors and acquaintances that night. As he had pointed out to Felicity earlier, the interests and outlook of most were not those of the Polite World, but that did not automatically make them poor company. Doubtless country folk had their share of human failings and foibles, but as a group they seemed more genuine and more warmhearted than city dwellers whose overriding desire to be seen as up to snuff in every aspect of the current culture often caused them to assume artificial manners at the least and sometimes to forget their basic humanity in the process. He found his spirits rising in the wake of the friendly welcome he saw about him, and he was pleased at their eagerness to accept Abigail into their midst.

Max had no complaint to lay against his pseudo-fiancée's behavior either. Abigail was possessed of an innate friendliness that could not fail to please, allied as it was with well-bred, unaffected manners. The touch of shyness she displayed at meeting so many persons together did her no disservice among conservative country people. It was not stretching a point to say that he was quite proud of the girl he'd coerced into posing as his intended bride.

Any dissatisfaction Max experienced that evening could be traced directly to Abigail's popularity. Having devoted hours during the afternoon to instructing her in the art of dancing, Max could not but feel he was entitled to grumble a bit when he kept finding himself just too late to secure her hand for a dance. He was not so unjust as to lay the blame for this state of affairs at Felicity's door, though no doubt his stepmother found the situation to her liking. A new face in the vicinity, especially one as pretty as Abigail's, would always prove a magnet to the able-bodied men of Sussex. For his own part he'd been rather overwhelmed by the enthusiasm of the welcome accorded him by old friends and former acquaintances on his return to his native soil. He had been pressed to pay any number of visits, most of the invitations including Abigail. It had been necessary to stress the brevity of his sojourn at Oakridge to soften the blanket refusal he'd been forced to give to all invitations at present. He'd despised himself for making vague, lying promises of another visit in the near future, but deemed it necessary to keep down any speculation about his plans from circulating in the area. He was surprised at the real regret he felt in having to refuse a number of the bids. Had his true situation been what it seemed on the surface, he'd have been more than happy to show off his future bride to all and sundry.

Max's eyes were trailing Abigail as she performed an unexceptionable reel with the younger brother of his old friend Jack Mockridge. Cyril had been a spotty-faced, sports-mad schoolboy when he'd left for the war. Now a budding dandy on the evidence of a wasp-waisted coat boasting platter-sized buttons and an intricate but not entirely successful cravat, the young man was exerting himself mightily to entertain his partner. Abigail was doing more listening than speaking, but she smiled frequently and generally presented a picture of a girl enjoying herself without reservation. As she separated from her partner and started to make her way down the line, Abigail caught Max's eye and broke into a dazzling smile before turning away again to play her part in the production.

"A lovely girl indeed, and with a disposition to match

from what I have observed of her thus far. She does you great credit, Max, and what is more to be desired, I believe your happiness will be safe in her hands."

As he assimilated the quiet words, Max turned and looked into the face that even he could see was an older version of his own. "Isn't that a rather sweeping statement, sir? Is anyone's happiness guaranteed in this vale of tears? I thought mine was once, but I was mistaken." Since his eyes never left his father's, he knew that shaft had gone home. Not a muscle in the earl's face moved, but his pewter eyes darkened with emotion—anger? regret? sorrow?—Max could not be certain.

After a brief hesitation Lord Dalmore said softly, "She was very young, and she did not know her heart. She did not really love you, Max."

"And does she really love *you*?" The sneering words were in the air before he could prevent them from escaping.

This time a muscle twitched in the earl's cheek, but there was no other reaction, and his voice remained quiet as he said, "I will not discuss my marriage even with you, Max."

"Don't you mean especially with me?" Max retorted.

Father and son were standing toe to toe. Max was blind and deaf to anything except his father's anticipated response to this challenge, but the earl merely pointed out that the music was winding down and he would be advised to move quickly if he hoped to secure the next dance with his betrothed.

Actually, Max was unable to do anything save watch his father's back retreating down the room during the crucial seconds it took for a swift-footed youth to lay claim to Abigail. Turning just in time to see her place her fingers on the arm of a reed-thin young man in an ill-fitting coat, Max heard the introductory strains of a waltz tune and exchanged a rueful glance with his fiancée before the spidleshanks in the oversized coat whirled her away.

To set the cap on his seething discontent, Felicity glided up as he was stepping back to clear more space for the dancers.

"There you are, Max darling!" she gushed. "Do you realize the waltz is the one dance we've never done together? Isn't it time we rectified that omission?"

There was only one thing to do in this situation, and Max did it. Wordlessly, he gathered her pliant body into his arms and moved into the stream of circling dancers, but not before Abigail and her partner barely avoided bumping into them. She gave him a startled look that told him Felicity's clear soprano had reached her ears.

My cup runneth over, Max reflected sourly as he whirled his stepmother around the perimeter of the great hall. It was no surprise to find her a perfect partner, and no pleasure either under the circumstances, although somewhere in the back of his mind he acknowledged that the fast, demanding footwork, though not as satisfying as punching something, was beginning to unknot his coiled muscles.

"That's better. You looked ready to bite someone's head off when I first spoke to you."

"I beg your pardon?" Felicity's voice brought Max's eyes to his partner's beautiful face. She was smiling, but curiosity looked out of her narrowed eyes. "Did your father have anything to do with the grim expression you were—and still are—wearing? What were you two talking about so intensely on the dance floor?"

"Nothing of earthshaking importance. He informed me that you never really loved me, but of course I had already reached that conclusion unaided."

"That's not true," she hissed, stiffening. "Dalmore had no right, no authority to make such a pronouncement!"

"I should have thought he had every right," Max retorted with mock innocence, "given our respective positions in your life today."

She bit her lip and averted her gaze. "You *know* why I felt I had to marry your father!" she protested in wounded accents. "I have suffered too, Max." She raised melting blue eyes swimming with unshed tears to his face in mute appeal.

"But you have had ample and varied consolations to ease your suffering, have you not?"

"What do you mean?"

"Must I enumerate? Your country house, your town house, a high position in society, the Waring jewels, an allowance the royal princesses would envy you, and of course your child, not to mention a collection of cicisbeos to dance attendance on you everywhere you go."

Fury had already dried her incipient tears, and she pulled away as far as Max would permit. "And you, Max, have you had no consolation at all, poor boy?"

"Not many until lately," he said cheerfully. "Oh, by the by, my father also congratulated me on my choice of a bride and assured me that with Abigail my happiness was safe."

Her laugh contained more scorn than mirth. "That is mere whistling in the dark. Dalmore is so jealous of what we were to each other that he is desperate to get you married, even to a little nobody who will bore you to extinction within the month."

"You have changed your tune radically in twenty-four hours. Yesterday you sought to convince me that my father would forbid the banns."

Again her mood underwent a rapid change, and she looked up at him in deep reproach. "You delight in tormenting me as a form of revenge, Max, but indeed it is very cruel of you. I wonder if your little fiancée is aware of this aspect of your nature?"

"Abigail doesn't bring out that side of my nature."

"Not thus far perhaps," Lady Dalmore rebutted, and she was allowed to have the last word; Max remained silent, steering her carefully around the room between the other couples enjoying the exhilarating dance. It was fortunate that his former fiancée attempted no further conversation before the music ended, for Max, mired in self-loathing, was too worn down from back-to-back clashes with his father and his former love to play his role in conventional dance-floor repartee.

He had certainly abandoned the high road in both encounters and without provocation, at least in the scene with his father. True, Felicity had probed into the substance of his set-to with her husband, but he could have fobbed her off with a civil evasion. Passing his side of the recent verbal skirmish under rapid mental review, he could only conclude that he must have been spoiling for a fight, seeking an opportunity to jettison the impersonal affability that had served him quite well in his dealings with Felicity earlier in this accursed visit. *Stupid really, but there it was.* He could not in honesty deny the truth of her accusations of cruelty and revengefulness. In extending this honesty into a probe of his conscience, he could at this slight remove discern no true contrition for breaking the code of gentlemanly conduct. Based on his observations since returning to England, he doubted that Felicity possessed a heart that could be hurt, but that did not lessen the cruelty inherent in seeking a measure of retaliation for the misery she had caused him by favoring her with his low opinion of her character. He'd lanced a long-festering wound by lashing out at her, but he was conscious of no appreciable relief by the time he and Felicity went their separate ways at the end of the dance.

Lashing out had proved even less efficacious in the scene with his father. The earl had not fought back, and he *had* been hurt, it had been there in his eyes. In the grip of brooding introspection, Max looked vaguely around the hall, again failing to act in time to cut Abigail out of the pack. By the time he spotted her wood-violet gown in the crowd, she had accepted Jack Mockridge's bid. His eyes locked onto his old friend's, and he returned his mocking salute with a grin.

As the music started up again and the lines formed for a country dance, Max looked around for a way to be useful that did not entail making small talk with a determinedly vivacious damsel on the dance floor. Noticing some elderly friends of his mother's sitting along the wall, he headed in their direction to pay his respects.

Max spent the next twenty minutes among the dowagers, renewing acquaintances and catching up on all the births, deaths, marriages, and other vital changes that had occurred during the years of his absence. Oddly enough, he rather enjoyed revisiting his youth in the anecdotal reminiscences of some of the matrons and one old gentleman who had visited on a recurrent basis an estate where Max and Tom Redding had spent many afternoons playing tennis in an outbuilding that had been a stable at one time. All the dowagers expressed a desire to become acquainted with his betrothed, and he promised to arrange this treat if he succeeded in prying her away from the local lads. One toothless lady of venerable years cackled merrily at this and predicted eventual success if he possessed even half his father's address. Smiling at her, Max excused himself to make arrangements to send refreshments to this sedentary group.

In the end it was Abigail who tracked *him* down and not for the sake of his *beaux yeux.* She found him in the breakfast parlor, where a long table had been bountifully supplied with foods guaranteed to replenish the dancers' strength, and a variety of libations to quench all manner of thirsts. He was selecting an assortment of lobster patties, cakes, and jellies for a waiter to take to those too stricken in years to wish to brave the horde of dancers who would soon be descending on the refreshment table while the musicians rested from their labors.

"Oh, Max, I've been looking for you everywhere!" Abigail said while her eyes darted to the waiter standing nearby bearing a large silver tray piled with delicacies.

Reading her anxiety, Max dismissed the waiter to his duty, saying with a concerned look as the man moved away, "What is wrong, Gail?"

"It's Roly. He has just gone into the card room, Max. Roly is not a . . . a skillful cardplayer, but he is determined to try to win back some of the money he owes you."

"Young idiot," Max said with cheerful brutality. "Who is the prettiest of the local girls who are here tonight?"

Abigail blinked at the irrelevant question, but replied mechanically, "Miss Elcott, but Max—"

"When the music stops, you waylay Miss Elcott and invite her to share a table with us while I extricate your brother from whatever pit he is digging for himself in the flush of this ill-founded optimism that something in the air of Oakridge has improved his cardplaying skills. Do not look so worried, my sweet. He cannot be far under the hatches in such a short time. I'll deliver him to the garden room, where there are a few tables set up."

"But . . . but suppose Miss Elcott is already engaged for supper or—"

Max grinned. "Have no fear on that head. If Miss Elcott has made other plans, I promise you her mama will speedily unmake them for her. It has ever been Mrs. Elcott's practice to store up any little signs of favor paid her and hers by the prominent families in the area for the future edification of her less fortunate neighbors in the town. I imagine she will make a round of morning visits tomorrow to relate that her daughter was singled out to sup with the son and future daughter of the Earl of Dalmore." Abigail was staring at him with a peculiar expression that might denote fascination or perhaps repugnance, and Max burst out laughing, his earlier good humor of the afternoon suddenly restored.

"Close your mouth if you do not wish people to think

you a simpleton," he advised her kindly, "and be off to find Miss Elcott. I hear the music winding down."

She firmed her lips, gave him an indignant look, and took herself off as requested.

Max had no difficulty in detaching Roland from the cardplayers since he was merely making idle conversation while awaiting an opportunity to engage someone in a game. He was quite willing to postpone his effort to recoup some of his recent losses in favor of eating with the lovely Miss Elcott.

Max eyed the naive young man walking beside him for a moment before saying abruptly, "Roland, why do you persist in the misapprehension that you will ever make a cardplayer when you do not even enjoy the activity? By the same token, you seem unaware that your, shall we say, sporting talent lies in quite another direction. I have only once or twice come across anyone with your skill at billiards. Perhaps it is that musician's touch of yours that makes the balls ring true."

Roland's eyes, nearly as dark a purple as his sister's, widened in surprise. "Are you roasting me, Max? I always beat Bertie and Percy, but I just thought they were no good at the game." He paused, plunged deep in thought, and Max was content to remain silent, telling himself that any slight exaggeration on his part had been in a good cause. At least Roland would have better than a fighting chance in a billiard contest on the basis of raw talent.

During supper Max repaired some of the omissions of the dinner table, grateful that congenial company made it possible to savor the food. Miss Elcott was a lively young lady with copper-colored curls, whose artless pleasure in the occasion was infectious. The Monroe twins also appeared to have a gift for enjoying the moment. Near-continuous ripples of laughter rose from their table, and Max could almost feel himself growing progressively younger in their company. Not since his mother had died could he recall a similar spell of pure pleasure in simply being.

This unusual lightness of being stayed with him for the rest of the evening. Abigail was still sought after by the local beaus, but Max took the precaution of engaging her hand for the last waltz while they were still at supper. Meanwhile he danced with Marjorie Grafton, the delectable Miss Elcott, and the daughters of some of his parents' friends. There was no difficulty in avoiding his father and Felicity, who were naturally preoccupied by their duties as hosts. He noted Lady Winter and Sir Archie mingling with the Sussex natives and spotted Mrs. Carmichael circling the floor with Jack Mockridge at one point. Miss Talant seemed to have retired early, and he experienced a twinge of conscience for not having invited her to dance, but recovered quickly under the sybaritic influence of music and good company.

By the time Max claimed Abigail for their dance, the crowd had thinned somewhat, the most elderly of the guests and those living at the greatest distance having taken their leave while the moon was still at its brightest. Abigail's eyes rivaled the moon for brightness, as did her smile when she glided into his arms. He started off carefully, but soon made the happy discovery that the novice of this afternoon had become proficient in short order. Throwing caution to the winds, he whirled her out of the sedately moving outer circle and proceeded to demonstrate that Wellington's officers were famed for more than their military heroics. Abigail followed the intricate footwork effortlessly, her cheeks aglow and her eyes sparkling with delight. Neither spoke until the dance ended, then Abigail said, "That was wonderful, Max. I shall be sorry to see this evening come to an end. I could dance for hours!"

"Where do you get your energy from?" Max asked, shaking his head wonderingly. "You were riding all morning and dancing most of the afternoon while the other ladies retired to their rooms before the party. Did you rest at all?"

"Not exactly. I was in the nursery playing with Lady Rose when Mavis came looking for me to get ready for the evening."

"And you'd still like more exercise?" Max was maneuvering her around the entrance opening into the corridor as they talked. "You stand in no need of practice, my sweet. That last number proved you are an accomplished waltzer already; in fact, if modesty did not forbid, I'd say we showed them all how the waltz should be performed."

"Thank you for the compliment, Max, but I fear I am too short to make you an ideal partner. You and Lady Dalmore made a truly beautiful pair earlier this evening."

Hearing the wistful note in her voice, he said bracingly, "Nonsense, a small girl can partner anyone. Ask Miss

Grafton how she felt dancing with Cyril Mockridge, who is half a head shorter than she is. You may commiserate together, but I am persuaded she will not readily allow you to claim the greater misfortune on the score of height."

Something in her smile, gratitude mingled with disbelief, caused Max to cast prudence aside yet again. There was nothing save a large Chinese urn holding a fern screening them from those passing the entrance to the great hall, but Max gave in to a desire that had been gaining in urgency throughout the evening, and kissed her parted lips, pulling her up against him as he did so. The element of surprise worked in his favor initially, and he savored the sweetness of those soft lips for a moment before two small but determined fists jammed into his chest and shoved with unexpected force.

"Th . . . that was not in our agreement, Max," she declared the instant he ended the kiss with great reluctance.

"I know, and I will apologize if you found it repugnant."

"That is not the point and you know it!"

A flash of white-and-silver at the periphery of his vision had Max turning away from Abigail's indignant face before he could mount a defense. His brain confirmed his visual identification before Felicity, framed in the entranceway, spun on her heel and strode back into the great hall. There was no doubt in his mind that she had seen the embrace through the scanty veil of greenery, and when he looked back to Abigail, he could see by her crimson cheeks that she had reached the same conclusion.

Chapter Twelve

Contrary to her expectations, Abigail slept long and deeply that night. It had been a marvelous day filled with pleasurable activity, and she had hated to see it end. Her head was stuffed with impressions of the countryside surrounding Oakridge and the people who inhabited it, and her spirit was filled with music, especially waltz music, as she wended her way to the Queen's chamber sometime after midnight.

Mavis, tired though she must have been at such an hour, had been eager to hear about the reception the violet gown had received. She had crooned over the creation while dressing Abigail earlier and confided that all the other ladies' maids had remarked on it with what she recognized as poorly disguised envy when they had all been ironing their mistresses' gowns that afternoon. Abigail had tried to recall some of the compliments she'd received during the evening for the young dresser's enjoyment. Mavis had already learned from one of the footmen that Abigail had danced every dance, and she was puffed up with vicarious pride in this proof of popularity. Abigail had laughed and demurred, then hurried the young girl off to her bed, but it had struck her that there was very little that happened at Oakridge that the servants did not know almost as quickly as the principals.

According to Mavis, the same footman had reported in the servants' hall that the young master had taken it upon himself to fill a tray with the choicest refreshments for the oldest guests at his father's party. This gesture had won the applause of the veteran members of the household staff who had declared the viscount a fitting son of his late mother. Abigail had understood from Mavis's chatter that the earl's first countess had been much beloved by all the servants, indoors and out. As the heir's intended bride she had murmured appropriately at the approval heaped on Max in the servants' hall and, she was in truth favorably impressed by Max's style of dealing with all the people she'd met in Sussex. His manners were invariably easy and pleasant, without height or condescension, and she'd discerned genuine liking and affection for many.

Max Waring was a surprising person altogether, Abigail concluded as she slid between sweet-smelling sheets. She'd been predisposed to dislike him sight unseen for playing cards with someone as young as her brother, and their disastrous first meeting had only reinforced this dislike. Of course it was her own fault that she'd found herself at such a disadvantage, but his supercilious air and high-handed treatment had created what she'd thought was immutable hostility in her breast. Somehow in the past few days this animus had evaporated, vanished almost without any awareness of the process on her part. Abigail could only regard this rapid reversal of dislike with amazement, not to mention chagrin that she had been so quick to pass judgment in the first place. In her own defense, she could mention, however, that until a couple of days ago she had not been exposed to the wealth of Waring charm, since Max had not expended any of this valuable commodity on her in London. She'd only just discovered that Max, like his father, could by some subtle emanation—for want of a more precise definition—make the person with whom he was communing feel important or clever or likeable, even all three at once. Abigail was unsure whether this potent quality should be considered a natural attribute or a weapon in the Waring men. On the other hand, it was plain as a pikestaff that Lady Dalmore's brand of charm was totally assumed to further her own ends. She certainly didn't waste it on members of her own sex. Though her manners could not be faulted, the countess never left the impression that one was regarded with anything warmer than tolerance.

Pushing aside the superficial issue of charm, Abigail felt she had discovered a vein of kindness in Max's makeup that appealed to her. She'd seen how he had eased Roly's entrée first into the house party and then tonight into local society, and she thought his shielding of herself from Lady Dalmore's unspoken contempt was not entirely to preserve the portrait of young lovers he was bent on painting for his family. Also, his tenderness toward his little half sister bespoke a kind nature.

She had no firsthand knowledge of other aspects of his character or morals as yet, although he had stolen a kiss tonight. That had occurred in a party atmosphere, however, and she hoped she was not so missish as to make heavy weather of the infraction. It was unfortunate that Lady Dalmore had witnessed such improper conduct, but it was highly unlikely that his stepmother would ever refer to the matter; after all, she and Max were supposed to be betrothed, and some license was permitted in such cases. Not that she meant to condone any future liberties beyond the scope of their agreement as she had made clear to him tonight. He had promised it would not happen again.

On the brink of sleep, Abigail stiffened and her eyes flew open. *Had* Max actually promised to amend his conduct? Certainly he had apologized, but she could not quite recall his words. A vague uneasiness crept into her mind. It was just as well that this visit would be over in a day or two. It would be idle to deny the possibility that she could come to like Max too much for her own peace of mind. And that must not happen! They came from two different worlds, and their stations were too unequal. She dealt firmly with the irrelevant thought that the earl seemed to like her quite well. It was the viscount's opinion that mattered, and he considered her a nonentity—he had made that clear from the first. A few pretty clothes would not change that. She must not lose sight of the fact that most men would take advantage of the peculiar circumstances to flirt a little. It meant nothing, but she would be wise to limit his opportunities for flirting in the next few days.

On this sensible resolution, Abigail closed her eyes again and slept.

She was awakened in the morning by soft sounds in her room, soft but impossible to ignore, she decided after trying for a few moments. She yawned hugely and rolled over onto her back, stretching her arms upward. "Good morning, Mavis."

"Good morning, miss. I'm sorry if I woke you. I came in before with hot water, but you was still sound asleep, so I left."

"Oh, my goodness, is it very late?" Abigail jerked upright, glancing out the window at brilliant sunshine.

"Not so very late. None of the other ladies had stirred by the time I came back upstairs."

"Well, I am stirring now and quickly. I am famished," Abigail declared, swinging her legs over the side of the bed.

It was scarcely twenty minutes later when Abigail entered the breakfast parlor, only to find it deserted. She stopped short in dismay, but was reassured by the sight of covered dishes on the sideboard.

"Good morning, Miss Monroe," said Wilkins, entering from the service door, carrying a fresh pot of coffee.

"Good morning, Wilkins. I hope I am not the last one up. I am dreadfully late."

"Not at all, miss. May I serve you something?"

"I'll serve myself if you don't mind," Abigail said, heading for the sideboard, "but I'd love a cup of that coffee. It smells heavenly."

"Very good, miss."

Abigail heard the welcome sound of pouring coffee behind her as she began to fill a plate. "Are all the gentlemen out riding, Wilkins?" she asked, trying to sound nonchalant.

"Yes, miss, except for Lord Grafton, who has a touch of the gout this morning, I understand. Do you have everything you require?"

"Yes, thank you. Everything looks marvelous as always."

Abigail ate her solitary breakfast slowly, all the while trying to convince herself that anything that curtailed the time she and Max spent together during the remainder of the visit was devoutly to be desired. There was absolutely no cause to feel so bereft when that had been the conclusion she'd reached before going to sleep last night, but it was a glorious summer day and she did so love riding and exploring the vicinity.

Miss Grafton entered the breakfast room as Abigail was pouring herself a second cup of coffee. "How nice to see a cheerful face," she said artlessly. "Papa is always grumpy when his gout troubles him, and Mama is still fatigued from the party, so she is keeping to her room this morning. No one said anything last night about riding this morning, so I didn't were my habit either," she added, eyeing Abigail's sapphire cotton gown. "I suppose the men are out riding?"

Abigail confirmed this supposition and fell silent while Marjorie greeted Wilkins and helped herself from the dishes on the sideboard. She sipped her coffee as the other girl proceeded to make a very good meal. They chatted casually about this and that, though the main topic, not surprisingly, was the previous night's dance. Being a Sussex native, Miss Grafton was personally acquainted with nearly all the earl's guests, and she was most helpful in supplying the proper names and histories for the faces Abigail recalled from the multitudes she'd met in the course of the evening. They lingered at table until Abigail realized that Wilkins was hovering and no doubt wished to clear away the debris. Marjorie joined her in an apology that was received with unruffled calm by the butler before the young ladies strolled out into the corridor.

"Would you care to walk to the village this morning?" Miss Grafton invited, and Abigail accepted promptly.

"It would be as well to make a quick departure lest we run across Miss Talant and be compelled by civility to ask her to join us."

"I doubt she'd come," Abigail replied. "She seems not to enjoy any of the activities; in fact, I find it very difficult to carry on a simple conversation with her."

"So do I, but did you notice how she and Lord Edgeworth had their heads together at dinner last night? I cannot imagine what they found to talk about." Abigail chuckled at Marjorie's expression as the younger girl shook her head in puzzlement.

"Shall I ask him?"

"Do, if only to gratify my vulgar curiosity. Well, I must tell Mama where we are going and get my bonnet."

"Yes, of course," Abigail agreed, and went off to fetch her own hat.

She reached the designated door before Miss Grafton and met her hostess coming away from the little room where the cut flowers were brought for arranging. "Good morning, Lady Dalmore," she said with a smile.

The countess, looking beautiful in a crisp gown of lavender jaconet muslin, returned the smile and greeting. Noting the straw bonnet perched atop Abigail's dusky curls, she lifted an arched brow. "Going somewhere?"

"Yes, Miss Grafton and I are going to walk to the village."

"It is certainly a lovely day for a walk." Lady Dalmore tilted her head and slanted an amused look at Abigail. "I saw that you were lumbered with the Elcott prattlebox at supper last night. Accept my condolences."

Abigail blinked, startled. "I . . . I found Miss Elcott very amiable, ma'am."

"Oh, yes. She may be a pea goose, but I believe Miss Elcott is considered by one and all to be very amiable. Max hasn't changed a whit in four years," Lady Dalmore added with a tinkling laugh. "He still must have the prettiest girl in the room."

When the ability to think rationally returned, Abigail became aware of gratitude that Miss Grafton's timely appearance had prevented the response that leapt to mind, since it was clearly ineligible. A well-bred young lady did not take umbrage at carefully calculated insults and demand, "How dare you?" of her hostess. She held her tongue as the other two exchanged greetings.

"Enjoy your walk," Lady Dalmore said and left them with a bright smile.

The girls' polite responses were the last sounds for the next few moments as they made their way out of the aromatic herb garden to a tree-bordered lane beyond the brick wall. Miss Grafton eyed her companion's still profile and remarked, "When I saw Lady Dalmore in the hall, I thought for a moment that she meant to come with us. I must confess that I was relieved to see she was bareheaded. I do not know why it should be so, but I never know what to say to her. She is always perfectly charming, of course," she added quickly, "and so beautiful, but somehow I always feel gauche and tongue-tied in her presence."

Feeling that some response was required, Abigail said in neutral tones, "I expect it is simply that her poise and assurance casts our own inadequacies into sharp relief."

"Perhaps that is it. When I told Mama how I felt, she said there was nothing to be done about women like Lady Dalmore and we must just be grateful there are so few of them. And when I asked her what she meant, she said I would figure it out by myself in time and meanwhile I was to mend my petticoat flounce and stop chattering like a magpie."

With real heroism Abigail subdued the strong temptation to gossip about her hostess and made a comment about the lovely pastoral scene through which they were walking that gave Marjorie's thoughts a new direction.

The village, like those Abigail had seen while riding, was neat and spruce, its cottages in good repair, their entrances abloom with summer flowers in a joyous rainbow of colors. There were not many people to be seen at this hour, but the girls stopped once to compliment a buxom housewife on the tall healthy delphiniums she was staking out. Later, they paused to watch the antics of a red-haired toddler in determined but clumsy pursuit of an understandably wary cat. The child's disappointed wails when the cat ran under a hedge brought a young woman with titian hair bursting out of a cottage to scoop him up, scolding and soothing in the broad Sussex dialect that was still strange to Abigail's ears.

She and Miss Grafton passed a pleasant hour in the balmy air, engaged in inconsequential talk that advanced the little tendrils of friendship sown in the early days of their acquaintance. Except for rare visits with Lady Basingstoke, Abigail had been cut off from any sort of female companionship by her mother's death. Marjorie Grafton, pampered, carefree, and gregarious, was a heretofore unknown species in her limited experience. She kept up an amusing stream of chatter, primarily tales of her experiences during her first London Season, that riveted her companion's attention and produced occasional bursts of merriment that were foreign enough to Abigail's own ears to startle her initially. Marjorie evidently harbored an unfortunate propensity for falling into embarrassing mishaps, mostly by virtue of an impulsive tongue, but her self-deprecating humor and the solid sense of her own worth installed by loving parents enabled her to bob back up to the surface after sinking to what she described as the depths of humiliation on numerous occasions. Abigail was so caught up in her friend's related escapades that it came as a surprise to her to see the wall of the Oakridge kitchen garden come into view.

The sound of drumming hoofbeats shattered their feminine communion and brought them back to full awareness of their surroundings as the returning riding party crossed their path on the way to the stables. One rider veered away from the pack and trotted toward the two young women.

"Good morning, ladies." Lord Edgeworth pulled his horse to a stop and dismounted in one fluid movement as the girls automatically stilled their steps in response. "I see your beauty sleep has been highly beneficial," he added gallantly, his smiling gaze embracing both bright-eyed countenances regarding him with pleasure.

As Abigail and Miss Grafton greeted him in unison, the viscount turned his well-mannered horse smoothly and fell into step with them, quizzing them about their morning activities. Abigail was content to let Marjorie take the lead during the short walk to the spot where the gravel path through the herb garden exited onto the lane. Something in Max's eyes when he'd smiled at her just now had played havoc with her breathing, and she was grateful for a moment in which to catch her breath, literally and figuratively. She had been secretly rather proud of the debonair fashion in which she'd dealt with the stolen kiss last night, so it was doubly disconcerting to find herself so unsettled by a mere smile today. What was happening to her and, more to the point, what was she going to do about it?

Simple denial was the only action that had suggested itself by the time Max left the girls at the garden path while he took Allegro on to the stables. That was still the case when the house party came together for the midday repast.

Abigail had spent the short period of privacy in her room before lunch in trying to evaluate her feelings for Max. To herself she could *not* deny that she was not as indifferent to him as she devoutly wished to be, but this deplorable weakness changed nothing when it came to carrying out her end of their bargain. She would simply have to ignore her feelings, keep them out of her mind for the rest of this visit. There would be ample time for reflection when she was back at Broadlands, but it was essential that she not dwell on this dismal prospect if she was to maintain the carefree image of a girl newly in love that Max required from her. And that she would do if it killed her, Abigail vowed, her pride rushing to the fore. It was entirely her own stupid fault if she could no longer distinguish real emotion from playacting. She must think of herself as on stage every minute at Oakridge and allow no thoughts beyond this visit. Her resolution thus bolstered, she ran her fingers through the curls her bonnet had flattened and applied a liberal amount of the French perfume with which Max had filled her scent bottle to her wrists and throat for additional courage before leaving the sanctuary of the Queen's bedchamber.

Luncheon at Oakridge was more lively than usual on the day after the earl's evening party. For many of those at table this was the first meeting with their fellow guests today, and the conversation kept returning to events that had occurred during the recent festivities. Miss Elcott's beauty was remarked in passing, and the Mockridge brothers' prowess on the dance floor. It seemed to be the general opinion that the local denizens were by and large a genteel and amiable collection.

The earl ventured on a little gentle teasing of his prospective daughter-in-law for a degree of popularity that had had her betrothed scrambling to win any share of her time. Max claimed it had been a diabolical plot on the part of his former friends to keep the affianced pair apart, and Abigail mourned the fact that her popularity would instantly wane when she was no longer the only stranger in the group. The earl, however, would not allow that familiarity would breed contempt in her case. This time she could not muster the aplomb to continue the agreeable game, and blushed and fell silent.

Max rescued her with a question to his father about Tom Redding's marriage. The heat faded from Abigail's cheeks as she listened idly to their exchange. The earl appeared gratified to see that his neighbors and his guests had mixed so well together. It was impossible to judge whether the countess was equally pleased at the success of her party because she had concentrated her attention on Mr. Talant during lunch to a degree that could not go unnoticed. Abigail slid a glance down the table beneath her lashes and saw Lady Dalmore place her hand on Mr. Talant's arm. She was laughing, and the gesture could be interpreted as playful, but what did the woman intend by singling out a male guest for her favor in front of her husband? Now that she came to think about it, Abigail could not recall that her hosts had traded even a glance, let alone a remark during the course of the meal. With the exception of Miss Talant, whose attention rarely left her plate, the others appeared to be in high spirits. Neither they nor the earl gave any sign of finding anything singular in the countess's behavior. Obviously, she would do well to imitate their blindness, but Abigail felt the gap between herself and these worldly people to be very wide at that moment. She did not really belong in such company.

When the meal ended, Abigail needed no persuading to join Max, her brother, and Miss Grafton in the billiards room. A pleasant activity performed in company sounded like an excellent prescription for passing as much of the time remaining at Oakridge as possible.

For the next couple of hours Abigail had no difficulty in banishing personal concerns. She had acquired some skill at billiards as with other dubious accomplishments of her youth by determinedly forcing her company on Roly and Percy Basingstoke at every opportunity and copying their actions without regard to danger or appropriateness for girls. Marjorie Grafton's upbringing as the adored baby girl of her family had been quite different. Billiards had played no role in her life thus far, but she confessed to a private hankering to become adept at this activity and instantly became the pupil of three competing teachers, each of whom was convinced that his or her method was the best. This did not augur well for speedy progress, but did provide moments of general hilarity and ensured that a good time was enjoyed by all the participants.

It was Miss Grafton who brought the interlude to a halt ultimately. Glancing at the mantel clock, she gave a squeal and dropped the cue stick she was holding onto the table. "Goodness, I promised Mama I would waken her from her nap fifteen minutes ago," she said, straightening up with a groan. "My back feels permanently bent. Thank you all for the expert tutelage. I cannot wait to show Papa my new skills," she chortled, taking a hasty leave of her companions.

After Marjorie left the room, Roland asked Max if he thought there would be any objection if he were to play one of the pianos for a while. On being assured that one was his for the taking, he too went off, whistling a tune or, rather, part of a tune over and over.

"That is a sure sign that Roly has an idea for a new composition," Abigail said into the silence that fell when the door closed behind her brother.

"He is very talented," Max said, putting away the cue sticks. "I hope he will continue to pursue his muse. Have you seen the gardens yet, or the roses?"

"No, somehow the days have been so filled with activity that I have had no chance to wander about in the gardens."

"Come then. I'll be your guide. My mother had an abiding love for roses, which should be at their peak now." Max held out his hand.

It would have been churlish to refuse, Abigail assured herself uneasily as they set off together, but she drew her hand out of his clasp once they were outdoors on the pretext of repinning a curl in Mavis's latest coiffure, avoiding Max's eyes with their knowing gleam as she did so. *Drat the man!* He was too clever at reading her mind and positively relished being able to tilt her emotional equilibrium. Determined to deny him this perverse pleasure, Abigail lifted her delicate chin and produced an intelligent comment about the design of the formal gardens through which they were strolling. Max chuckled, but followed her lead. He proved a surprisingly informed guide, able to identify nearly every bush and flower in the extensive and diverse gardens. Abigail doubted if either of her brothers could recognize more than a half-dozen of the most common plants in England if their lives depended on the knowledge.

She wandered about the grounds in a state of pure contentment, vaguely aware of occasional soothing insect noises as her eyes darted from one lovely combination of plantings to another. Dainty white mounds of sweet alyssum bordered a bed that featured feathery pink carnations scenting the air with clove. Along another path gorgeous multicolored fuchsias nodded their heads before upstanding clumps of pristine daisies. Everywhere she gazed was loveliness; all lines of sight led to some new visual delight, be it statuary, a tinkling fountain, or a quiet green corner where a bench beckoned beneath shady branches.

Max allowed her to wander at will, good-naturedly supplying information and seeming to enter into all her enthusiasms with an indulgent smile for her expressions of rapture. He saved the rose garden for last, ushering her through an arched opening in a tall hedge wall.

"Oohhh!" Abigail let out an ecstatic breath. "Such beauty and such perfume!"

These were the only words she spoke for the next few minutes as her eyes took in the large sunny area divided into beds of different shapes, lined and separated by grassy borders. Almost at once her feet followed where her eyes had gone. She was unaware of Max's presence as she feasted her eyes on the array of mature bushes, most of them bearing a profusion of heavy, many-petaled blooms. She recognized her mother's favorite Rosa Gallicas and gave in to recurring temptations to stop and breathe in the perfume of unfamiliar species. Every shade between purest white and darkest red was represented in this enchanted space, and when Abigail turned to look back toward the wing of the house, she spotted a yellow rose climbing the stone wall that drew her forward with an exclamation of delight.

"That is my mother's crowning achievement," Max said proudly, reaching out to cup one of the velvety blossoms. "She and Cadbury, the head gardener, struggled mightily to establish a yellow rose and finally found that planting this against a southern wall provided enough protection through our winters. I'm happy to see it has flourished while I was away."

"Oakridge is so beautiful, Max," Abigail said softly. "How fortunate that you are not a younger son; this wonderful property will be yours one day. I can see how much it means to you."

"Yes." Max stepped away from the wall and took her hand again, directing her gaze toward the high wooden arch spilling over with hundreds of pink ramblers that stood across the garden from the opening in the hedge through which they had entered. "The herb garden and kitchen gardens are beyond that archway."

"Oh, I had not realized that Marjorie and I were so close to the rose garden this morning." The words were commonplace, but Abigail found it difficult to look away from Max as they bent their slow steps toward the flowery arch. Gone was the haughty and supercilious man who had foiled her incredible essay into housebreaking in London. Also vanished was the brooding and moody creature of the uncomfortable journey to Sussex. She had caught fleeting glimpses of a different man beneath these masks once or twice at Oakridge, but each time the guardedness was quickly resumed. Was *this* version, younger, more contented, uncomplicated and open the real Max Waring? Or would he be submerged in the cross currents she sensed at Oakridge? At this moment he was looking at her as if he would be content to go on doing just that forever, and Abigail's pulse rate began to creep up in response.

Until this moment they had not encountered another soul during their sojourn in the gardens, but now as they stepped under the archway that was actually a short pergola, a groom walking toward the house through the herb garden glanced their way and changed direction, calling out, "Gibbs sent me to look for your lordship. He thinks Allegro may have picked up something in his hoof this morning, and mebbe you'd wish to take a look at it yersel'."

"Very well. Tell Gibbs I'll be there directly."

The end of the idyll, Abigail thought, noting the little frown on Max's sun-burnished brow, and a good thing too for her peace of mind. She summoned up a cheerful smile. "Go ahead to the stables, Max. I can't get lost from here."

The frown vanished and he laughed, leaning over to pinch her chin. "I should hope not." The smile stilled and his eyes glowed as they searched hers. "Do you have any idea how very sweet you are?" he murmured.

Abigail could not excuse herself on the grounds of surprise this time. She saw the kiss coming and did nothing to evade it. In fact, her depravity must have included outright cooperation because the kiss that began as a featherlight touch deepened to something closer to a branding, judging by the burning sensation left behind when Max raised his head at last, saying with a slightly dazed look, "Don't move a muscle. I'll be right back."

As she watched her "betrothed" hurry down the length of the pergola, turn, and disappear up the path to the lane and stables, Abigail was conscious that her knees had lost their stiffening. With a vague idea of returning to the shady bench she'd seen earlier, she turned around and almost walked smack into Lady Dalmore, who had entered the pergola from the rose garden. The word "trapped" bounced around in her brain as she scrambled mentally to recover her composure.

"I see Max's technique hasn't suffered in the years he was off in the military."

"I . . . I beg your pardon?" Abigail tried to make sense of words uttered in seeming amusement while looking into the icy blue eyes of her hostess standing less than two feet away. She fought a mad desire to beat a craven retreat; the urge to run away was nearly overpowering.

"When Max and I were engaged, his kisses used to turn my knees to jelly too, but I assure you, you'll survive."

"When you and . . . Max . . . were . . . ?" Abigail struggled to produce words that could be heard above the roaring in her ears, but she faltered to a stop as Lady Dalmore's eyes opened wide in pretended surprise.

"Oh, dear, do you mean that Max neglected to mention that he and I were betrothed before he went into the army? How very . . . naughty of him."

Abigail knew by the malicious satisfaction in Lady Dalmore's face that she'd been unable to conceal her shock at the woman's callous disclosure. That was past mending, but the blatant intent to wound had the effect of releasing an incendiary anger that burned up all cowardly impulses.

"What happened?" she asked baldly.

Those frigid blue eyes narrowed at the tone, but the countess replied airily, "Max introduced me to Dalmore, and I discovered that I preferred the father to the son." She shrugged pretty shoulders in a sprigged muslin gown.

Abigail regarded the lovely-looking blond woman without blinking. "How very fortunate for Max," she said with precise articulation, "but it really cannot be wondered at that he should prefer to conceal his youthful folly."

As the words registered, two spots of color flew into Lady Dalmore's cheeks. "Your manners are atrocious," she snapped, "but no more than one might expect, given your low origins."

"You would be the authority on atrocious manners, of course," Abigail replied with spurious cordiality, never taking her eyes from the other woman's, though her muscles tensed as if to repel an imminent attack.

Lady Dalmore conquered any impulse toward physical violence, though her voice shook with rage. "Be so good as to let me pass," she commanded. "I find your company quite intolerable."

"Delighted to oblige you, ma'am." Abigail stepped back, unmindful of possible thorns on the rose boughs twining up the supports of the pergola as the countess brushed past her on her way to the kitchen entrance.

Not until she heard the loud closing of a door did Abigail venture the smallest movement of any part of her body; then she whirled about and raced off in the opposite direction.

Chapter Thirteen

No thought of shady garden benches occurred to Abigail as she retraced her path to the side entrance she and Max had used earlier. In the roiling mass of pain and protest that was her brain only one thought—escape—and its corollary—avoidance—could be identified. She saw nothing of the gardens that had so delighted her a few minutes ago in another lifetime, but her senses, like those of a hunted animal, were on the alert for any alien presence that might impede her flight. Fortunately, the gardens were still deserted.

Within five minutes Abigail was in her room, her back pressed up against the closed door, her sides heaving from the exertion of racing up the stairs. For countless heartbeats the only sounds in the large room were her gasping breaths as she stood by the door, contemplating the ruins of her hopes. Not that she had ever admitted to herself that she'd committed the ultimate folly of cherishing the faintest hope of a future with Max, but surely this numb desolation was unwanted proof of their existence. How abysmally stupid she had been!

Her father had been right after all, Abigail acknowledged, moving away from the door and wandering over to a window that looked out toward the low, tree-covered hill in the distance that gave Oakridge its name. She had put herself in a position to invite the condescension and contempt of the so-called Polite World. A chill feathered down her spine as Lady Dalmore's face, rigid with contempt and enmity, flashed before her eyes. It was not fear that chilled her or even humiliation, she realized, but the manifestation of the petty and vindictive nature behind that beautiful facade. At least her embittered parent would be relieved to know that his daughter had not allowed herself to be trampled upon without a show of spirit, though she would never claim credit for her own behavior, which would have covered her gentle mother with shame had she been alive to witness it. She should be ashamed of sinking to the countess's level, but at present she was still too angry to care that she had sunk herself quite beneath reproach by attacking her hostess.

Oddly enough, though she considered Felicity Waring eminently capable of twisting facts to suit her purpose up to and beyond prevarication, Abigail did not doubt the truth of the countess's claim that she had once been betrothed to her stepson. How could she when this one crucial fact explained so much that she had questioned about the strained relations existing between Max and his family?

From the outset the reason Max had offered for perpetrating the hoax of an engagement on his family and friends had struck her as inadequate when weighed against the possible adverse consequences should the farce be discovered. He had not struck her as the sort to allow himself to be embarrassed by situations of someone else's contriving. Once at Oakridge the seething resentment she'd detected in his attitude toward the earl and countess had troubled her, but after the incident of his mother's missing portrait, she'd assumed that his animus was a grieving son's resentment at his mother's replacement by a young and beautiful woman. She'd pitied his heartache when he'd shown her his mother's portrait; in fact, that had been the moment when she'd first felt any positive emotion toward the man who had coerced her cooperation in a scheme she deplored.

Abigail flung herself away from the window and began a furious pacing as anger spread through her veins, chasing out the initial numbness. What an idiot she had been! And what a waste of compassion hers had been, poured out not on a wounded son but on the spurned lover of a worthless woman! He must have been laughing at her the whole time because he'd *known* what she was thinking—he always seemed to read her thoughts with ease.

Well, now *she* knew that his real intention had been to flaunt a new love before the woman who had rejected him, with the object of arousing her jealousy, and he had succeeded to a fare-thee-well, as evidenced by the confrontation Lady Dalmore had just forced on her. Did Max care at all that the unwitting instrument of his revenge was being subjected to the increasingly spiteful attentions of his former lady love?

Abigail slowed her angry pacing and applied her intellect to considering the question without prejudice, coming at last to the conclusion that Max did have a conscience on her behalf. He had tried to insinuate himself between Lady Dalmore and his supposed fiancée on several occasions when it became evident that the countess would not be displeased to see her guest stumble in unfamiliar social situations. Furthermore, after reviewing the hours they had spent together in active pursuits or simply wandering around Oakridge, Abigail did not think it presumptuous to assert that Max actually did enjoy her company. Most likely, he had not considered the feelings or position of his catspaw when he'd conceived of this masquerade, but she must acquit him of any conscious intention of harming her. It was cold comfort, she thought wearily, dropping into the comfortable chair Mavis had supplied, but at least she could trust Max to shield her from his stepmother's hostility in company.

But who was going to protect her from Max? This afternoon marked the second time he had kissed her, and Lady Dalmore had been a witness on both occasions. There were fourteen people staying at Oakridge at present in addition to an army of servants, but Max had managed to conceal his actions from all but one person. Could pure malevolent chance account for Lady Dalmore's presence, not once but twice? Desperate though she might be to have it otherwise, Abigail knew it would be a fatal exercise in self-delusion to hope that *she* mattered more to Max than his stepmother. Whether it was love or hate he felt for Felicity Waring now, the passionate history they shared made this conclusion inevitable. This Abigail must accept as she must accept that his seemingly lighthearted dalliance with his pretended fiancée these past two days was irresponsible behavior at best, if not downright cruel.

Max Waring's character had always been a mystery to her with so many contradictory elements. She'd been intrigued and eager to plumb its depths, the more fool she, but no longer. Today's disclosure had been sufficient to satisfy her curiosity on that subject forever.

Oh, Lord, she had to get away from here soon! Surely he had achieved his object by now. She would beg him to leave tomorrow.

Without warning, tears began to slip down Abigail's cheeks, slowly at first and then streaming down. Her hands proving totally ineffective in stemming the flow, she rose and began a search of the armoire for a handkerchief.

Detouring by the small mirror on her way back to the chair, Abigail gazed in horror at the puffy-eyed, red-faced image therein. She could not go down to tea looking like this. Although it galled her to let Lady Dalmore assume she had vanquished the nobody, she would have to plead a headache until she was fit to be seen in company.

When Mavis entered the room shortly thereafter, Abigail sent her downstairs with her excuses while she lay upon her bed with a cold cloth over her eyes until it was time to change for dinner.

All traces of tears had been erased when Abigail entered the saloon that evening, dressed again in the white gown she'd worn the first night at Oakridge. This time, however, she had not permitted Mavis any latitude in dressing her hair, directing the maid to pull the curly mass back into a simple bun at the back of her head. She declined to recognize this action as a rather feeble symbol of her refusal to enter into a competition with her hostess for Lord Edgeworth's affections, telling Mavis only that her scalp was tender after her headache and she wished the simplest arrangement possible. She was unaware that the severity of the style cast the delicacy of her profile into a cameo relief and emphasized the smooth slenderness of her graceful neck. Nor was she aware that the fatalistic acceptance of the situation that had succeeded her self-indulgent bout of tears had lent a hard-won serenity and an added maturity to her bearing.

Abigail included everyone in the saloon in a general greeting and headed toward the spot where her brother was talking with Sir Archie Rhodes.

Max lost no time in joining the small group, his concerned gaze searching Abigail's countenance. "I'm sorry you weren't feeling quite the thing earlier, my love. Is the headache gone now?"

While nursing her fictitious headache, Abigail had had

time to decide that the way to get through the rest of this visit with the least pain was to keep Max from discovering that she knew the real motive behind the charade. Bestowing a careful smile on him, she said, "Nearly gone, at least. I should not have ventured into the garden without a hat in the middle of the afternoon with the sun at its hottest."

"You are a little wan yet, but I am persuaded you'll feel right as rain after a good dinner."

Abigail rewarded this optimistic prophecy with another brief smile and turned the subject to the men's experiences that morning during their ride. She pretended an interest she did not feel in the conversation that followed, which, thankfully, took them up to Wilkins's announcement that dinner was served. She had not expected to find a private moment with Max in which to begin pushing for an early termination of their stay at Oakridge, certainly not until the men rejoined the ladies after dinner. Her hostess had not so far seated her within earshot of Max at any meal, so Abigail was unsurprised to see that pattern continued this evening.

She was conscientious in doing her duty by her dinner partners, Mr. Carmichael and Mr. Talant, though she found the latter dull company, his hapless infatuation with Lady Dalmore rendering him incapable of concentrating on any idea long enough to sustain something resembling an impersonal conversation if his inamorata was in the same room. From time to time her eyes trailed his to the foot of the table, where the countess, resplendent in a diamond necklace sparkling above a low-cut gown of black silk trimmed in silver lace, kept Lord Grafton and Sir Archie well entertained, if their frequent laughter could be considered a good measuring stick. Abigail took care to keep her expression pleasant when her glance drifted down the table, but she need not have put herself to the trouble since her hostess took equal care to avoid meeting her eyes. Even in her present state of heightened sensibility, Abigail was confident that none of the others would have noticed anything untoward in the lack of intercourse between Lady Dalmore and one of her guests at this point in the evening, but that could change if the countess pointedly ignored her in a setting of more general communication among the members of the house party than that presented by dining-room seating arrangements.

It was in the anticipation of possible awkwardness that Abigail accompanied the other ladies into the saloon after dinner, but her concerns were soon set at rest. She acknowledged a disinterested admiration for the easy way Lady Dalmore disposed her feminine guests about the room without once looking or speaking directly to the girl she despised. Abigail and Marjorie flanked Lady Grafton on a sofa, with Miss Talant and her pile of tatting seated in a nearby chair, able to distance herself from their conversation should she choose, without spoiling the cozy appearance of the group. Mrs. Carmichael, who had acquiesced to her hostess's suggestion that she might like to select some music, was contentedly looking through piles of sheet music at the pianoforte and occasionally trying out bits and pieces of some new discovery. These arrangements left the countess free to conduct a low-voiced conversation with Lady Winter at a little distance from the piano with no fear of being overheard.

Seeing Abigail's eyes linger on the twosome, Lady Grafton said, "I believe Lady Winter and Lady Dalmore are quite old friends who are often seen together in London."

Abigail's lips moved in a faint gesture of acknowledgment as Marjorie said artlessly, "They had their heads together all during tea this afternoon also. I am happy to see you have recovered from your headache, Miss Monroe. I hope it wasn't trying to teach me the rudiments of billiards that brought it on."

Abigail laughed at her anxious expression. "Of course not, that was most enjoyable. Now that you have made such a propitious start, I am persuaded Lord Grafton will be happy to continue your instruction."

"Oh, yes. I have warned Papa that I mean to plague him to death until he teaches me properly. He shall have no peace until I am an adept at the sport."

Abigail smiled at Marjorie's sunny confidence and, not wishing to give the impression of evading an explanation for her reported headache, said with a fair assumption of ease, "I did not take the precaution of putting a hat on when Max offered to conduct me around the gardens after we finished our billiards session. The gardens are so glorious at Oakridge, and Max was such a well-informed guide that we strolled about for close on an hour. I did not give the sun a thought *then,* but regretted my imprudence later. A short rest did the trick, however, and I am quite recovered."

Miss Talant actually raised her head from her eternal tatting on hearing the gardens mentioned and ventured a comment that launched a lively discussion of horticulture that was still going strong when the gentlemen returned to the saloon.

From her vantage point on the sofa Abigail had an unrestricted view of the men as they straggled into the saloon. Max, almost the first to enter, was listening to something Mr. Carmichael was saying. For an instant she permitted her eyes the pleasure of roaming over his lithe, athletic figure and finely chiseled features. Regret speared through her, but she suppressed it, steeling her fluttering heart as Max caught sight of her. The quickened pace and eager look that came over his face were an actor's tricks, she reminded that unreliable organ in her breast, assumed in an unworthy cause. Their existence made it imperative that she don her own actor's armor.

Abigail flashed Max a smile as he made a beeline to the group of which she was a part. This circumstance would rule out any private conversation at present, she realized, curbing her impatience. She would have to find a way to get Max alone for a few minutes during the course of the evening.

That was easier said than done, Abigail gradually apprehended in the course of a musical evening. Though Max remained at her side throughout the entertainment, the audience was simply too small to permit the discourtesy of conducting even a whispered tête-à-tête to go unremarked. Lady Dalmore had begun the program by inviting Abigail to sing since, as she recalled, her performance had been so well received before. She contrived to introduce and thank her least favorite guest without actually looking or speaking directly to her, a feat that Abigail could appreciate with detached amusement as, after singing two Mozart arias, she smiled and accepted the enthusiastic applause with a composure she flattered herself was no less accomplished than that of her hostess. Max had asked her to sing the Bononcini love song again in a hasty aside as she'd left her place, but she had made no sign that she'd even heard the request and merely gave him a bland smile on her return to her seat.

Any complaint he might have made at the omission was derailed by Lady Dalmore, who said, as if a happy thought had suddenly occurred to her, "Max, I have not heard you play the violin in ages! I am persuaded I would not be the only one who would enjoy hearing a selection or two. Do say you will play for us!" The beautiful blonde was all hopeful anticipation, inviting those present to second her request by an inclusive gesture of her hands.

Abigail, sitting beside Max, could detect nothing save lazy amusement in the voice in which he replied, "Since I have not held a violin in more than four years, I very much doubt that even my own mother could derive the slightest enjoyment from such reckless presumption were I to make the attempt. For my part, I would greatly like to hear Mrs. Carmichael play something sweeping and grand on the pianoforte."

Abigail was only vaguely aware of laughter and the swell of agreement at Max's suggestion that shortly resulted in Mrs. Carmichael taking her place at the instrument. It had just forcibly come home to her how vastly different must be the interpretation of seemingly innocuous remarks that had been made these past few days in the light of what she had learned this afternoon. There was no doubt in her mind that Lady Dalmore's gay reference to Max's musical talent had been intended for her ears alone, to let the upstart know that she would never be the first to share such little intimacies with Max. They had met scarcely a fortnight ago. The countess had as good as said that though they might proclaim themselves to be in love, *she* was much more intimately acquainted with Max than was his betrothed.

It was no more than the truth, after all, Abigail acknowledged grimly, but she'd be hanged if she'd contribute one scintilla to the woman's satisfaction by exhibiting any reaction to this latest jab. She favored the rocky-jawed man at her side with her sweetest smile before settling back to enjoy the music.

Abigail gathered from the audience's reception that Mrs.

Carmichael's performance had indeed been superior, but the greatest artist in the world could not have commanded her continued concentration this evening. Errant thoughts kept winging back to situations and conversations that had played out earlier in her stay at Oakridge. She recalled that she had been talking with Lady Grafton on the very first evening when the men had rejoined the ladies after dinner. Max had made a polite application to Lady Grafton to excuse them so he could show his betrothed his mother's portrait, and she—Lady Grafton—meaning to offer a compliment to his intended bride, had said something to the effect that Max had as discerning an eye for feminine beauty as his father. She clearly remembered Max's reply, "one might even say the same eye," only because there had been something in his voice, a dryness perhaps, that did not accord with the lightness of his words. In the exciting bustle of entertainments and new experiences of life in a gilded setting, the odd remark had quickly moved into the dimmest recesses of her memory.

Not so dim, evidently, that it had not shot like an arrow to the surface to add to her torment tonight, she realized, sitting nearly shoulder to shoulder with Max but no less alienated mentally than at their portentous first meeting in his London house. This was inestimably worse, however, following as it did upon the heels of that magical hour of nearly perfect happiness they had spent together in the gardens this afternoon. At least that was how she had regarded the interlude at the time. Obviously, she must accept that she was incompetent to judge of Max's feelings. Nothing was as she had believed it to be with him.

Abigail's loosely clasped hands in her lap tightened against each other with ever increasing pressure among the folds of her skirt as she concentrated on the physical pain, increasing it, using it to fight against the stupid tears again threatening to undermine her control. That she'd been a credulous idiot was past mending, but the period spent in a fool's paradise was over. In order to get through the rest of this ordeal without revealing the wounds inflicted on her heart and spirit by Max and the woman he had loved, perhaps still loved in a twisted fashion, she required all her faculties: brain, guile, endurance, and courage. In short, the stiff-necked pride she had frequently deplored in her father.

By calling upon every ounce of resolution, Abigail sat quietly through an interminable program of music, none of which she could have identified five minutes after the last notes had died away. She smiled and applauded, smiled and agreed with Max's assessment of various performances, smiled and responded at random to requests for her considered opinion; in fact, her jaws ached from smiling, and her mythical headache threatened to become real by the time the tea tray finally arrived.

Among so much smiling and enduring, Abigail had kept her purpose in sight. After some little reflection she'd decided that a light approach would serve her best as long as she managed to convey determination along with the regret she might be expected to feel at bringing such a rare treat to an end. Seeing Wilkins and one of his minions approaching with refreshments, she donned her mental armor for the coming battle.

As was her wont, Lady Dalmore recruited Max to help supply the guests with tea and slices of her pastry cook's justly famed lemon pound cake. Abigail had taken advantage of the shifting around of the group to work her way to the edge of the area where her hostess presided under the pretext of examining a charming Dresden figurine reposing on a side table whose elegant design was made up of intricate marquetry work in many shades of wood. The table stood near the double entrance doors and promised some slight degree of privacy.

When Max approached carrying a cup and saucer in one hand and a plate in the other, Abigail dropped quite naturally into the chair set against the wall next to the table, where he placed the plate containing a large piece of cake.

"Thank you," she said, accepting the cup he extended with a smile that changed to a grimace of comical dismay as she looked down at the plate. "Goodness, I could not possibly do justice to this enormous slab of cake, Max."

"The cake is for me, though I can be coaxed to share," he said, giving her the familiar smile that started in his eyes, inviting—and generally receiving—her complicity. "I'll be back directly with another cup. Meanwhile, don't move from this spot." This command was issued with an assumption of sternness that widened her eyes in surprise.

"Where would I be going?"

"That's what I wondered this afternoon when I rushed back to the garden from the stables to find you gone."

Abigail's eyes flickered and shifted momentarily as she realized he was referring to his similar command after their kiss under the pergola. She made a quick recovery and said on a little laugh, "I promise not to budge this time. I'd like to speak with you privately for a moment."

"Except for the woefully inadequate time frame, you have expressed my sentiments exactly," Max assured her before retracing his steps to the tea table.

Abigail trained a wary eye on his resolute back as he wove his way smoothly through the small groups of people. She took a sip of her tea and then a gulp, experiencing a welcome rush of warmth. She had felt herself congealing over the course of the evening as the iciness of her thoughts spread through all parts of her body. For the moment at least the process was halted by the beneficial effects of the hot brew. Her mind was fixed on her purpose with a tenacity born of desperation. She was convinced that neither tact, diplomacy, nor roundaboutation would serve her in this instance. Max was too used to getting his own way with that insinuating address of his; he was expert at wheedling and charming stupid females like herself. Keep it light, but be direct, she repeated mentally as she watched him come toward her.

"This tea is delicious," she said by way of an introduction as he pulled another chair from the wall close to where she sat.

"Cozy," he said with a devilish grin, waggling his eyebrows in a villain's leer.

She produced the requisite laugh at this nonsense. "Cake?"

Seeing the plate poised under his nose, Max absently broke off a corner of the cake and put it in his mouth. Abigail set the plate back on the table and plunged. "This has been an absolutely delightful visit, Max. Oakridge is a marvelous estate, and I've enjoyed every minute of my stay, but I fear it is time to bring it to a close."

He was chewing with pleasure at the start of this speech, but he made short work of the cake as he stared at her in frowning surprise before snapping, "Nonsense, we've scarcely arrived! There is talk of driving to the coast in the next few days and other excursions of pleasure that I am persuaded you will enjoy."

Abigail's sigh of regret was not entirely feigned. "I was afraid you would not be quite pleased, Max, since you have said nothing about leaving, but indeed this is our *fourth* night at Oakridge. I think perhaps you do not quite understand how very reluctant my father was to give his permission for even a very short stay. I promised him I would be away for only a few days." Nervously aware that Max's scowl had not diminished as he fixed her with a piercing stare, she concentrated on aiming for a note of rueful earnestness. Not wishing to overstate her case and set him wondering, she closed her lips and regarded him with a limpid expression, though her nerve ends were sizzling with apprehension. She had nearly reached the screaming point when Max's face softened.

"Why was your father so very reluctant?" he asked, puzzled. "He knew you would be well chaperoned at my home."

She hesitated briefly, then opted for a version of the truth. "I thought you were aware of our situation. As I told Lord Dalmore, my parents made a runaway marriage when my grandfather refused his consent because my father, though a gentleman, was neither wealthy nor well connected socially. Her family cut my mother off from that moment. She never complained, but her sadness and his own guilt at being the instrument of her alienation perhaps, combined to produce in my father an implacable resentment against my grandparents that swelled in time to include all the upper class."

"And you say my father is aware of this story?"

"He vaguely knew about the elopement, but not that my grandparents never relented in their decision to have nothing further to do with their daughter or her children. I told him nothing about my father's attitude toward your class."

"You have had an even more difficult time of it than I had apprehended," Max said with a sympathy that nearly destroyed Abigail's reserves of composure. "Naturally, I am very disappointed, but I would not for the world have you fall under your father's displeasure at my hands. Only say when you wish to leave, although tomorrow would be rather awkward with so little notice."

"Then may we leave the day after tomorrow?"

"Very well. Meanwhile, we must contrive to enjoy tomorrow to the fullest, agreed?" His smile contained an element she would have described as tenderness, did she not know better.

Abigail agreed with a forced smile. She must be grateful of course that she had obtained her objective without a nasty scene, but the sick shakiness within could not be said to resemble gratitude. She dropped her eyes to her cup and raised it to her lips for something to do with her hands, knowing even before she tasted the now cold beverage that its therapeutic properties had already been exhausted.

Roland came ambling over to the engrossed pair at that moment, cup in hand. Abigail was glad to leave telling him of their decision to depart to Max as she attempted to gather the rags of her courage about her in preparation for the last day of her private purgatory.

Chapter Fourteen

Following a night of regretful reflections and fitful periods of sleep in roughly equal proportions, Abigail had to battle a smothering weight of lethargy on waking in order to summon up an appearance of good cheer. Last night, relief at getting Max to curtail the visit without the necessity of an acrimonious scene had carried her through the remainder of the evening. Though she was reasonably satisfied that nothing in her demeanor had betrayed her basic unhappiness, the artificial boost supplied by relief had seeped away by the time she reached her room, and it had been beyond her powers to present a cheerful face to Mavis. The little maid's hovering concern had nearly overset her precarious composure, but Abigail had desperately pleaded the remnants of a headache to excuse her want of spirits as she endured the nightly routine with gritted teeth until the maid left her to the solitude she craved.

In the morning she applied herself determinedly to the task of demonstrating her complete recovery, encouraging Mavis's chatter and pronouncing convincing platitudes expressing her enjoyment of the pleasures attending a stay at Oakridge. She had herself well in hand by the time she made a smiling entry into the breakfast parlor, arrayed again in her habit since Max had spoken last night of riding west toward Arundel.

In the midst of a general welcome, Abigail obeyed the invitation in the earl's beckoning hand and dropped onto the chair next to him at table.

"Good morning, sir," she chirped after remembering to send Max a special smile.

"I must tell you that I have sustained a severe disappointment this morning," Lord Dalmore said by way of greeting. "Max has told me that you and your brother will be leaving with him tomorrow. I shall be very sorry indeed to lose you so soon, my dear child, especially since my duties as host to a sizable gathering have preempted time I would have preferred to spend improving our acquaintance. My consolation is that this is only by way of a short postponement. You and Max will be returning soon and often to Oakridge, of course."

"Y . . . yes, sir, of course." Abigail inserted the expected agreement into the little pause, although her conscience jabbed her at the lie in the face of the earl's patent sincerity.

"Meanwhile, we must steal some time together today to discuss your wedding plans at least," her host continued with a smile that made him look more like Max's elder brother than sire.

"Y . . . yes, sir," Abigail murmured again, hoping she did not look as nauseated as she felt at this prospect. A timely interruption by Lord Grafton addressing a question to his host gave her a reprieve as she slanted an involuntary glance across the table at Max.

There was no comfort to be expected from that source. Max was pretending to listen to Marjorie Grafton, but his hooded gaze was fixed on his father. As if feeling her eyes on him, he shifted his, and Abigail could almost feel the heat from two smoldering coals. She comprehended with a jolt that Max was jealous of his father! If she had not been so consumed with licking her own wounds after Lady Dalmore's disclosure yesterday, she might have realized sooner that the very natural jealousy he must have experienced when the girl he loved jilted him for his father had become so irrational years later as to include the bogus fiancée he did not love. It explained the previously obscure hostility she'd sensed when he'd questioned her about his father's friendly attentions the first morning they had gone riding.

Abigail experienced a wave of intense irritation toward Max. Did the stupid creature really believe that the earl would try to seduce every female his son professed to love? That would argue a truly loathsome nature and a want of affection in the earl that was clearly not the case. Could he not see how proud his father was of him and how much he loved him? Even though a blind man could see that in losing Felicity to his father, Max was well out of a bad bargain, Abigail could appreciate what a devastating double blow that must have been at the time. However, she still had no patience with this extended period of puerile sulking.

Abigail continued to regard Max dispassionately, and presently the conversation became general as the meal progressed. She maintained a pleasant expression while listening with half an ear, grateful for a respite from role playing.

"Yes, an early start is advisable. Wilkins says today is a weather breeder," Lord Dalmore said, rising from his chair. "There will be fog before many hours."

The scraping of chairs on the wooden floor roused Abigail from her reverie, and she rose hastily, looking around for her hat and crop. "Oh, dear, I've forgotten my gloves," she said to Max who had come over to her. "I'll run up and get them. You go on ahead, and I will meet you at the stables."

"No, I'll wait for you here, and we'll catch up with the others. Let me hold on to your hat and crop for you."

"Thank you, I won't be long." Abigail returned his smile and hurried out of the room.

A few minutes later she was about to round the last corner leading to the back entrance hall when movement on her left brought her head around. Max stood in the doorway to a small sitting room, smiling at her.

"That was quick. There is a mirror in here for putting on your hat," he said, stepping back.

Abigail obeyed the invitation, passing him to enter the room. As she turned to reach for the hat he was holding, Max pushed the door closed with his foot and pulled her into his arms, grinning down at her in triumph.

"The troll under the bridge always exacts tribute for holding a hat, you know," he explained to the surprised girl. "One hat equals one kiss."

"Don't be silly, Max," she said with a light laugh. She put her hands on his arms and pushed down, stepping back at the same time to free herself as she pulled her hat from his slackened grasp. "There is no point in kissing me when Lady Dalmore is not here to witness it, and we agreed that our bargain doesn't include kisses."

Abigail fancied that she'd hit just the right note with her laughing rejoinder as she headed rather blindly toward the wall mirror above a pier table, but her satisfaction in her quick thinking was short-lived. Max, frowning slightly, followed her, standing where he could see her face in the mirror as she made a production of adjusting the hat.

"You did not object to my kissing you yesterday, bargain or no, and there was no witness then," he said quietly. "What has made you change your mind today, Gail?"

Too late Abigail saw that it had been a mistake to mention a witness and a graver mistake to mention Lady Dalmore, but it was her only chance to carry off the situation with a light touch. She widened her eyes and said with an assumption of surprise, "But of course there was a witness. You must have seen Lady Dalmore near the pergola. There, the hat is on—shall we go? Everyone will be wondering what has happened to delay us." She turned from the mirror, but Max did not oblige her by stepping away, and she was forced to stop to avoid walking smack into him.

"I told everyone we'd catch them up," he said absently, taking care of her objection as he searched her face with serious eyes. "I didn't see Lady Dalmore yesterday, but that isn't really the point, is it? Did I frighten you, my dear? I had not intended it to become so intense, but when you are in my arms I forget how young and inexperienced you are. Gail—"

"No," Abigail said, holding up a hand to ward him off when he moved as if to gather her into his arms again. "You didn't frighten me, Max, but . . . but with Lady Dalmore there, I cooperated too well perhaps. It's over now. You have done what you set out to do, and tomorrow we will go our separate ways—"

"Is that what is troubling you?" His brow cleared before an expression of reproach settled over his features. "How could you think I would toy with your emotions for my transitory pleasure? You must have seen, you must *know* that everything has changed between us these past few days."

"No, nothing has changed, Max. You accomplished your purpose in bringing me to Oakridge, and we shall part tomorrow. Let us leave it at that. Please."

The tender look that had nearly been her undoing faded from Max's countenance to be replaced by chagrin as he shook his head. "No. I have told you that all is different with me, so when you say nothing has changed, you must mean that *you* have not changed; you still dislike me as much as you did in London." He paused, his dark eyes probing hers. She looked away and moistened her folded lips with her tongue, knowing she must utter the lie, but before she could frame the words, he went on slowly, "But how could I have been so wrong about you, about us? When I kissed you under the roses, I thought . . . You said you cooperated because Lady Dalmore was there . . ." Again he paused on a note of inquiry.

"Max, we should be heading for the stables," Abigail burst out. "Why must you try to analyze a simple situation. Indeed—"

"Be quiet!" he snapped, and the harshness in his voice stopped hers. "*I* did not see Lady Dalmore when I went through the kitchen garden to the stables. If she was near enough to the pergola to witness that kiss, then she must have been in the rose garden behind you. You could not have seen her, therefore she could not have prompted your 'cooperation.' Do you still claim she was a witness?"

"Yes," said Abigail, too angry now to retreat in the face of his inquisition.

"Thank you for respecting the truth," he said with a glimmer of humor lightening his eyes briefly. "I believe we may now dismiss Lady Dalmore's presence as a contributory factor to your 'cooperation,' but I strongly suspect her presence has somehow prompted your sudden desire to be quit of Oakridge and me. I apprehend that she told you we were once betrothed." One eyebrow quirked upward in inquiry.

"Yes. Shall we leave now?"

"Not yet," Max replied, eyeing her set features. "Let us clear the air, my dear. Obviously I regret that you should have been the victim of Lady Dalmore's spitefulness. I know that she has been less than gracious to you from—"

"She's been actively hostile," Abigail corrected forthrightly.

"Yes, although you've more than held your own." A little smile tugged at the corners of his mouth before he went on in a serious vein. "Perhaps you think I should have told you that I was once engaged to her, but when we made our bargain a fortnight ago, we were complete strangers, and I did not feel you were entitled to know my life history. Afterward—"

"I quite agree," Abigail cut in ruthlessly, "but I *was* entitled to know the purpose our arrangement was to serve, and you lied to me. You made it sound as if this betrothal farce was a simple little ploy to avert any potentially embarrassing matchmaking attempts on the part of your family when all the time you were using me to revenge yourself on the woman who jilted you by pretending to love *me* to inflame her jealousy! It was cowardly and contemptible, but it certainly worked! I suppose I should be grateful that your Felicity didn't have a dagger to hand when you were kissing me—"

"Enough! You've said quite enough," Max cried, cutting off her spate of invective. "So this is your opinion of me? I am glad to know it and agree that there is now nothing more to be said between us on the subject. Shall we proceed to the stables?"

"*No*! I do not wish to ride! You go," Abigail said, quivering with yet unreleased fury.

"A capital idea," Max agreed in silky tones. "It will spare you the trouble of being civil to me for a few hours at least. I shall tender your apologies to the others. A return of your 'headache' should serve once more, but if you wish to avoid having my father send for a doctor, perhaps you should employ your time in creating a new excuse for any future derelictions. Your servant, ma'am."

The exaggerated bow that accompanied this salute was a masterpiece of ironic grace that had Abigail clenching her fists in impotent rage as he left the room.

For uncounted minutes she stood rooted to the spot, shaking with what she assumed was anger. This sick feeling in the pit of her stomach *must* be anger at the way matters had turned out. She had worked out her course in a sensible fashion, deciding what to say and how to act for the best, only to have that hateful, infuriating wretch with his persistent questions force her to say what she had never meant to divulge and act in a manner totally at odds with her careful plans. She had vowed to stay cool and controlled, but then that fiend had made her lose her temper and fling accusations she had never meant to air. And he, when taken indisputedly at fault, had remained disdainfully calm, not even deigning to deny the charges or defend his conduct. He'd simply looked affronted and left her to stew in her own juices, as the saying went.

Some remnant of functioning intelligence suggested that a period of quiet reflection would be the wisest course to pursue, but Abigail's taut muscles and thrumming nerves screamed a protest against inactivity. The mere thought of hiding out in her room as she had done for a couple of hours yesterday drove her to scoop up her crop and gloves and rush frantically from the room, down the hall and out the kitchen garden entrance. Not until she was safely past the herb garden on the lane did the question of what she should do with herself until lunch move to the front of her mind.

She stopped abruptly and glanced around to take her bearings, noting that she'd automatically turned in the direction of the stables. Well, why not? She was dressed for riding, after all. Suddenly, there was nothing she wished more in the world than a good gallop! Riding had always been her consolation and escape from her tribulations. She was in the habit of taking long solitary rides. Many's the time she'd go off for hours on end. Of course, that was in

Richmond, where she was familiar with every hillock and bush and, if the truth be told, where the Monroes were held to be a rather eccentric lot by the locals, thanks to her father's reclusive practices following her mother's death.

Abigail's steps slowed as she conceded mentally that it was not quite the thing for a young woman to ride about the countryside unattended by a groom, but she resumed her brisk pace almost immediately, aware that she did not intend to let that stop her. Her brow creased in concentration as she tried to think what she would say to achieve her goal.

In the event, there was little difficulty. The stable yard was deserted when she entered except for a lad about to unsaddle Dolly.

"I see I got here just in time," she called out to the lad, who jumped at the sound of her voice and spun around. Dolly whickered and tossed her head in welcome as her mistress drew near. Abigail gave the attendant a breezy smile as she said casually, "It took me longer than I expected to get ready. Thank you for keeping Dolly company. Will you give me a leg up, please?"

"Beggin' yer pardon, miss, but I was told to unsaddle the mare."

"Yes, if I didn't get here in time," Abigail said, voice and smile taking on an even brighter character. "Will you assist me to mount, please," she repeated, getting into position beside Dolly.

The stable boy cast a worried eye about for someone in authority to rescue him before he succumbed to the habit of obedience and tossed Abigail up into the saddle. Fortunately the stirrup needed no adjustment so she was able to effect a conventional exit before her impatience to be gone broke through the nonchalant manner she'd adopted.

As always, riding liberated Abigail's spirit, and she was able to close her mind at first to the personal disasters that had so overset her. The mare was eager to be off, and she let her set her own pace more or less as they headed away from Oakridge toward the Downs. It was another in the series of lovely days she'd experienced in Sussex, perhaps a trifle cooler, which made for perfect riding weather.

Abigail would have denied in all honesty that she'd had any prior destination or plan in mind when she'd gone to the stables, but her first glimpse of the town of Steyning in the distance instantly decided her on her course. Still laboring under a strong sense of ill usage induced by Max's cowardly flight from their argument, she recalled that he had promised they would climb Chanctonbury during this visit, but obviously without any real intention of obliging her. Applying her intelligence to the practical aspects of the situation, she concluded that if she followed the path along the meadows westward, she could leave Dolly in one of the groups of trees clustered here and there at the foot of the hill while she climbed to the top for a look in all directions. It was her last chance after all, and Chanctonbury Ring wasn't a real mountain but a rounded grassy hill less than eight hundred feet high. Had Max not said children climbed it? The others had made an early start for a longish ride to Arundel. In all likelihood she would return before they did with no one the wiser. Persuaded by her own reasoning, Abigail turned Dolly westward to put her plan into action.

All went smoothly at first. She left the bay mare in the shade of a clump of trees and began her upward trek along a recognizable path. She deliberately refrained from looking behind her until forced to pause to catch her breath. The view was definitely rewarding from her increased vantage point, although objects in the distance appeared a bit hazy. Glancing up she saw that the sky was rather hazy too and the sun was partly obscured. Better for climbing actually. The slope ahead of her was much steeper now; in fact, she could not even see the top of the hill from under the slope to gauge her progress.

No thought of abandoning her quest entered Abigail's mind as she set off again with renewed enthusiasm, firmly in the grip of the fierce single-mindedness that Mr. Percy Basingstoke, with a lifetime of exposure to the volatile Monroe twins at his service, would have recognized and deplored as being impervious alike to the claims of common sense and the threat of potential danger. It was more climb than walk now, and Abigail was obliged to test her footing frequently to avoid slipping backward or falling. She was grateful for her leather gloves, for she found the underlying limestone, where it was exposed, sometimes crumbly to the touch. The challenge was exhilarating, and she continued to make steady progress. She had long since lost all sense of time, but what did time signify in the middle of an adventure? She was aided now by the lessening in the sun's heat because the exercise was sufficiently demanding to have made her uncomfortably warm during the early stages of the ascent.

The period of exhilaration gradually gave way to increased effort as Abigail's muscles, unused to the type of physical exertion climbing required, began to protest. She must be near the top now because it was growing colder, and the little breeze that had cooled her cheeks at first had strengthened until it became a force to be reckoned with as she had to struggle to cling with hands, feet, and often knees to her footholds. She gave a passing thought to the disheveled appearance she would present in her now dirt-stained habit upon returning, but the concerns of the moment were fairly all-encompassing.

Abigail pressed on with dogged determination, trying to ignore increasing weariness, and only realized that she had achieved her goal when the ground cover beneath her feet thickened, and she no longer needed to find handholds. She plodded forward until the ground leveled, then raised her eyes, turning in a circle.

And saw—*nothing*!

Mindless panic shafted through her, and she heard her involuntary gasp loud and sharp in her ears. She could see her feet on springy turf beneath her and her hand at the end of her extended arm, but beyond was a swirling cloud of mist that erased all physical objects near and far. There was no visual evidence of the crown of beeches she knew shared Chanctonbury's flattened top with her, and no trace of any landscape feature below or beyond the hilltop. She would never have believed that she could have remained unaware of the fog coming in during her climb had the irrefutable evidence not been surrounding her, blinding her, and, she divined without being told, soon to be seeping into her bones with a damp chill that she did not wish to contemplate.

A very few minutes of frenzied consideration of her predicament—miserable—and her options—nonexistent—served to convince her that only one course remained open to her if she were to have any hope of finding Dolly again when the mist eventually lifted. Knowing with shaming certainty that her inevitable reflections would provide her with abundant cause to rue her impulsive nature and censure this morning's imprudent conduct, Abigail sat down on the soft turf, gathered her skirts about her knees, and waited.

Max rode into the stable yard in a frame of mind only marginally improved over the black humor in which he'd ridden out two hours before, after presenting Abigail's excuses to the assembled riding party in what he hoped had been a convincing fashion. He had chafed impotently under the obligation to maintain a civil demeanor during the excursion and was probably the only person who was disappointed when his father had advised cutting the outing short since the incipient change in the weather seemed to be a bit ahead of Wilkins's predicted schedule.

There was already a noticeable lowering of visibility as the riding party dismounted and dispersed. In the attendant bustle of activity in the yard a young stable lad sidled up to Max as he alighted from Allegro and said diffidently, "Begging yer pardon, sir, but did the lady not come back wi' ye then?"

"What lady?"

"The lady what rides the little bay mare. She come in here after everyone left when I was about to unsaddle the mare and ast me to help 'er mount."

"You mean she went out riding—alone?" Max's sharp question caused the lad to blanch, but he answered manfully in the affirmative. "Where did she go? Why did you let her go out alone?"

"There was no one in the yard but me, sir, and the lady seemed to know what she was about. When I told the other grooms after she left, they reckoned as how she meant to catch up wi' the rest o'—"

"Hold him," Max ordered, thrusting Allegro's reins into the boy's hand as he set off to catch Roland who, with the earl, was about to follow the others out of the yard.

"Roland, stay," he called. He cursed under his breath when his father stopped also and walked back with Roland, but swiftly realized that he'd need some story or the whole household would soon know Abigail was missing.

"That young stable hand told me that Abigail went riding

just after we left this morning and hasn't returned. Roland and I will have to find her before the fog gets worse. I'd rather keep this between us at present if possible."

To Max's infinite relief, his father asked no embarrassing questions, though he directed a piercing look at him before saying, "I'll set it about that you took Abigail and Roland somewhere for lunch, the Reddings perhaps?"

"Thank you, sir." Max turned away, but the earl said hastily, "Wait, Max. Which way will you go? I'll send some of the grooms out in another direction to cover as much ground as possible."

At this point Roland intervened. "I have an idea where she may have gone, sir. Max, do you recollect how eager she was to climb to the top of Chanctonbury Ring? It's my guess that, with this being our last day at Oakridge, she decided to try it."

"She couldn't be that foolish!" Max expostulated.

Roland laughed. "You don't know Abigail when she gets the bit between her teeth."

"Don't send any of the grooms out yet," Max said to his father. "If she returns in the next half hour or so, send someone after us."

"Very well. I'll see you later. Take a canteen of water," the earl added as the young men headed back to their horses.

Roland held his tongue in the face of Max's grim silence as they rode away from Oakridge a moment later. When they'd traveled a mile or so thus, Max, eyeing the younger man's serene profile, snapped, "I sincerely hope the fabled mental communication between twins is more than a myth, because I haven't the slightest idea where to look for your sister if she should not be on Chanctonbury. Is she in the habit of going off entirely on her own like this?"

"Since our mother died, no one comes to call at Broadlands, so Gail has no social life to speak of. She is used to riding about the locality alone. She knows every family for miles around."

"She knows no one in this locality, however, nor any of the hazards such as our sudden mists," Max pointed out.

"Gail is like a cat, Max. She always lands on her feet."

Max refrained from promising that this particular cat would have one less life to rely on when he caught up with her, knowing he should be taking comfort from Roland's optimistic view of the present situation. Brother and sister both wanted a keeper in his opinion. Neither had enough sense to foresee adverse consequences from their blithe rashness. They rode on without speaking for a while in a world gone eerily silent, such muffled noises as reached them sounding otherworldly when visual clues were removed.

"We turn here to intercept the path around the foot of the hill. She would have to leave Dolly somewhere before beginning to climb. The terrain is a bit uneven. Is Mozart surefooted?"

"Very," replied Roland, following his guide.

Suddenly, trees loomed up in the mist on their left. Max drew up, lifting an arm in warning. "Quiet. Did you hear anything?"

They both concentrated on listening, and then Mozart snorted and sidled. An answering whicker led them into the small stand of well-grown trees where the little bay mare signaled her delight in having company.

"Thank God." Max was off Allegro in a flash. "In the interest of saving time, we can ride uphill as far as the going is reasonable, then I'll do the rest on foot," he said, untying Dolly. "Can you hold the other two until I bring her down?'

"Yes."

"My real fear is that she may have tried to find her way down in the mist," Max continued as they started up the slope leading Dolly. "Do not expect us back in under an hour. I'll keep calling while you can hear and respond."

Max was impelled up Chanctonbury by a combination of anxiety and the anger that had been simmering ever since their quarrel, demanding a physical release. He'd been so shocked by learning what Abigail really thought of him that he had not dared permit himself to respond. He'd quickly put as much physical space between them as possible, though not before saying something cold and cutting that had driven the color from her face. He'd spent the next two hours trying to conceal his foul humor from the rest of the riding party. Then to prove that matters can always get worse, he'd gotten within striking distance of attaining a modicum of privacy in which to think, when the news of the little idiot's latest start had greeted him.

What had possessed her to attempt a stunt like this all alone, especially with the weather due to change? He found himself praying that she'd at least had the sense to stay put once the fog had closed in. If not, she could be anywhere on the slopes by now. This thought drove him to beat his own record up the ridge, though he stopped from time to time to call her name.

At last he heard a faint reply. "Keep calling," he yelled, correcting his course as he tried to gauge her position above him.

Max's first reaction on seeing Abigail bedraggled but unhurt was a surge of pure relief, but that had barely registered when she said tremulously as he strode toward her, "I am very glad to see you, Max."

"Well, I could throttle *you*!" All the seething feelings of the past several hours were reflected in his harsh tones. "Of all the stupid, irresponsible, inconsiderate antics, this takes the palm! Was it your intention to set the whole household by the ears before leaving, or was this simply another of your 'mad impulses'?" He stopped, appalled, but before he could begin to frame an apology, Abigail, her eyes stricken, put out a hand as if to ward off an assault.

"I know I deserve to have a peal rung over me, and I am truly sorry for any worry and inconvenience I've caused, but *please,* Max, if there was ever any kindness in your heart for me, please, I beg you, do not say anything more."

No stinging rebuttal could more thoroughly have reduced Max to the status of a loutish bully in his own eyes than the sight of the petite, valiant girl clutching the rags of her dignity about her to endure what she must. He held out his hand.

"Come, Roland is waiting halfway down with the horses."

"Dolly too?"

"Yes."

The only words exchanged by the pair during the difficult descent were Max's occasional directions about where to put her feet or queries as to whether she needed to rest awhile before going on, and Abigail's repeated assurances that she was fine. She had refused his offer of his coat on the summit, although she'd been shivering, but had gratefully taken a drink from the canteen he carried over his shoulder.

The first sound of her brother's voice replying to Max's call visibly put new life into her, relieving Max of any doubts of her ability to ride back unaided.

Roland was still astride Mozart, controlling all the horses, who were understandably restive by now, but his smile for his sister was unclouded. "None the worse for the experience, I see."

"Yes, I'm fine, but I am sorry to have put you both through the ordeal of rescuing me." Abigail's contrite words were for both men, but she avoided looking at Max as he lifted her onto Dolly's back.

"That's all right. May I have a drink, Max?"

Max turned the flask over to Roland and mounted Allegro.

"Did you see anything of the view from up there?" Roland asked his sister.

"No, it was completely blanketed in mist when I got to the top. I had not been aware of it as I climbed."

"Too bad, another time then."

Max caught the agonized look Abigail sent her brother, who subsided. "Shall we be off home?" he said briskly, marveling at the tacit communication that existed between sister and brother, often obviating the need for words. His parents had had it too. For a brief time he'd thought he was coming to know Abigail in the same intuitive fashion, but he'd been wrong. She had made it very clear this morning that she considered him cowardly and contemptible.

This unrewarding line of thought was derailed by Roland's prosaic announcement that he was starving.

"I'm afraid lunch has been over for some little time," Max said, consulting his watch.

"Besides, his lordship was going to tell everyone we were going to the Reddings for lunch, remember?"

"What is this?" Abigail looked alarmed at the prospect of paying a call in her present state.

"Nothing to concern you. My father just wished to give us time to find you before letting anyone else know you were missing." He felt her quick glance, but turned his attention to Roland. "We might stop to eat at an inn in Steyning, but Abigail is chilled and needs a hot bath."

"No," Abigail protested. "You both must be starving. The exercise of coming down the hill warmed me. I do not require a bath. Let us stop at an inn by all means."

"You are going directly into Felicity's new bathtub, my girl, if I have to put you there myself," Max said flatly before turning to Roland again. "Don't worry about food. Mrs. Howell will see to it that we dine royally in the housekeeper's room with no one to carry tales."

Abigail had not deigned to argue with his masterful pronouncement, but Max was not gulled into believing she would meekly acquiesce to his dictates, so he took her rebellious nature into account when making his plans. As the trio pulled abreast of the kitchen garden some ten minutes later, he leaned over and seized Dolly's bridle. "Abigail and I will dismount here, Roland, if you will be so good as to take the horses on to the stables. I'll meet you in the little flower room off the back hall after I've conducted her to the bathing chamber and spoken to Mrs. Howell."

A grinning Roland watched as Max lifted his sulking sister down from Dolly's back and propelled her up the walk with a firm hand on her elbow. Abigail did not open her lips all the way to the bathing chamber, where Max knocked and opened the door.

"Here we are," he said, stepping back. "By the way, if you are not in here when Mrs. Howell or Mavis comes presently to assist you, I shall make it my business to track you down and carry you back to personally supervise your ablutions. Is that understood?"

Abigail, still stubborn of spirit but obviously weary, put her straight little nose in the air and flounced past him, closing the door with a bang.

A half hour later, his outlook somewhat improved by a sustaining lunch eaten by the fire in the housekeeper's room, Max drank the last of his ale and put the tankard down, smiling across the table at Roland, who was finishing the last of a meat and potato pie, an expression of bliss on his face.

"There's nothing like a good meal to put heart into a man," Max observed lazily. "I hope Mrs. Howell does as well by Abigail when she comes out of the bath."

"Mmmmmm," his companion contributed with a full mouth just as a knock sounded on the door.

Wilkins entered and addressed Max. "His lordship's compliments, sir, and he requests the honor of your presence in the library as soon as it should be convenient."

Chapter Fifteen

With a sense of inevitability Max made his way to the earl's library. He'd known from the start that this meeting must occur sooner or later; that was one reason he'd hoped to put off a visit to Oakridge. He had not been sure how he felt about his father. Did he know now? He was always stopped by the paradox. What his father had done to him required an apology, but he didn't want an apology from his father. What he wanted was for it not to have happened, but it had happened. It had happened more than four years ago, and he had not moved on. Obviously it was more than time he stopped playing the ostrich.

Max halted in the middle of the stairway as it hit him like a *coup de foudre* that he'd never once examined the situation except with himself as the central figure. He'd been badly hurt, but it did not necessarily follow that hurting him had been the wish of his father or Felicity. As was the case with him, they were the center of their own universes and made their choices, as he did, primarily to secure their own happiness. Through no personal virtue, his had been the only choice that had not been made at the expense of someone important. It had not secured his happiness, but on the other hand, it had not caused him the corrosive sort of suffering that a bad conscience provides. He was not actively unhappy four years later, and he had many choices open to him.

Felicity had tried more than once to convince him that she had acted under compulsion, moral if not physical, in throwing him over for his father, but he did not believe this version of past events. She had taken what she wanted most at the time, but four years later her behavior offered convincing proof that she was not completely satisfied with her decision. She had choices open to her in the future, but the honorable ones didn't make her happy, and the others could destroy her reputation in society, which would make her actively unhappy. She seemed determined to try to keep him in love with her, and that would be a certain recipe for disaster. It was almost beyond his comprehension that vanity or a desire for conquest could make her foolhardy enough to risk all she had chosen by the exercise of a cool intelligence.

He was tired of thinking about Felicity, but he would have to acknowledge that once she'd really accepted that she could no longer command his devotion, the odds were high that she would become an implacable foe who would not scruple to use underhanded tactics to spoil any rapport he might achieve with his father. She'd already managed to bring the regard that had been growing between Abigail and himself to a crashing halt.

Max stopped staring at the stairwell wall and resumed his slow climb. His father was the unknown factor in the original situation dating back four years. From the moment when Felicity had given him his *congé,* he'd permitted no real communication, replying with stilted formality to the earl's letters announcing the birth of his half-sister and the death of his maternal grandfather while he was in the Peninsular. He'd repulsed in a fairly boorish fashion his father's tentative attempts to reestablish some slight intimacy during this visit; in fact his behavior might be termed downright childish. Still playing the ostrich, he acknowledged with self-disgust as he reached the landing and headed for the library.

Max squared his shoulders and gave a quick tap on the door before entering.

His father, seated behind his massive desk, smiled and gestured toward a leather wingback chair in front of it. "Come in, Max, and sit down. I gather Abigail was on Chanctonbury as Roland thought and has taken no harm, though it must have been an unsettling experience in the fog, to say the least."

"Yes, but she didn't lose her head or give way to hysterics. She's pluck to the backbone, but too damned reckless by half."

"Why did she go off like that, Max?" When his son hesitated, the earl pressed him. "Did you two quarrel?"

The earl's expression was sympathetic, but Max resisted instinctively. "Why should you think we have quarreled?"

"Because women tend to act recklessly when they have quarreled with the men they love, even your mother."

"Mother?" Max was intrigued by the notion and his father's grimace. "I didn't think you and Mother ever quarreled."

"We weren't perfect people, son. Of course we differed occasionally, especially if your mother felt I was being too domineering or dismissed her opinions without reasonable consideration. Did you and Abigail have words, if you prefer the softened version?"

"In a manner of speaking, though not because I—"

"Max, did it have anything to do with Felicity?"

Max could feel his facial muscles freeze. "Of course not. Why should you assume that?" he snapped, knowing he sounded defensive.

"Because I thought Abigail seemed a bit . . . subdued at breakfast, and I have not been unaware that Felicity has behaved in a rather condescending manner toward her. Abigail is young and inexperienced in society. I . . . I hope she hasn't felt unwelcome at Oakridge."

Now it was the earl who hesitated, and suddenly Max abandoned his defenses and admitted, "She found out that Felicity and I were once betrothed. I hadn't told her."

The earl nodded. "Women always do find out what we men for our own comfort prefer they not know, and invariably they throw it in our faces when we are unprepared to deal with it, so *we* invariably make bad worse. But Abigail loves you, Max, so take heart. This may not be the ideal atmosphere in which to mend your fences, so perhaps it is fortunate that you are to leave tomorrow. I am persuaded she'll come around soon, and you will have a better understanding thereafter."

Max shifted in his chair, hoping the interview was over, but his father, who had dropped his eyes to his desk and begun to toy with a pen, looked up again. "Wait, Max. You have avoided any private conversation, which is understandable, given that you believe I have betrayed my own flesh and blood in the foulest way imaginable. I cannot deny this or excuse it," he added, meeting his son's burning gaze squarely, "but it is vital that you understand the context—"

"You need not make me any explanations or apologies," Max shot out. "It doesn't signify—at least, it no longer signifies," he amended, trying for truth.

"Yes, Max, it did and does, and I must make you explanations and apologies, not on my own account—I have confronted my demons and accepted my guilt—but for your sake. If I can ease some of the burden of bitterness that has tormented you these past years, you might be able to begin your married life in better case to give it your best efforts."

Max's eyes flickered, but he made a deliberate effort to relax his muscles and settle back in the enfolding wings of his chair.

"You know that your mother and I were very happy together," the earl went on. "It was a minor sorrow that we didn't give you brothers or sisters, but we had you and we were content, even smug, until your mother became ill, and no efforts of mine, no amount of love could keep her in the world. We both mourned deeply at her death, but you were young, with your life before you. I felt I was already dead in every way that mattered. You tried to be a comfort to me, and I appreciated it on some level, but even after nearly two years it was too much effort to go through the motions of living most days.

"Then one evening when I'd returned to London from the planting, you walked into the house with Felicity on your arm and announced that you had met the girl you would marry. I gazed at that beautiful face and it was like . . . like the dawn of creation. Suddenly I was alive again, throbbingly alive."

Max could read nothing in his father's face, not elation or regret, and the voice in which he resumed his story was controlled and even.

"I called at the Stantons' house the next day, to meet her father, I told myself. He was away from home, and Felicity received me in his stead. It didn't occur to me to wonder where her mother was. We were alone, and it soon became apparent that if I chose to pay court to her, my suit would not be rejected. Yes, I know it is despicable to claim 'the woman tempted me,' " the earl conceded as his son straightened in his chair and let out an inarticulate protest.

"And crude," Max flashed.

"That too," his father agreed calmly, "but nonetheless true. In the most ladylike fashion, Felicity let me know she realized the state I was in and indicated that she would welcome my addresses. She accepted my offer two days later. You could not have been under the impression that I abducted her, compromised her, or falsely claimed I controlled your purse and could forbid your marriage?" He cocked an eyebrow and waited for a denial.

"No . . . no, of course not . . ." Max mumbled, "but—"

"But the most important emotions and motivations have a habit of being untidy, ungenteel, even unpalatable, I know."

Max leveled a scorching stare at his sire's calm countenance. "Are you trying to tell me that you and Felicity fell under the all-consuming spell of a grand passion?"

"I cannot speak for Felicity, but I was certainly under a spell of a sort. As best I can explain it long after the fact, I was blind and deaf to anything except that here was a chance for me to rejoin the living, a second chance at loving again, and I seized it with both hands. The last thing in the world I would maliciously do is hurt you, Max, but in those few days I did not allow myself to think of you consciously. I rationalized the situation, of course. Since Felicity obviously didn't love you, my giving her up couldn't spare you pain. You were young, you would soon recover; but nothing can alter the central fact that I grabbed for happiness at my son's expense. When you left for the war without telling me or confronting me, I knew that you must have considered yourself cruelly betrayed by the two people you loved most."

"Did you expect me to hang around and dance at your wedding? Give you my blessing?"

"No, one doesn't expect altruism from the grievously wounded. Perhaps the worst thing is that nothing I could do for you now or in the future can be considered altruistic either; it would simply be to assuage my guilt, because your ruination would be entirely and deservedly laid at my door."

"Rubbish," Max scoffed. "I'd be a pretty poor specimen if I went to hell in a handbasket because of a disappointment in love."

"I fear it would be because of your father's heinous betrayal. I know how much I hurt you, Max. It is beyond apology—nevertheless I have to keep hoping that you will be able to forgive me one day."

"I . . . I might have felt that way once . . . at first," Max admitted, awkward and embarrassed in the face of such raw emotion, "but time passes . . . things change."

"Thank you, son, your eloquence unmans me."

The words were solemn, but Max grinned, well acquainted with his father's sly sense of humor.

"You are quite correct about things changing. Sometimes I believe change is the one constant force in life, for good or ill makes no difference."

Eyeing his father's face, wiped clean of any expression now, Max was tempted to inquire if it had all been worth the pangs of conscience he'd been living with these past years, but the fleeting thought was swamped in an instantaneous conviction that he did not wish to learn the answer.

After a few seconds, the earl blinked and focused on his son's face once more. "I fear I may have blundered this morning by telling Abigail that we would discuss your marriage plans before you leave. She must regard that as more threat than promise under the circumstances, poor child. Don't press her, Max. Give her time to come to grips with the situation."

It was with unbounded relief that Max soberly, if not entirely truthfully, indicated his agreement with his father's assessment of the present situation.

"We should be at Broadlands in another hour if all goes well."

Abigail mustered a polite little smile in acknowledgment of Max's observation before redirecting her blind gaze out the carriage window, where it had rested for the entire journey, except when civility demanded a show of attention. Her pretense of interest in the passing scenery would not have fooled the most simple-minded creature breathing, but she was beyond acting at this stage, almost beyond pride.

No, not quite that, some remnant of spirit protested. When Max had found her on top of Chanctonbury yesterday and erupted into a tirade of condemnation without even the courtesy of an automatic inquiry into her physical state after her ordeal, it had been the stiff-necked Monroe pride that had saved her from being reduced to a blubbering wreck. That same pride and the realization that her plight was entirely her own fault had denied her even the transitory satisfaction of verbal retaliation then or later when her pretended fiancé had ordered her about like the stern parent of an unruly child.

At this point in the adventure, Abigail reflected wearily, she must make do with whatever satisfaction she could extract from the knowledge that she had fulfilled her part of the distasteful bargain right to the bitter end to the best of her ability. She'd emerged from the sybaritic bathing chamber warmed, cleansed, fragrant, and determined not to crumple under the strain of continuing the farce when she and Max were so out of charity with each other. Later, Mavis's pampering, plus her insistence that her mistress should indulge in a short nap, had completed Abigail's physical restoration at least.

It had taken more than an ounce of resolution to face the other guests at tea and dinner with her chin up and a smile pasted on her lips, but some of her anxiety had eased when it became apparent that her shocking solo ride and its aftermath had not become common knowledge, thanks to Lord Dalmore's and Max's early precautions to explain her absence at lunch. Oddly, today's disaster had served to take some of the sting out of Lady Dalmore's careful unawareness of Abigail's existence, which if continued would prove awkward over time but had the present benefit, no doubt unintended, of preserving her victim from those little slights the countess had indulged in early in the visit. After Abigail's escapade, Max and his father must think her a deplorable hoyden, but there was some measure of comfort in what one might almost term a conspiracy of silence to protect her from exposure to more general censure. Honesty required acknowledging a small guilty pleasure in the secret conviction that the countess would not learn of Abigail's misdemeanor from her husband or Max.

Honesty also compelled the admission that her convincing performance as an adoring bride-to-be on that last evening had had as its inspiration the impotent annoyance she knew it caused both the recipient of her attentions, who had made no bones about wishing to strangle her, and his jealous former fiancée, who would like to claw her eyes out. As with most retaliations it provided only tainted satisfaction, however, and she'd experienced a twinge of shame when she encountered the earl's thoughtful gaze late in the evening.

She'd gone to bed exhausted by unhappiness and regret, and had arisen unrefreshed but resigned and eager to be safely home. Knowing, as they did not, that she would never see them again had made it difficult to strike the right note in saying good-bye to Mavis and Lady Rose, but it was the earl who had nearly overset Abigail's precarious composure.

At breakfast, Lord Dalmore had asked her to come to his library when the meal was over. Perforce she'd accepted, hoping she'd masked her sudden trepidation, but the fear that her host had discovered the scheme that had brought her to Oakridge, or even suspected that all was not as it seemed with his son's betrothal had robbed her of all appetite. Max left the table before his father to check on the horses, so she had been on her own. Her palms were sweating and her knees had been knocking as loud as her knuckles on the library door when she obeyed the earl's summons to enter.

Lord Dalmore had expressed no suspicions about the authenticity of his son's betrothal. He'd reiterated his delight at Max's choice in generous phrases that would have warmed her heart had her sore conscience not rendered this impossible. Even worse, he'd pressed upon her what he'd called a "small token," an exquisite gold hand mirror with beautiful enameling that he had given his late wife to commemorate an anniversary. Abigail's panicky protests that she could not possibly accept such a valuable gift, at least not until she and Max were married, had been brushed aside with gentle insistence. In the end, she had left the library in reluctant possession of the mirror, her inflamed conscience now further weighed down by the fear that her stammering appreciation had been totally inadequate and ungracious.

There had been only one bright spot in the ordeal of leave-taking and one that should by rights have covered her with shame. When they were getting ready to climb into the carriage, Lady Dalmore, after wishing the trio a safe journey, had added dulcetly that she comprehended that Miss Monroe would be relieved to be back in her own home again. The subtle insult had wiped out all Abigail's vows to abide by her mother's social dictums. With horror she heard herself outdoing this spurious sweetness as she assured her hostess that she looked forward to her next stay at Oakridge for the pleasure of becoming more intimately acquainted with her future mother-in-law. This gushing insincerity had tightened the countess's lips and brought a spark of humor into Max's eyes as the travelers entered their coach.

Abigail had taken advantage of this softening of the facade of absentminded affability he'd presented to her since her mountain-climbing escapade to describe her discomfort at his father's gift and implore him to take possession of the mirror so it might be saved for the girl who eventually became his bride. She'd had no more success with Max than with the earl, and the son's manner had contained none of the father's gentle courtesy. Quick resentment at his refusal to concern himself with the delicate matter lent pugnacity to the tones in which Abigail had then set forth her intention of changing into her own clothes and abandoning the new wardrobe wherever they stopped for lunch, but again she was taken at fault. Max had blandly stated his entire indifference to the subject, after which he had proceeded to initiate a conversation with Roland that was clearly meant to exclude her.

This altercation and her subsequent silence had set the tenor for the long hours of travel. Roland, bless his heart, had engaged Max in sporadic but easy conversation. All that was demanded of her was the nearly impossible but heroic exercise of endurance.

Abigail sat up straighter as she recognized the brick wall of an estate near Broadlands. Her downcast eye lighted on the faded blue cotton gown she'd donned two hours before, and her lips thinned. Mentally she lashed out at the weak, acquisitive side of her nature that had quailed at parting with all the beautiful clothes she'd grown accustomed to wearing in six short days. Better to mourn the wardrobe than the man though! Neither was necessary to her existence, she reminded herself for the fiftieth time in four-and-twenty hours. Broadlands might not be paradise, but it was infinitely preferable to a marriage where one party did all the loving.

The moment she had longed for and dreaded arrived, and the horses came to a stop in front of her home. Max assisted her down from the carriage. Feeling worse than gauche suddenly, Abigail held out her hand and faced him with as much of a smile as she could manage. "Thank you for everything, Max, all your consideration for me. I had a very nice time at Oakridge, which is indeed a beautiful house. Good-bye and good luck." Having delivered her little speech in passably steady tones, she tried to withdraw her hand, but Max retained it in both of his.

"First of all, it is I who should be thanking you. I had indeed been a coward about this first visit to my father's house, but thanks to your good sportsmanship and generous spirit, I had a rather nice time too," he said with a smile that began in his eyes. "And this is not good-bye but *au revoir,* unless you plan to cut my acquaintance in the future?"

"Of . . . of course not," she murmured in confusion when he paused with a lifted brow.

Roland came up to the pair then, saying casually, "I'm taking Max down to the stables to see the chestnut pair Bertie has been training, Gail. I'll see you presently."

"Of course," she said again, tugging on her hand to no avail. Max raised it to his lips and pressed a kiss on her fingers. "*Au revoir,* Gail."

"Good-bye, Max."

The men turned aside, and Gail quickly went in the door the manservant had opened, determinedly holding back the threatening tears until she could reach the haven of her own room.

Inactivity was anathema to Abigail in the fortnight after her homecoming. She very sensibly resolved not to dwell upon what might have been—scores of times, in fact—but continued to catch herself recalling some joking remark Max had made to her at Oakridge or the way he had looked at her during the waltz lesson. When her errant thoughts inevitably reached the kiss in the rose garden, she clamped down on them, reinstating the smashed resolution, and looked about for a project to engage her attention, or at least occupy her hands. She took ruthless advantage of the surprisingly warm reception her father had given her to badger him into permitting some long overdue refurbishing of the main rooms in the house. He blanched at the cost of some green, cream, and gold striped fabric she bought for new draperies in the drawing room, but recovered somewhat when she announced that she'd unearthed a trunk in the attics that was full of old curtains from her grandfather's time that could be salvaged and recut to begin life anew in the dining room and the small room she used as a morning room. She explained that she was doing the sewing herself with the help of the laundress and the maidservant to save money. Her father's interest in the domestic affairs of his household, never great, rapidly waned, and he escaped to the stables to avoid further discussion.

Stable lads sent up to the house to do the actual painting had been willing enough but unskilled, Abigail concluded with a sigh when she inspected the drawing room after their departure one afternoon. In several areas the old ivory paint still showed through the medium gold color she'd chosen to contrast with the white moldings. The wisdom of hindsight now told her she should have remained to supervise the boys' slapdash efforts, but she'd been reluctant to bring the beautiful fabric she was sewing into the room while the painting was going on.

Seeing that they'd left a ladder and the paint in one corner, she began to drag it over to the place with the most glaring errors.

Attracted by the noise, Roland stuck his head in the archway a moment later. "What are you doing?"

"Just what you see me doing," his sister retorted. "Help me move this ladder over there to the right of the fireplace."

Her brother obeyed mechanically, holding his end of the ladder at arm's length. "Why do you want it over here?"

"The lads missed a few spots. I suppose you would not be so kind as to touch up the areas that need repainting?" she asked without much hope.

"What, wearing my best leathers? You suppose rightly. I'm off to the stables. Shall I send one of the boys back to finish the job?"

"No, I'll do it myself, then I'll know it's done right."

"When you wish something done right—" Roland began, and then jumped back, dodging the rag she threw at him. "That thing is full of paint," he protested, adding on his way out, "Don't fall off the ladder."

Abigail was near the top of the ladder, painting an area under the ceiling molding after taking care of all the easily reached spots when she heard boots on the wooden floor again.

"Roly? Would you hand me that rag I threw at you? I'm nearly done."

"Roland said he thought you were in the drawing room and to walk right in, but he didn't tell me you were pretending to be a bird."

"*Max*! What are you doing here?" Abigail held onto the ladder tightly until her wobbly knees resumed their function. Her heart was beating in her throat as she gazed down into laughing grey eyes.

"If you come down from your aerie, I'll be glad to enlighten you."

"I must just wipe a smear off the molding if you'll hand me that rag." It was a wrench to break eye contact when he handed it up to her, but Abigail turned away and applied herself to her task, her mind a swirling mass of confusion. She must be calm. Horses . . . he was here because of the horses. When she had herself well in hand again, she began to descend the ladder.

"I remember now. Roland mentioned that you were buying the young chestnuts for your curricle, or was it your phaeton?" she said, proud of her recovery.

"That was one reason. The other is that I've come to begin the lessons."

"Lessons?"

"The fencing lessons I promised to give you. I am here to carry out my obligation." Her eyes followed his to where a long, bulky package leaned against the wall near the archway.

Abigail burst out laughing. "Max, you idiot!"

"Ah, that's better. Are you glad to see me, Gail?"

"I might be," she admitted, "if I were not looking a perfect mess in the oldest rag I own, with my hair all wild and—"

"And a paint smear on your cheek," he finished, pulling out a handkerchief. "You never looked lovelier to me." His eyes smiling down at her in that intimate fashion that caught at her breath every time, he took the bemused girl's chin in one hand and wiped the paint off her cheek with the other. "When we marry, I'll talk my father into letting Mavis come to us if she would like to be a lady's dresser. She turns you into a perfect work of art every time."

"Max, wait, you are going too fast." Abigail stepped back where she could think better and breathe easier. "We've known each other only a few days really, and some of that time has been spent in quarreling. You cannot be in love with me so soon, and I won't marry a man who isn't sure he's gotten over a previous love."

"Your courage and honesty are two of the things I love most about you," Max replied, "but let us address these objections in turn, starting with my infatuation for Felicity. I thought I was madly in love with her and those feelings certainly would have settled into an enduring love if she had been the person I believed her to be. I was shocked, hurt, and exceedingly bitter at both of them. Running off to join the army may have been cowardly, I don't know anymore. It certainly was the response of a romantic young fool. The really cowardly action was engaging you to be a shield during the visit to Oakridge. I freely admit that, but I had not seen Felicity in four years, therefore her image had remained unchanged in my memory. I was afraid of how I would feel being around her on a daily basis. The situation seemed fraught with potential embarrassment for everyone that the presence of a fiancée could defuse, but I swear to you that I was not seeking revenge or trying to make her jealous. I simply had not thought the matter through because I'd spent years refusing to let myself think about it. I still believe the basic plan was sensible, but I hadn't expected that you would be exposed to such malice; I hadn't known Felicity's real character at all."

"And you think you know mine after an even shorter acquaintance?" Abigail asked softly.

"Shorter perhaps but much more intense." Max's smile became tender. "I know you are a hotheaded little termagant with the tongue of an adder when aroused and an impulsive streak that disregards sense or danger, and that you stand in great need of a strong guiding hand to curb your rebellious nature."

"My word, with such an opinion, I wonder that you should wish to marry me at all," Abigail declared, taken aback by this frank and unflattering depiction of her character.

"So do I, but there it is. I told myself I couldn't possibly be in love with you. I purposely stayed away this past fortnight to give myself a chance to forget your physical charms and appeal—I'd gone blindly down that road once before—but I've missed you so terribly, your gaiety of spirit, your sweetness with my little sister, your transparent honesty and moral courage, not to mention the complete absence of affectation and artifice that sets you apart from the crowd. But most of all," he added, pulling her into his embrace with a deliberation that she could have thwarted if she chose, "I missed the look in your beautiful eyes when I kissed you in the pergola, like this."

Wild elation bubbled through Abigail's veins as what began as a gentle kiss escalated into an assault on her senses that she responded to with all the surprising strength of her small person.

"Yes, that's the look I meant," Max said unsteadily when he'd released her mouth at last. "Do you love me, Gail?"

"Oh, Max, of course I do, though I certainly had not intended to fall in love with someone so domineering. I fear I do have an independent nature and resent it when men discount my opinions only because I am female. We shall probably lead a cat-and-dog existence."

"There are worse existences by far. Honest and fair combat with no underhanded tricks or simmering resentments, who could ask for better?" He kissed her again lingeringly. "When would you like to marry?"

Abigail's dreamy expression disappeared, active alarm

taking its place. "Max, we've forgotten my father! He is so terribly prejudiced against the nobility. Oh, what if he refuses his consent? What will we do? I could not bear it if I were never to see you again!"

Max detached his beloved's clutching fingers from the lapels of his coat where they were wrecking havoc on one of Weston's newest creations and cannily sandwiched them between his own. "As a matter of fact," he replied in soothing accents, "while your father and I were dickering over the price of his chestnuts, I did happen to mention that my father had been very fond of your mother when she was a girl and had nothing but contempt for Sir Charles Fellowes's unfeeling treatment of his daughter. I got the distinct impression that Mr. Monroe thinks I come of good sound English stock despite the irrelevance of the title."

"Oh, Max," Abigail said, untroubled by any considerations of underhanded tricks, "how clever of you!" She threw her arms around his neck in joy and relief.

Max did what any clever man would do in such promising circumstances. He kissed her.